EXTREME EVICTION

RYAN WILSON NOVELS

Hell's Hora (2014)
Depraved Destiny (2013)
Extreme Eviction (2013)
Sudden Shadow (2012)

EXTREME EVICTION

A Ryan Wilson Novel

CHRISTOPHER WATERS

Rev. date: 05/23/2013

To order additional copies of this book, contact:
Xlibris Corporation
1-888-795-4274
www.Xlibris.com
Orders@Xlibris.com
128122

To Laura; my mother.

The extraordinary woman
who gave me the ability to write.

"The forces of retribution are always listening. They never sleep"
–Meg Greenfield

CHAPTER 1

THE RAINY WEEKEND was over and Monday morning broke through with a Chicago sunrise that was both warm and bright. The rain had not been a negative facet of Tom Murphy's weekend. His girlfriend had expressly asked for a day in bed on Sunday and he was more than happy to oblige when they awoke to the sound of raindrops on the window panes. Susan had been a godsend to him and she could have anything she desired as far as he was concerned. The strange thing was that she was not a greedy girl at all. She enjoyed a good deal of things that he liked to do. If she wasn't so beautiful he would have thought she was doing all those things to get him to like her. She didn't need to, he had liked her from the minute she had walked into the bank to open her account and transfer her funds from her old bank. He was never happier to have had to fill in for his mortgage and mutual funds manager than the day Susan strode up to his counter thirty-three days ago. As a Bank Manager, numbers were important to Tom so it was easy for him to keep track of the days since she had arrived in his life. Afflicted with a slight case of OCD Tom liked everything to flow methodically and he was very organized with his daily routine. His alarm was set for seven-o-five every weekday morning giving him one hour and ten minutes before he needed to leave the house to get to work on time. During the week his routine never changed, Susan only stayed over on Friday and Saturday nights. His daily routine was shower, shave, coffee and toast, brush teeth and then out the door. Each day of the week he had his own distinct added functions that he would perform on top of the normal daily ones. On Monday it was nasal irrigation, on Tuesday it was nail clipping, and today, Wednesday; it was nose and ear hairs. He left the house at eight fifteen as usual even with a slight headache bothering him. Being late for work was not an option for Tom as it would mess up his world and ruin his inner chi. On his drive to work Susan called to say good morning. They exchanged the usual lover's discourse and then he told her that he had a headache.

"Did you take anything for it?" she asked.

"Not yet. You know I don't like drugs."

"Okay. I will call you later. Hope your headache gets better."

By lunchtime not only had his headache not receded but it had been joined by a stiff neck. His stomach was telling him it was not interested in food so he took an antacid tablet from the bottle in his desk drawer. He barely made it through the day before leaving. His determination to lead by example and his stubbornness as a man made him stay to the end of the day before heading home. By the time he got home he was vomiting even though he had not eaten anything all day. He did not want to go to the doctor and against all logic he decided to drink a hot lemonade drink for cold relief. Susan called and offered to come over but Tom said he would be a miserable patient. They both laughed at that and for a moment he felt better.

The next morning his stiff neck was more subtle but his forehead was hot and the headache pounded in his head. His coffee tasted more bitter than normal but he assumed that his taste buds were affected by this flu bug. He knew that he had to keep drinking despite the old wives tale about fevers and colds. He poured the last glass of orange juice from the container in his refrigerator and thought about asking Susan to bring him more. As much as he deplored missing a day of work he could not take a chance of spreading this flu bug through the bank. He let everyone at the bank know, via email, that he might be off work the next two days. At lunchtime he opened a can of chicken noodle soup hoping for a homemade cure. He managed to get half a bowl of soup into him before he had to race to the bathroom to vomit it back up. The process wiped out all his energy and he crashed on his couch and fell asleep. Hours later he awoke starving and made some plain toast praying his stomach would cooperate. When he didn't feel the urge to throw up he took a chance on a glass of warm milk before heading to bed. When Susan called to check up on him and to say goodnight his spirits lifted and he went to bed with pleasant thoughts of time they would spend together when he was over this flu.

On Friday morning when Tom poured his coffee he noticed that the wonderful aroma, that usually greeted him each time he poured it into his cup, was not there. In fact he could not smell anything significant not even the toothpaste when he brushed his teeth. His bad sinuses were always an issue but the flu seemed to have cut off all his olfactory senses. He liked to stick to his daily routine and despite the flu's influence on his nasal passages he would not use his neti pot to irrigate his sinuses again until Monday. The fever was still there as was his headache but the stiff neck had dissipated and Tom took that as a positive sign. He rarely became sick. At work he would make sure to wash his hands often to avoid the germs that customers bring into the bank. He tried to replay in his head when he might have touched someone and not washed his hands afterwards, but he kept losing his concentration and his train of thought would be gone. With the exception of losing his sense of smell Friday was a carbon copy of Thursday.

On Saturday morning Susan called Tom to check on him again.

"No I don't feel up to going out yet," he said.

"Shall I go shopping for you?"

"I was thinking that but I have enough milk to get me through the weekend and I am not exactly ravenous about food."

"I feel so bad that you don't feel well enough to get out."

"It's not your fault Susan. I probably picked it up from a customer at the bank. There is nothing you could have done to prevent it."

"Okay I will check on you later. Try to rest up."

"I will trust me. Resting is at the top of my list of things to do today."

They both laughed and it made Tom felt good, if only for the moment. His naps were eating up most of his day and he easily confused morning with afternoon. Susan called him later in the day and he barely had the consciousness to speak to her. She expressed her concern but he assured her he would be better in the morning. It felt to him that the fever was breaking and he would be his normal self soon. Carrying his cup of warm milk to the bedside table he lost his grip and the milk spilled all over the carpet. He was too tired to clean it up and besides it was hardly noticeable in the beige carpet. He fell asleep as soon as he pulled up the covers.

He was awakened by a noise coming from his kitchen. He didn't know what time it was but it didn't feel like morning. He rose and barely had the strength to put on his robe and slippers.

"Who's there?" Tom called out, thinking Susan must have convinced the building super to let her in. No one answered him so he shuffled down the hall to the kitchen. The kitchen light was on and there definitely was someone in there making noise perhaps cooking. When he came around the corner and looked at the person in his kitchen he was both shocked and elated at the same time. Suddenly he was not feeling sick; he was feeling a different kind of warmth inside.

"Mom?" he cried.

"Yes Tom. I am making you something to eat. Would you prefer pancakes or French toast? I have the eggs ready."

"Mom," he said again, not understanding what he was seeing. His mother had died two years before and yet he could see her and hear her and even smell the eggs she was beating. He was about to ask for pancakes when his body began shaking like there was an earthquake but the shaking was only inside of him. The kitchen was not shaking and nor was his mother and then he felt the heat emanate with the shaking. Tom lost his balance and fell to the floor reaching up to his mother for help but her image disappeared as did the kitchen and darkness slowly enveloped him like a warm but fatal blanket.

CHAPTER 2

SOMETIMES LIFE IN the morgue is anything but a normal routine and tonight was one of those times for nightshift Medical Examiner Dr. Fred McLaughlin. A drive by shooting in the south end had added to the daily workload of autopsies and had pushed more work into the nightshift and of course that meant a long night for Fred.

They worked feverishly to get caught up on the potential criminal deaths so the DA could start their workday tomorrow with the needed paperwork on their desk.

With an average of over one hundred autopsies being performed each week in the Medical Examiner's Office in Chicago sometimes there is little opportunity to pause and reflect but the next corpse Fred saw would require him to do just that. He read the report from the paramedics.

Name: Thomas Rupert Murphy
Gender: Male
Age: 47
Notes: No vitals – DOA

The man's body showed no apparent signs of a cause of death, leading to the assumption that he died from a possible heart attack. The poor man been home with the flu and was alone when it happened. The building superintendent and the man's girlfriend found him Monday after she was worried because he had not answered his phone.

Fred continued with the paperwork details of the body including taking pictures. After his assistant had opened the torso he started the removal and assessment of the organs. The healthy lungs were not a surprise as the man was not a smoker but the healthy heart was a shock. Fred laughed at himself, reminded of the little ditty of the word assume. *U makes an ass out of me.* He had jumped to a conclusion about the heart attack but it now appeared that the reported flu may be the culprit after all and if that was the case they would need to be careful going forward. It might be more than just the flu, conceivably a case of spinal meningitis. He inserted a needle into the spinal canal to extract the cerebrospinal fluid for later examination. Next they would check the brain which will show swelling if meningitis or encephalitis was the cause of death. When he removed the skull cap from the back of the head he could distinctly see the cerebral edema. The brain itself was inflamed not unlike a case of Reyes Syndrome but this one had a hidden surprise when he finished removing it. At the base of the brain there was a puss like substance that should not have been there under any conditions that he had considered. Fred's eyebrows furrowed and then he looked at the body again ascertaining if there was a possible spider bite on the skin. He found nothing noteworthy except for the redness of the nasal passage. Murphy was a bank manager but that did not preclude him from snorting drugs, in fact it may have been asset to acquiring those drugs. Fred snared a sample of the puss from the brain and a sample of nasal mucosa to go along with the spinal fluid and marked them for viewing later to determine the cause of the brain swelling.

Five hours later when the day's gunshot, stabbing and poisoning victims were autopsied and reports sent upstairs Fred looked at slides of the samples he quarantined from the Murphy corpse. At first he thought he was too tired to concentrate on the tiny images in the ocular lens of the microscope but then something on one of the slides of the mucosa caught his attention. He immediately put in the sample slide of the spinal fluid and adjusted the objective lens, the iris diaphragm and finally the fine focus until he saw it again. He stood up blinked several times wiped his eyes and looked one more time to confirm it was there. Fred sat back on his stool and took a deep breath. Tiny amoebas called trophozoites were floating on the slide. The rest of the puzzle now fit together. The flu like symptoms were masking a more deadly body invader, a strain of bacterial meningitis called Primary Amoebic Meningoencephalitis; PAM for short.

Murphy had no chance. By the time he thought he had the flu he was already past help. The amoeba enters the body through the nasal passage and then using nerves like a ladder they climb their way up to the brain where they begin to feed on the brain cells. This in turn causes the inflammation of the brain and over the course of a few days nausea, headache, stiff neck, and vomiting. That is followed by changes in smell and taste, bouts of confusion and clumsiness and finally hallucinations, seizures and inevitably death. This all takes place in three to seven days after being infected and very few people survive. There were two obvious ways for Murphy to ingest his killer. He either went swimming in a pond or stagnant lake recently or used tap water in a neti pot to irrigate his sinuses, or he could have done both.

Fred called Officer Andy Campbell who had first responded to the call.

"Campbell here."

"Andy, Fred here."

"Hey doc what can I do for you?"

"I am wrapping up my autopsy report on Tom Murphy, the DB from this morning, and I need you to check something for me."

"Sure thing."

"Check his place for a neti-pot."

"A what?"

"It looks like a small ceramic tea pot. It should be in his bathroom."

"Okay."

"I am hoping there is some water in it. I will need that for testing so please seal it in an evidence bag."

"Will do doc."

"And check if he has a day planner perhaps showing where he has gone on the weekends."

It was a long shot but might as well be thorough while he is there. Fred sat down to finish off the rest of his paperwork and an hour later in walked Officer Campbell holding a beige neti-pot sealed in clear plastic evidence bag.

"There is only a little bit of water in it so I have kept it upright even in the bag," said Campbell.

"That's great. It should be enough to tell me what I need to know."

"Oh, the super wanted to know if it was contagious. I told him it was not a virus."

"No it won't be contagious. Thanks Andy."

"Anytime doc." Campbell turned and left.

Fred readied a sample slide of the water from inside the neti pot to view under the microscope. The same trophozoites that he found in the body appeared in the new slide. Murphy had definitely used tap water instead of distilled water or a saline mixture as was instructed on the original packaging. It was such a shame that he had taken a short cut and used tap water for irrigating his nose. Over two hundred people worldwide have died from PAM, some from swimming and some from doing the same thing that Murphy did. It seemed like an innocent mistake for anyone to make and as unfortunate as it was at least Fred could now give the family the real reason for the death.

CHAPTER 3

THE TRANQUILITY AT six a.m. was one of the things that Dr. Emmett Brennan truly enjoyed when he started his morning rounds. He was typically the first one in and he relished the quiet environment. Smitty, the guard at the front gate could write down his arrival time a week ahead because Dr. Brennan was so punctually consistent that it varied by no more than a minute each day. His routine of turning on the lights and releasing the animals was almost therapeutic. To Dr. Brennan it was like watching a new birth each day. Ever since he had developed the concept for the Genesis Research Lab he felt like he was repeating some of the evolution that happened over a billion years ago when plants first started to appear on earth. His theory was to take what Mendel had done and go to the next step. He didn't just want to make plants and crops resistant to weeds as had been done with corn and rice, he wanted them to have the same growth capabilities and ideally make them even stronger than the weeds. They were experimenting with both the Gene Gun method and the Agrobacterium method of transforming genes in an effort to spawn new species of virile crops that would have the strength of a weed and the plushness of a produce. If above ground crops and root vegetables could grow as effectively in the same sparse conditions that weeds can endure then the food shares of third world countries could double or triple in less than a decade. The lab had been built on a fifty acre farm just south of Kelby that had been acquired in a bank foreclosure. The original barn, equipment and a small herd of cows were kept for the aesthetic value as much as the necessity. Furthermore, the office and research labs were built to look like an extension on the house and an additional barn, so that environmentalists would have a hard time finding the lab if by chance they chose to demonstrate about the work they were doing.

Every morning he came to work Dr. Brennan greeted the cows by singing to them before he turned on the rest of the lights in the barn. He enjoyed letting the cows out to pasture each morning, listening to their brays and moos as they marched down the passageway to the open field. He would unlock the first gate at the barn and leaving it open just a few inches while waiting for the first cow to notice he walked down the twenty yards of the coral chute to open wide the gate to the back pasture. If the cows were undistracted and sedentary and did not try the first gate right away they would eventually begin their march when they saw him open the second gate.

Today was a landmark day. Dr. Brennan did not arrive at the lab until six-thirty five. Smitty, was almost concerned enough to consider calling Dr. Brennan had he been any later.

"You had me worried doc," he said with a chuckle when Dr. Brennan pulled up to the gate in his silver beamer. "I thought you must have been sick today."

"Good Morning Smitty. It was the strangest thing; I had a flat tire this morning. Luckily service was there in fifteen minutes and he changed it in another fifteen minutes. I will of course have to pick up the repaired tire on my way home tonight."

"Well I'll keep my fingers crossed that you don't have another one before you get your spare back."

"Thanks. I certainly hope not."

"I wonder if your cows can tell that you are late," Smitty inquired.

Dr. Brennan smiled back, "An interesting thought, they just might."

The security guard raised the front gate baton and Dr. Brennan drove through to the office parking lot that was hidden behind the house. As Smitty watched Dr. Brennan's car disappear behind the house he reflected that their conversation this morning was the longest one he'd had with the doctor in the year he had been working at the front gate. Very few of the scientists stop to talk at the front gate when they arrive at the lab in the morning. They all seem to be in a trance that mutes their ability to have a normal conversation with another person. While Smitty hoped his kids would get a university education he also hoped they never become a zombie like scientist like the ones that passed through his gate each morning.

After flicking all the required light switches to the on position Dr. Brennan headed out to the paddock to release the cows. He walked around to the back of the barn and squeezing between two of the horizontal rails of the chute he started sing to his audience, "And the corn was as high as an elephant's eye . . ." Apparently his lateness had not unsettled the morning routine as far as the cows were concerned. They greeted him with the usual amount of braying. He opened the first gate from the outside and started his walk down the chute to the second gate. A couple of the cows slowly pushed the first gate open and watched the doctor walking away from them before moseying towards him. That was when they heard the bull horn coming from somewhere inside the barn. Dr. Brennan stopped and turned back to face the barn trying to understand what he had just heard. It wasn't a fire alarm. It was more like a horn that you would hear at a sporting event to initiate cheering from the crowd. At the same time that he was trying to decipher the cause of the noise the cows had started a stampede to get out of the barn paddock. The cows were jarring each other trying to get down the narrow chute to the second gate. They were coming straight toward Dr. Brennan who realized what was happening and he ran for the second gate as fast as he could. All he had to do was get the second gate open and dart to the right to avoid the stampede. The cows were closing fast but he had reached the second gate. Then when it appeared all was going to be fine, a strange experience happened to Dr. Brennan. It was the same experience as when you hear a noise in the parking lot while you are trying to get your keys into your car door lock but you panic and your dexterity leaves you, and you drop your keys on the floor. Even though he had unlocked that gate hundreds of times he missed unlocking it on the first attempt and then he slowed his second attempt to ensure success. The gate lock released and Dr. Brennan began to push it open but he was a second too late and the cows rammed into him and one after another they trampled him into the ground. He would never reach his goal of genetic food improvement. The animals he had greeted and sung to every morning had become the executors of his death.

CHAPTER 4

IF THERE WAS one thing that Medical Examiner Dr. Fred McLaughlin enjoyed about his work it was the diversity. Even with deaths that are obvious there are never two exactly the same and because of that there is little opportunity for boredom to creep in. When he reviewed the list of tonight's autopsies one case stuck out far more than any other, first because it was a doctor, Dr. Emmett Brennan, and second because it was listed as "crushed by cattle stampede." He needed to work through a couple of stabbings from a bar fight before he was able open the file of the crushed doctor. When he opened the body bag with the doctor inside it was a terrible mess as he had expected. There were so many broken bones that determining which happened first and was the cause of death was virtually impossible. It was most likely that the crushed skull had killed Dr. Brennan but there was no way to be sure that the shattered ribs didn't happen first. Either way it was as strange an autopsy as he had seen in quite some time. Finishing up his report he read over the State Trooper's notes again. He remembered when the Genesis Research Lab opened up about two years ago. After some serious lobbying Dr. Brennan had received a government grant to work on plant genetics. Fred wondered what would happen to his projects now but presumed it likely that the other doctors on staff will be able to keep the farm tasks running until a new lead manager could be hired. Sitting at his desk he turned to his computer and searched the internet for news release of the opening of the lab. When he found it there were the usual blarney about what exciting times these were and pictures of people from the governor to the mayor and others holding the red ribbon while Dr. Brennan using oversize scissors cut through the middle of the band. He was about to close the search window when he saw something that made him look twice. He stared at the picture for a few more minutes before saving the page. It was almost seven a.m. so he called instead of texting.

"Wilson here."

"Good Morning Detective Wilson."

Wilson recognized Fred's distinctive voice, "Hey doc, what's up?"

"Are you very busy right now?"

"No, not especially, just some court cases to attend to later. Why?"

"I was wondering if you could drop by my office on your way in today. I have something that might interest you."

"Okay. I should be there within the hour doc."

"Good." Fred's mind was already wandering.

Click

Wilson looked at his phone and wondered what could make Fred so curious that he would call him at seven a.m. Forty five minutes later Wilson was rapping on Fred's office door.

"Oh great you're here. Have a seat I want to show you something."

Wilson pulled an empty metal chair to the side of the desk and Fred put a file in front of him.

"Take a look at that file."

Wilson skimmed through the notes about a bank manager that had died from a brain eating amoeba.

"Take a look at the picture." It was the usual cold, morgue picture of a dead man.

"Okay now read this file." Fred handed Wilson the doctors file.

Wilson read through the second file quickly and frowned. These were two completely different, natural deaths. Fred was smiling at him causing Wilson to frown more.

Fred clicked his mouse and a picture came on his computer screen.

"Okay now take a look at this picture."

Wilson leaned forward and squinted.

"The guy cutting the ribbon is my crushed doctor."

Wilson looked at Fred waiting for more information but Fred was waiting to drop the other shoe.

"Look at the picture again," said Fred pointing to the screen.

Wilson examined the ribbon cutting picture again noticing the mayor and the governor. There were also a couple of attractive smiling women and between them a man in a suit. Wilson grabbed the first file, looked at the black and white morgue picture and then back at the ribbon cutting ceremony photo on the screen and read the caption. The man in the suit was the same man in the black and white morgue photo in the first file.

"Wow. And these two guys died two days apart?"

"Yep."

"Well that is interesting."

"I know that you don't like coincidences so I thought I would bring this to your attention rather than let it go through system."

"Can you email that link to me?"

"I will do it right now." Fred said as he pounded his keyboard.

"So the bank manager and the head of the lab accidentally die two days apart," said Wilson. "I wonder if anyone else in the picture is due to have an accident."

"Well that I will leave up to you to figure out."

Wilson closed the two files and tucked them under his arm.

"Have a great day."

"Thanks Fred."

Wilson didn't wait for the elevator at the precinct; he raced up the three flights of stairs to the bullpen and walked to Nelson's desk. He dropped the M.E. file of Murphy the bank manager in front of her and said, "Read Please."

She looked up at him with a curious look and inspected the file carefully. When she was finished she walked over to Wilson's desk and handed back the file. Wilson was uploading the link that Fred had sent him.

"Take a look at this."

She looked that the ribbon cutting picture Wilson had brought up on the screen but didn't see the connection. Wilson opened the second file and showed her Fred's report.

"That is the man cutting the ribbon," said Wilson as he waited for her to notice anything pertinent. "They were killed two days apart."

Nelson looked back at the ribbon cutting picture trying to see the link. She was about to ask what she was supposed to be looking for but then she saw it and said, "Oh."

"How about that," said Wilson.

"That is a bit weird. You think it's too much of a coincidence and that the deaths might not be natural," she asked.

"I don't believe in coincidence when it has anything to do with murder."

"I concur."

"My first concern is, if two people in this picture have died, how much time we have before someone else in the picture dies."

"There is no way to know if any of the other people are being targeted until we know why."

"We need to talk to the mayor and the governor first. Have Dixon find out who the rest of the people are in the photo. I'll go talk to the Captain about this and see how he wants to handle the mayor and governor."

Nelson grimaced knowing the bristly relationship between the Captain and Wilson.

"Good luck," Nelson said as she left to go see Dixon.

Wilson emailed the picture of the ribbon cutting ceremony to Nelson and Dixon simultaneously then grabbed the two M.E. files and headed to Captain Stone's office. The issues between Wilson and Captain Stone go back to when Wilson was a beat officer and Stone was a Lieutenant. Wilson had butted heads with him on a couple of cases and Captain Stone has not let him forget. Wilson had mended his ways and tried very hard not to cross Lieutenant Trentini as he needed a buffer between him and Captain Stone. Trentini was not in today so he was on his own in speaking to the Captain on this issue. Wilson tapped lightly on the open office door.

"Sir," he said.

"What is it Wilson?"

"I need some advice and Lieutenant Trentini is not in today." He thought that was a good way of easing into the subject but with Captain Stone you never knew.

"Again Wilson, what is it?" His stern voice unchanged.

"Sir I have two dead people who were in a picture with mayor and the governor from two years ago and I was wondering if we need to advise them about it."

"Dead people. We are talking about natural causes and not murder."

"Well yes sir but they both died this week, just two days apart."

"Were both by natural causes?"

"Well more accidental than natural and I was concerned that there might be another one, perhaps in two days."

"Give me the files."

Stone studied the ME files almost as briefly as Wilson first done and then he looked up at Wilson. "You think this warrants an investigation and that we should alert the mayor and the governor."

"Yes sir."

"Are you out of your fucking mind," Stone blurted out.

"I . . ."

Before Wilson could finish his answer Stone laid into him.

"You want me to go to the mayor and say excuse me Mr. Mayor Sir, but could you please be careful not to have an accident tomorrow. And then you want me to tell the governor the same thing."

"Well."

"Well nothing Wilson," he said as he tossed the ME files across his desk. "I didn't get to be the Captain because I go off all half-cocked all the time. I thought you had settled down now that you are a Detective-Sergeant but I see I was wrong."

"But sir," Wilson tried to explain.

"But nothing Wilson. You said the picture was two years old and the deaths were accidental. That doesn't sound like murder to me. It sounds like a hair brained idea. We are here to close cases Wilson. We don't need to make up a "*who done it*". Solve the ones you have open. You do have open cases don't you."

"Yes sir." Wilson stood still.

Stone stared at him "Anything else."

"Sir, my concern is that if these are not just accidents then the killer is very smart. He didn't just shoot them and leave us a trail. And if someone else dies in two days and I did nothing."

Stone cut him off, "Fine, fine. You have two days. If no one in the picture dies in the next two days then the case is closed. Do I make myself clear?"

"Yes sir," Wilson replied with mild surprise.

"I will advise the Chief and he can decide if he wants to tell the mayor and the governor." Stone looked down at the paperwork on his desk. "That's all Wilson."

"Thank you sir."

Wilson picked up the files and left.

CHAPTER 5

NELSON ARRIVED BACK at the bullpen minutes after Wilson had returned. She regarded at Wilson to see if he had been ripped a new one by the Captain but it appeared everything was okay.

"How did it go with the Captain?"

"Better than I thought it would. He gave us two days. If no one else in the picture dies in two days we have to drop it."

"Good. I mean it's good that he gave us two days to work on it."

"Any luck with Dixon?"

"There are seven people holding the ribbon in the picture and eight in the back row not holding it. Two are now dead and minus the mayor and governor leaves us three to talk to. Two women and one man. We have the women's information now. Dixon and Anthony are still checking out the other man holding the ribbon and also the people in the back row."

"If there is another target it would seem likely that it will be someone in the front row."

"The two women are Deborah Webster the president of the local Chamber of Commerce and the building contractor Melissa Green."

"Okay. Let's call them and find out if they know about the deaths and where they are going to be over the next two days."

Nelson called the Chamber of Commerce and asked for Deborah Webster.

"This is Deborah Webster," was the reply from the woman who answered the phone. "How may I help you?"

"You are on speaker phone with Detective Wilson and Detective Nelson from Chicago PD."

"Really."

"Yes ma'am. We would like to ask you a few questions," replied Nelson.

"Well anything you need to know about Kelby I can tell you. Did you know the city was originally called *Ratatoskr* after a Norse god's pet squirrel because we had so many squirrels?"

"No ma'am I didn't."

"We have two types of squirrels here; the Eastern Grey Squirrel and the Franklin Ground Squirrel."

"I am afraid we have more pressing questions we need to ask you. We are looking at a picture of a ribbon cutting ceremony."

"Oh. Does this have anything to do with the death of Dr. Brennan from the research lab?"

"Yes Ms. Webster, it does. However there was also another death this week that has our interest. Tom Murphy from the First Chicago Savings and Loan Bank died two days ago."

"Oh my," her voice dropped off.

"I take it then that you remember him."

"Yes of course. He was instrumental in arranging the finances for the project. Dr. Brennan was turned down by other banks before Tom went to bat for him and convinced his bank to back the construction part of the project."

Wilson asked, "I thought that Dr. Brennan had a grant from the government for his project."

"The grant money barely covered the equipment and employee budget."

"I see," Nelson reflected. "Ms. Webster have you had any threats made against you or the Chamber of Commerce?"

"No, of course not. Who would want to do that?"

"That is what we are trying to determine."

"But I thought that Dr. Brennan's death was an accident?"

"It could have been but Mr. Murphy's death put it in a different light."

"I am not sure I follow you."

"We think that it's possible someone might have a vendetta against some of people in the picture."

"Oh wow."

"We just don't know who or why yet?"

"But that's crazy. That was two years ago and there were no demonstrations or letters of protest about the lab."

"I understand. It may not lead to anything but just to be safe I would suggest that you work from home tomorrow if that is possible."

"Why tomorrow?" she asked.

"Well the other two deaths were two days apart and if it is a pattern then tomorrow might be the day."

"Yes I can do that. I can forward all the calls to my cell phone."

"Great. Hopefully nothing will come of all this but if you see anything unusual please call us immediately."

"I most certainly will and thank you for the advice."

"Thank you for your time," Nelson said.

Detective Anthony entered the bullpen waving a list in his hand printed out by Dixon and handed it to Wilson. The other man in the front row was identified as Robert Gregory, the Mayor of Kelby.

The back row was comprised of the other five employees of the research lab, the Police Chief, the Mayor's executive assistant, and finally the insurance underwriter for the project.

"We'll stick to the original idea that the front row will be the target. Nelson and I will go see the Mayor and his assistant; we have already talked to the Chamber of Commerce lady. Anthony you go to see the contractor lady and the insurance guy. They are both in the Chicago area."

Everyone agreed.

Detective Michael Anthony arrived at Rothenberg and Snyder Insurance in less than twenty minutes. The offices were on the second floor but there was no elevator. He was slightly winded when he reached the second floor lobby. He looked back down the stairs and wondered how handicapped people were expected to get up here. Ernie Taylor was five – five with short black hair and green eyes and glasses. He looked exactly the way Detective Anthony thought an insurance agent should look like. He was waiting at reception for the detective.

"Good Morning Detective."

"Thank you for meeting with me Mr. Taylor."

They sat down in the lobby chairs and Anthony pulled out the picture of the Genesis Research Lab ribbon cutting ceremony. Taylor had heard about the accident to Dr. Brennan but did not know about Murphy's death.

"Who did you know in the photo?"

"I met Mr. Murphy and Dr. Brennan and of course the contractor Melissa Green. I only needed the numbers to get the insurance policy approved. The other people just showed up that day for the picture."

"And you have never dealt with any of them since that day?"

"No not at all."

"Do you work out of your office or do you travel each day?"

"I work here most of the time but I do have client meetings out of the office occasionally."

"Do you have any meetings scheduled for tomorrow?"

"Why?"

"Just in case they are not accidents we are just trying to reduce the possibilities of another one in two days. It is quite possible that all this is circumstance but better safe than sorry."

"I see. Okay let me check," Taylor said as he pulled out his cell phone and scrolled through his apps. "No I don't. I will be in the office all day."

"Good. If you see anything unusual please call me right away," said Anthony as he handed Taylor his card. "And don't go anywhere alone."

"Of course," Taylor replied eyeing the card as if he was trying to memorize it.

Anthony thanked him for his time and left to go see Melissa Green at Green and Associates Contracting. He had called her earlier to ascertain if she was in the office or on site somewhere. Fortunately for Anthony she was at her office today, he wouldn't have to walk through a mud laden construction area to talk to her.

Melissa Green was a tall woman with a persona that left no doubt who was in charge. Her eyes evaluated you with a skill usually seen in a criminal attorney.

"What can I do for you Detective Anthony?"

"We are following up on the death of Dr. Brennan."

"Yes it is very sad. He was a very nice man. But what do you need from me?"

"It may or may not have been an accident."

"I don't understand. I thought that he was trampled by the cows in the barn?"

"Yes he was, but after we found out that Tom Murphy was involved in the Genesis Research Lab project we are covering all the bases."

"What do you mean?"

"I am sorry, I guess he didn't hear. Tom Murphy died two days ago."

"Oh my god," Melissa said, sounding more woman than boss now. "That's terrible."

"So you knew Mr. Murphy."

"Of course, he arranged the financing for the construction of the buildings."

"Who else did you know in this picture?" he said as he handed her the ribbon cutting picture.

"I met the Mayor of Kelby and Ms. Webster from the Chamber of Commerce and Mr. Taylor the insurance guy and of course Dr. Brennan."

She handed back the picture to Detective Anthony. "But I didn't meet any of the other people except to say hello, and shake hands on the day that picture was taken."

"Are you planning on working from the office tomorrow?"

"In the morning but I have a couple of jobs to inspect in the afternoon."

"Is it possible for you to postpone that for one more day?"

"I suppose if you feel it is that important."

"We do. And try not to be alone tomorrow. We don't want to take any chances."

"Okay. I will work from here tomorrow and have others with me all day."

"What about driving home?"

"I will leave my truck here and get a ride home with my brother."

"That would be great," said Anthony. "Thank you for your cooperation."

Melissa shrugged her shoulders almost conceding that she didn't have a choice. Her company was founded on a structure of stability. They didn't take on risky projects and she wasn't about to start now.

"You're welcome," she responded.

Anthony headed back to the bullpen.

Nelson's cell phone rang and she had a short conversation while making some notes. She hung up and turned to Wilson. "That was Tim. He's the Tech I gave the footprint pictures to for analysis. It turns out it is a hiking boot that most wilderness stores carry called a *Caprina*. It's a men's size nine. It's fairly common but he mentioned that farm mud in the treads would prove that it is a match."

"Good to know," said Wilson.

CHAPTER 6

WILSON AND NELSON arrived in Kelby and went straight to City Hall to see Mayor Gregory and his executive assistant, Caryn Olson. Before leaving Chicago for Kelby Nelson had called to inform the Mayor that they needed to speak with him about Dr. Brennan's death. Miss Olson was waiting for them at reception. Caryn Olson was in her late twenties, blonde with the cherubic smile of a girl right off the farm. She escorted them directly to the mayor's office where Mayor Gregory greeted them with a handshake. Nelson noticed that Olson watched the Mayor like a hawk, but not in a boss-employee type of way, more like in an adoration way.

"How can we help you Detectives?" asked Mayor Gregory. The Mayor of Kelby was a tall, thin man in his early forties with slight resemblance to an actor that Wilson couldn't quite grasp the name of. He made a mental note to ask Nelson later if she made the connection also.

"We are investigating the possibility that Dr. Brennan's death might not have been an accident."

"But he was trampled by the cattle."

"Yes we know. The reason we are suspicious is the death of Tom Murphy two days ago."

"I hadn't heard about that," the Mayor replied. "But you are right that is an odd occurrence." He turned to Olson. "Please look into sending flowers to the Murphy family."

"Yes Mr. Mayor."

Wilson put the ribbon cutting picture on the table.

"Two years after this picture was taken two people in the front row died two days apart. That is way too much of a coincidence for my liking."

The Mayor looked at the photo reminding himself of who the people were and then looked at Wilson and said, "I would have to agree with you."

"We are contacting all the people in the picture starting with the front row. If these are not accidental deaths and this is a pattern we want to avoid another accidental death tomorrow."

"That makes good sense."

"We would like you and Miss Olson to never be alone tomorrow. Especially if you go outside for any reason."

"I see."

"And I know this could be a bit tricky based on your position but it would be a good idea if you didn't meet anyone new tomorrow."

"Yes that could pose a problem. Although I am in a council meeting that will take up most of the morning and most visitors come in the mornings so I won't be able to say hello."

"That's good. And can someone else greet and afternoon visitors for you?"

"Yes. The assistant Mayor can take over that for the day."

"Good," Wilson said. "We are hoping that this will be resolved without incident but I don't want to take any chances on another mishap."

"I would not want one either. Caryn and I will make sure we are never alone," said Gregory as he and Olson nodded to each other. Nelson shrewdly observed the look that passed between them.

"And make sure your staff know to watch for anyone unusual hanging around."

"We will inform everyone."

"Call us right away if you see anything that doesn't look right."

"We will," Gregory said. "And we appreciate the time and effort you have taken to brief us on this issue." Spoken like a true politician.

When they were back in Wilson's white SUV Nelson said, "They are having an affair."

"Who?"

"The Mayor and his assistant."

"Wow. Are you sure."

"Yes they gave each other *the look* when you told then to stay together."

"Well I meant for them to always be with someone not necessarily each other."

"Trust me they would be together whether you had told them to or not."

Wilson snickered, "You do have nose for romance."

"That is an assignation"

"It's still romance," he countered.

"Perhaps," she said. "But it is not with the right person. He's married."

"Maybe his wife is having an affair also."

"Two wrongs won't make it right."

"Okay you win. Let's go talk to the Police Chief Caswell."

Aiden Caswell had grown up in Kelby and knew almost everyone who lived here which helped him immensely in winning a second term as Police Chief. His staff had grown as the population increased and what was once a one cop town was now a bustling team of over sixty police officers. A visit from the Chicago PD was both interesting and irritating to him. Did they think he couldn't have handled this with just a phone call?

Knowing that they were treading on sensitive ground Wilson showed impeccable discretion and respect.

"Detective Wilson and Detective Nelson to see Chief Caswell please." He asked at the front desk.

A moment later a female policewoman came to the lobby and said, "This way please."

All this formality in a small town surprised Wilson. They followed her down the hall and when she opened a door there inside was Police Chief Aiden Caswell.

"Detectives please come in and sit down," said Caswell without offering a handshake.

Wilson smiled, small town after all. Nelson decided that she would play the submissive role and just watch this play out.

"So what brings you out to our humble city?" he said dripping with derision.

Wilson ignored the obvious mock and showed him the ribbon cutting picture and started his speech. He had already informed Chief Caswell about the death of Tom Murphy.

"We are concerned that the two deaths may be linked and that a possible third accident might happen tomorrow."

Caswell picked up the picture and laughed, "This picture was taken two years ago."

"But the deaths this week were two days apart."

Caswell tossed the picture back to Wilson.

"These are accidents. What proof do you have that they are linked?"

"So far nothing except this picture."

"Then why are you here?" His self-absorbed tone sounded eerily similar to Captain Stone's.

"This is just an inquiry since the first accident was in my backyard. If there is a pattern and another accident is going to happen tomorrow we want everyone to be aware."

"And you don't think we can take care of things here?"

"We only want to be sure everyone is availed of the same information."

"Who have you talked to?"

"We have now spoken to everyone in the picture except the lab people."

"You spoke to the Mayor without talking to me first!" Caswell was now clearly upset that Wilson had by-past him.

"It was just that City Hall was closer than you."

Caswell glared at Wilson.

"And then you came here to tell me in person because you don't think I can't protect myself?"

"No. It was to keep you in the loop."

"So if nothing happens tomorrow then this is a dead issue," Caswell said. "No pun intended."

"I hope so." Wilson stood up taking that as his cue to leave, "Thank you for your time Chief."

"No problem always happy to help out our big city friends."

Nelson watched Wilson use his most passive face during the meeting observing that he has learned to deal with these situations in a different manner than when he first started on the force. She nodded her goodbye to Caswell and followed Wilson out the door.

"Well, that went well," Wilson said once they were outside the building.

"I was impressed with your reserve."

"More like self-preservation. I don't need Caswell calling the Captain and complaining about the way we handled the visit. But he was right that I should have gone to see him first. Don't let me do that again." Wilson snickered.

Nelson smiled back, "Do you mean in Kelby or if we are in other small towns?"

Wilson did not reply.

CHAPTER 7

THE GENESIS RESEARCH Lab looked like any other farm in the area. It was rectangular in shape with the narrow section facing the road being about one third the width of the length. Except for the sight of a security guard shack and baton at the beginning of the driveway, fifty yards from the house, there were no outward signs that the house, barns and crops were anything but a regular farm. Wilson pulled up to the gate.

"Good Morning. I am Detective Wilson and this is Detective Nelson."

The guard's name tag was Smitty and he was not surprised to see the detectives.

"I was wondering when you guys were going to get here."

Wilson and Nelson looked at each other puzzled by that comment.

"We are from Chicago PD."

"Even better. Glad they have independent cops on the case."

"We are here to talk to the staff," offered Wilson.

"They can't help you. None of them were here when it happened."

Wilson was even more befuddled now. He asked if he could pull inside the gate so they could talk. Smitty raised the baton and they drove through and stopped.

"This could be interesting," Wilson mused.

Wilson and Nelson got out of the SUV and shook hands with Smitty.

"We think that Dr. Brennan's death may not have been and accident."

"Of course it wasn't," Smitty spouted out. "Those guys in Kelby haven't a clue.

"About?"

"About Dr. Brennan's death. It was not an accident. Someone killed him."

Nelson blinked in surprise.

"Explain why you think so."

"Well first of all cattle don't stampede unless provoked."

"Good to know. Go on."

"I thought I heard a noise just before the cows started going crazy."

"Crazy?"

"Yeah, mooing like mad."

"What kind of noise?"

"A horn or an alarm. Like a fire alarm from the barn. That's why I went to see what was going on and found Dr. Brennan."

"But you didn't see anyone else there."

"No. Dr. Brennan was the only one on the premises. He is always the first guy here in the morning. Except that morning he was thirty five minutes late. He said he had a flat tire. What do you think the odds are that the only day in all my time here that he is late is the day he dies?"

Wilson nodded and looked at Nelson. Another coincidence.

"That does seem strange."

"It was!" said Smitty. "The other strange thing was that we had a nice talk that morning. Normally he is itching to get inside so it was just the usual good morning wave as he drove in but that day he stopped to talk. It was nice."

"Is there anything else?"

"There was a white car parked down the road last week for about an hour. Someone got out and walked over to the bushes on the property next door." He pointed east of the gate. "At first I thought they just stopped to take a piss but the car was there too long for that."

"You have a good eye Smitty," Nelson said as she wrote down his observation.

"Yeah but a bad leg. Can't run. Couldn't pass the physical to get on the force. Then again I wouldn't want Caswell as my boss."

"Thanks for your input," Wilson added.

"Anytime. You know where to find me," Smitty laughed.

As Wilson drove up to the house Nelson looked over at the bushes Smitty had pointed to. The field of the farm and the bushes of the adjacent property were separated by a six foot high wooden fence. It was too high for a cow to climb over but not too high for a human being to scale. When they parked their vehicle in the parking spots behind the house it was completely hidden from view by anyone driving down the country road.

A Swedish looking man was waiting at the back door for them. He introduced himself as Ivar Ericson. He was one of the three lab technicians. Aaron Goldstein and Alex Chung the other two were in the lab that he directed them to. The other two staff members were Dr. Gil Ackermann and Dr. Kathleen Shearer. When the doctors saw the detectives they instructed everyone to adjourn to the lunch room presumably because there was more room there but also perhaps to keep them away from the lab work. Wilson started the meeting.

"I am Detective Wilson and this is Detective Nelson. We are from the Chicago PD."

There were a couple of murmured *good mornings* and perplexed faces.

"We are investigating the death of Dr. Brennan. You may not be aware but two days ago Tom Murphy died also." More confused faces.

"And we think that they are related. Did anyone here know Mr. Murphy before the day this picture was taken?" Wilson held up the ribbon cutting picture. Everyone shook their heads negatively.

Alex Chung asked. "How did Mr. Murphy die?"

"A brain eating amoeba."

Muffled shock.

"The reason we are here is that if these were not accidents then there may be another accident tomorrow. So far two people died two days apart and they were in the front row. The fact that you are all in the back row and did not know Mr. Murphy suggests that you may not be a target."

Sighs of relief.

"But we are suggesting, to be on the safe side, that you do not come to work tomorrow."

The doctor's nodded in agreement.

"Detective Nelson and I are going to look around the barn now. If anyone has more questions you can catch us out there."

Heads nodded but no one said a word.

The big, rusty red, barn where the cattle were kept was directly behind the parking lot and the right hand side of the barn was not much more than a hundred yards from the tall wooden fence that separated the properties.

They unlatched the front door and went inside walking past the paddock where the cows were forced to remain since the accident. There was straw and hay on the ground but no footprints. When they looked out the back of the barn the gate from the chute to the pasture was still wide open. It was about twenty-five yards to the second gate.

"Let's take a look at the path from the barn to the fence and the neighbour's bush," suggested Nelson. They went back out the front barn door that they first entered and turned towards the fence line. There was a shorter fence leading from the front of the barn to the fence along the side of the property. It was just three horizontal boards high but enough to be used as a screen, for someone bent over, to hide their movement. When they reached the boundary fence they saw marks on the wood railing indicating someone had climbed over it recently and footprints in the ground going both directions. Someone had been here but it would be almost impossible to confirm who, although the prints were fresh so the *when* was recently. Nevertheless it was concerning to the detectives that they found it so easily. Nelson took pictures of the prints to take back to the Techs for identification. The word *accident* was now out of the equation. Someone had been here and it was probably the same someone who instigated the stampede. This was murder.

CHAPTER 8

THE DRIVE BACK to Chicago was sombre. Wilson and Nelson were going through all the information they had acquired and mulling it over in their heads. It was reasonable to assert the probability that someone else in the ribbon cutting picture might be the next target of an accident and possibly as early as tomorrow. The problem was proving it. The other question was the motive. It was plausible that somewhere in the picture was a disguised motive. If they could determine a hidden connection between Murphy and Dr. Brennan then they could uncover a motive and that might help them to surmise who the next victim could be.

Wilson said, "The spot where those footprints were at the fence line leave a clear view of the front gate and the parking lot behind the house. Smitty would not be able to see if someone was watching him from there."

"Watching?"

"Watching and waiting. Perhaps Smitty went to the washroom and gave them a moment to get over the fence. At six in the morning the light would not have been bright enough for him to see someone along that fence."

"The perp could have flattened the doctor's tire to give them more time to get to the barn and hide," said Nelson.

"And they could have parked their car further down the road so Smitty could not see it."

"Another reason they needed to slow down the doctor. They would have needed the extra time to walk through the bush, climb the fence and get to the barn and hide."

"After the stampede they could have snuck back to the fence and waited for Smitty to pass by the house. He's a slow walker so they would have about ten to fifteen seconds to climb the fence before he came into the parking lot."

"Even then his focus would have been on the cows. He said they were mooing crazily."

"That would leave the killer with a nice distraction for his getaway."

"I wonder how many people could pull off a stampede murder."

"Someone with farming and livestock experience."

"That might include half the population of Kelby."

"So we are looking for the proverbial needle in a haystack."

"Whoever it is must have intimate knowledge of the people in the picture. They know details that they are using as a cover to make the murders look like accidents."

"That makes it all the more difficult to figure them out."

"I just had a scary thought. What if the next target isn't in the picture?"

"Explain," said Wilson.

"What if someone like a spouse is the next target?"

"Well it would confirm that the accidents are not accidents but open up another line of possible targets.

"I'll call Dixon and have he and Anthony track down all the spouses attached to our picture."

"Good. We also need more information on Murphy. Like how did the killer get him to snort bad water?"

"Yes. If it is murder how do we prove he did it?"

"Let's go have a talk to the M.E. about that. Fred isn't in yet but the C.T. on the day shift should be able to help us out."

"Even if the killer is on a two day schedule we still don't know if there is an hour of the day he will strike."

"The first two, whether by accident or design, were in the morning."

"That means we might have less time than I was thinking we did."

They arrived back at the morgue and found C.T. Cindy Matheson at Fred's desk writing up a report. Fred had filled her in on the two deaths.

"How can we prove that Murphy's death was murder?"

"Wow. That is a tough one," Cindy said. "Once the tap water was inserted into his nasal passage his death was inevitable so why did he use it."

"So if he was out of the sea water he should have used distilled water," Nelson asked.

"Yes. Did you check Murphy's sea water bottles or distilled water bottles to see if they were filled with tap water?"

"Not yet."

"That would be a good start to proving he didn't do it to himself. We know the neti pot had tap water in it and it had to have come from somewhere. If this was a murder I doubt he filled it up himself straight from the tap."

"Thanks Matheson."

Following up on Cindy's suggestion, Wilson and Nelson drove to Tom Murphy's place and looked for any of the water bottles that he may have used. There were no video monitors in the hallways that would show the detectives who had entered Murphy's apartment prior to his death but they did find an empty water bottle in the recycling bin. It had a 'distilled water' label and some residual water inside. They sealed it and dropped it off at the morgue for Fred to test it against the water found in the neti pot.

When they entered the bullpen Detective Anthony was waiting for them with the additional information that Dixon had dug up about spouses of the people in the picture. Wilson brought him up to speed on the visit to the farm.

Anthony was eager to add to the investigation, "Okay so here is what we have on the spouses. The governor is home now and our mayor is out of town for a family function so we are covered on them. Unless the killer plans on waiting for them to come back."

"At this point we can't be sure what the agenda is so we have no idea if they are safe until we catch him."

"Or her," added Nelson.

"Okay or her." Wilson shrugged.

Anthony continued, "Continuing with the front row, the mayor of Kelby is married. Dr. Brennan was not. Deborah Webster, the president of the Chamber of Commerce is single, very single if you get my drift. Tom Murphy was not attached. Melissa Green is married."

"Okay that covers our first row. We'll talk to the mayor and Green again."

Anthony said, "The back row goes as follows. Goldstein is married but his wife is still in New York running her own business." He shook his head and smiled. "Chung is engaged to be married. His fiancé is in her last year at the University of Colorado. The rest of the staff members are divorced. Police Chief Caswell is married and so is Taylor, the insurance agent but the mayor's executive assistant is not married."

"Okay. I think we can assume for now that out of town people are safe. Everything we know so far indicates that the killer is local to Kelby. Anthony you call Green and Taylor back and give them the update."

"I'll call Caswell and then you can call the mayor," Wilson said to Nelson.

She nodded while Wilson redialed Caswell's number.

"Police Chief Caswell," he answered the phone.

"Chief, this is Detective Wilson."

"Well I thought we were all finished with our business detective," his tone was civil but cool.

"I was hoping so too sir but we may have uncovered something that affects the investigation."

"I wasn't aware that it was an official investigation. I thought you said it was just an inquiry."

"Well it was until we found evidence of a possible intruder at the research lab."

"So someone trespassed. That doesn't make them a murderer."

"I realize that sir but we don't want to leave anything to chance and that is the reason for my call. We forgot to consider that some of the people in the picture have spouses."

"So now you think your mystery murderer might be out to kill people that are not in the picture?"

"We don't want to rule anything out just yet sir." Wilson could imagine that Caswell was rolling his eyes.

"Fine detective. I will tell my wife to stay home tomorrow."

"Thank you sir."

Click.

"That went well," smirked Nelson.

"Your turn," he replied.

Nelson called to speak with Mayor Gregory.

"Hello Detective Nelson. What can I do for you?" the voice came over the speaker phone.

"I am sorry to bother you again Mr. Mayor but after some reflection we have considered that perhaps the spouses of the people in the picture might also be at risk."

"I see."

"We don't mean to alarm you."

"No I understand and I appreciate your concerns."

"Does your wife work?"

"She doesn't have a vocation but she does volunteer work in the community."

"Well perhaps she could stay home tomorrow."

"I will make sure she does. Thank you for the call."

"You're welcome sir. We will keep you informed of our progress."

"Good luck detective. I will say a prayer for your success."

"Thank you sir."

Click

"Well that sounds like you have a new friend," said Wilson.

Nelson glared at him.

CHAPTER 9

ANTHONY FINISHED HIS calls and advised Wilson about his conversations with Green and Taylor.

"Green has decided that a trip out of town is warranted. She and her husband are leaving tonight for Dayton, Ohio. Her in laws live there and they will stay with them until they here from us."

"Good," said Wilson. "One less thing to worry about."

"Now Taylor is a different kettle of fish. He seems oblivious to any danger. He said the odds that he is a target are slim as he came into the picture at the very last. Everyone else was involved earlier in the project."

"Lucky him then. Okay that is all the additional potential accidents covered."

"So where do we go now?" asked Anthony.

"That is a good question. We need more information on the connection between Murphy and Dr. Brennan. Go see Dixon and have him check phone records for those two going back all the way to the date of the picture and see if there were any numbers the same."

"Okay I am on it," said Anthony.

Wilson was in deep thought but then noticed Nelson staring at him.

"You and I need to go see if Fred had a chance to look at that water bottle," he said as he took off walking out the door.

Fred had been as excited about seeing the water bottle on his desk as the two detectives now standing in front of him were to hear his results.

"Well I have good news and semi bad news."

Wilson frowned at him and Fred pretended not to notice.

"The good news is that water in the bottle is the same as the neti pot water. So even though the bottle you found has a label 'distilled water' the water inside was switched. The semi bad news is that the Techs found no finger prints on the bottle."

"Semi bad," Nelson pondered.

"He's messing with us," said Wilson. "If there were no prints it means that the killer wiped it down after switching the water otherwise there would have been all the prints of everyone who had handled it from the stock boy to the cashier. But why weren't there any of Murphy's prints on the bottle? He would have had to pick it up to put it into the neti pot."

"Ah, I leave that conundrum to you Mr. Holmes," said Fred teasingly. "But I have more work for you. I looked at the flotsam in the water and it was the same as the neti pot, but!" He paused for effect.

Nelson urged, "But what?"

"I tested it against the tap water here and it wasn't the same as the neti pot sample so I was wondering if it was really tap water from Murphy's taps or did someone bring their own water."

"So you want a sample of Murphy's tap water to test."

"Yes please," he said as he held up a plastic container.

"Okay. Right now we need anything that will give us some insight to our victims. We don't have much time to find a lead."

Wilson turned to Nelson. "Pick up the water sample and I will meet you back in the bullpen. I have a couple of calls to make."

She nodded and took the container from Fred and called Officer Campbell to come and pick her up.

Wilson headed back to the bull pen to make calls from the landline. He wanted to keep his cell phone free in case anyone from Kelby called.

His first call was to his new mentor and his late father's best friend, Professor Jim Maltby.

"Hello?"

"Hi Jim, Ryan here."

"Good evening Ryan. It sounds like you have something on your mind."

"Why do say that?"

"Your voice sounds strained, tense like you are under pressure."

"Good call. We are investigating a murder and we might only have until tomorrow to prevent another one."

"Yes I'd say that was pressure."

"I need to run something by you. Two people in a ceremonial ribbon cutting picture from two years ago died in strange accidents. They were both in the front row." Wilson described the two deaths to him. "There are five more people in the front row." Wilson went through the people in the front row for Jim. "We haven't found any reason behind the deaths and the only link is the picture. We are not as concerned about the people that are out of town."

"And you think a person in the front row is next on the list."

"Yes that is our focus but we have talked to everyone including the eight in the back row."

"Who is in the back row?"

Wilson gave said the names and Jim wrote them down so he had an idea of what the picture looked like.

"Okay. You have eliminated the Governor and our Mayor because they are far enough away."

"Yes."

"Well your killer is very smart but not egocentric."

"Why do you say that?"

"The first death was not the man in the middle. He isn't necessarily killing them in a specific pattern. Also he is not letting his anger control him otherwise he might have made a few forensic mistakes and would be easier to catch."

"Yes, I see what you mean."

"It appears he could be choosing them by opportunity incorporated into a design. That will make it very difficult to determine who is next on his list."

"And by having Green go out of town I may have upset his apple cart so to speak."

"Perhaps. But that would presume that Green is on the list. If she isn't then nothing has changed for him."

"Great."

"What you have done by warning everyone may have more influence on who is his next victim. He may not be able to get at the intended next target if they don't leave their house tomorrow. If he has specific accidents planned he may need his prey to be somewhere other than at home."

"That makes sense."

"That is unless he wants someone to be at home."

"Shit."

Jim understood Ryan's frustration. "You can't cover all the bases unless you know who the actual targets might be."

"Exactly but how to I find that out."

"Well you already have some of that information. You know it won't be out of town people. More importantly you can eliminate some people or at least put them at the bottom of the list."

"Really, who?"

"Well, it is likely that the accidents will be aimed at the core of the issue."

"He's targeting the people he is most angry at."

"Precisely. We can deduce how many of the people in the picture fit the parameters."

"Those who live in Kelby for starters," said Ryan.

"Yes. They go to the top of the list and out of town people go to the bottom."

"Okay."

"The picture tells a story. Take the people at the top of the list and find out why they are in the picture. Eliminate those at the bottom of the list who have no connection to the original victims. Whoever is strongly connected to your first two victims will be a possible target. I doubt he is going randomly after everyone on the list. He seems to have a method no matter how erratic it may appear."

"Thanks Jim."

"I hope it helps. Coffee when you are done?"

"It's on me next time."

"Good luck."

Click.

His next call was to Jennifer Lewis his girlfriend. Her job as a photographer gave her some independence that had allowed them to develop a good relationship.

Again he used the landline.

"Hello," she answered.

"Hi Jen. It's me."

"Oh Hi. That's strange. The call display said unknown number?"

"I am calling you from the bullpen."

"So I guess that means you are working tonight."

"Very much so. That's why I called from the bullpen, I need my cell phone free just in case."

"Oh. This sounds serious."

"Yes. We have a short window to see if we can stop another murder."

"Oh my. Okay give me a call me when you get a chance."

"Will do. Goodnight."

"Good luck. Night."

Click.

Wilson's cell phoned pinged to tell him he had a text message. It was from Fred.

'Looking at water'

Nelson must have returned with the tap water sample from Murphy's place. Fred was referring to looking at the water through the new electron microscope they installed in the basement last year. Wilson ran down the stairs to get to the parking lot, too anxious to wait for the elevator.

Ten minutes later he joined Nelson in Fred's Office.

"What have you got?" Wilson said eagerly when he reached Fred's office.

Nelson smiled indicating it was good news. Fred had already copied the images and loaded them onto his computer.

"Okay this is an image of our tap water here. See the amoeba with the little feet. Those are called false feet because they are merely the cell wall extended so it can move."

Wilson and Nelson nodded but weren't sure what they were looking at.

"Okay now this is the water sample from the neti pot. Notice that this amoeba has a pair of tails to make them move. That is called a flagellate state. It's what happens when this amoeba comes in contact with distilled water. These are the brain eating amoeba."

Again Wilson and Nelson nodded.

"Okay now look at the sample from Murphy's tap. It is virtually the same as our tap water."

Wilson and Nelson understood immediately.

"The killer brought his own tainted water to Murphy's apartment."

"If you can find the source of that water you might find where they are from."

"Well that is promising but it is unlikely that we can find the source by the end of tomorrow," Nelson added.

"Well it doesn't live in oceans or salt water bodies. It is generally found in warm water like ponds or lakes or even a stagnant untreated swimming pool."

"Good to know."

"I'll tag all the samples in case you find something to compare it to."

"Thanks Fred."

With an obscure piece of the puzzle in their possession Wilson and Nelson left and went back to the bullpen where Wilson pulled out the *Big Board*.

"Okay," he said, "we need to make a list of most likely to most unlikely."

Nelson grabbed a black marker to write with.

Wilson continued, "There are fifteen people; anyone with a spouse will get an asterisk."

"Okay," Nelson replied and wrote the numbers one to fifteen down the left column.

"The first two are Murphy and Brennan," said Wilson.

Nelson noticed that he had dropped the use of doctor from the victim's name.

"The bottom two will be the Governor and our Mayor. With asterisks."

"The next on the list is Mayor Gregory and asterisk"

Nelson wrote the name on the board with the asterisk after the name.

"I think the front row is still a key so Webster is next."

Nelson added the name and then asked, "Green next?"

"Actually no for two reasons. She is out of town now and I think Kelby residents should be higher on the list. Next is Olson because she is connected to the Mayor and then Chief Caswell."

"That takes care of all the Kelby residents."

"Yes it does."

"Now Green?"

"Yes and then Taylor."

"That just leaves the lab staff," she said as she wrote their names randomly and then stepped back to view the list with Wilson.

1 — Tom Murphy

2 — Dr. Emmet Brennan

3 — Mayor Gregory *
4 — Deborah Webster
5 — Caryn Olson
6 — Chief Caswell *
7 — Melissa Green *
8 — Ernie Taylor *
9 — Kathleen Shearer
10 — Alex Chung *
11 — Ivar Ericson
12 — Aaron Goldstein *
13 — Gil Ackermann
14 — Mayor of Chicago *
15 — Governor of Illinois *

They were standing looking at the list when Anthony came back.

"What is that?" he asked.

"That is our potential list of victims in order of priority."

"Whoa."

Wilson looked at Anthony, "What did you find?"

"There are no phone numbers the same between the two of them going back a year."

"Well it was a long shot."

"Brennan had called the bank a few times but not Murphy's cell."

"So it was just business."

"Seems so."

"Okay check the calls for the Mayor and Webster and Olson."

Wilson picked up his cell and called Chief Caswell.

"Good evening detective," Caswell's voice still had that tone in intolerance. "Good news I hope."

"Sorry Chief, I don't have that. However we have considered everything we know and we think that the Mayor or Deborah Webster is the next target."

"Really."

"Yes sir. I was wondering if you would consider it prudent to post a patrolman to watch them tonight." Wilson used his most contrite voice he could muster so as not to rile Caswell.

"Now."

"Yes sir. We don't know if the killer considers one minute after midnight as tomorrow but the first two accidents happened in the morning."

"I see." It sounded as though he was taking this a little more seriously now. "Well we don't want anything happening to the Mayor or our Chamber of Commerce lady, do we?"

"Not to anyone sir."

"Yes agreed. I will post a patrol car outside their house tonight and have an officer watch them all day tomorrow."

"Thank you sir."

"Good night detective."

Click

As much as Wilson deplored kissing ass, if it saved a life tomorrow, it was worth it. The three of them sat in silence looking at the board. The Mayor and Webster appeared to be the next most important people on the list. Had they guessed right or did the killer have an agenda that they weren't able to see? Those were the type of questions that will take away a needed night's sleep.

CHAPTER 10

AT SEVEN A.M. Wilson was back in the bullpen with coffee for everyone. None of them had slept much anticipating a call they hoped they would not get. Thirty minutes later he called Deborah Webster.

"Good Morning Detective Wilson," she said.

"Good Morning. Are you working from home today?"

"Yes I am. I see I have a body guard also. You must have been very persuasive with the Chief. Thank you."

"We want to cover all the bases even if this is a false alarm."

"But you think it is real. That there is someone out there and they are going to kill again today."

"Yes I do believe that."

His matter of fact tone was not as reassuring as she had hoped to hear.

"If you leave the house even with your body guard please be careful and try not to do things the way you would normally do them."

"How do you mean."

"If you walk to work normally have the officer drove you instead. Don't have your morning coffee when and where you normally do. Don't go out for lunch at your normal time. Switch everything up."

"Oh I see now. Thank you for the advice."

"And call me if anything unusual happens."

"I shall. Bye for now."

"Good bye."

Now it was Nelson's turn to call the Mayor.

"Hello."

"Good Morning Mr. Mayor."

"Ah Detective Nelson. Do I have you to thank for my body guard?"

"We didn't want to take any chances. Detective Wilson convinced your Chief it would be a good idea."

"Well thank Detective Wilson for me. Perhaps he should consider politics; it is difficult to get the Chief do something that isn't his idea in the first place."

"Yes we noticed that."

"So no news then."

"No sir not yet but we have some leads that we are working on," she was trying to be positive.

"Well that is encouraging."

"We want you to be careful today and as much as possible don't follow your normal daily routine."

"Oh. You don't want me to be predictable."

"Exactly sir. If you change your normal pattern it might reduce the chances of a planned accident."

"I see. Well I will have my police escort with me so that should disrupt my normal course of duties although the council meeting this morning is a planned weekly event."

"So far the accidents have been in the morning and when the person was alone."

"Well I will not be alone at all this morning. My wife is here now and the patrolman will accompany me when I leave the house."

"Good. And call me if you think anything isn't right."

"I will. Thank you."

"Good Bye."

Click

A few minutes later Anthony came back from checking phone logs with Dixon.

"We checked all three and no phone numbers in common for anyone."

"Well it was worth a try," Wilson said. "Go find Murphy's girlfriend and let's see what she can add for us."

An hour later the Mayor was inside the council chambers and perhaps safe for now. No news about Webster yet but no news is good news.

Detective Anthony came back to the bullpen just before noon with a confused look on his face. He stopped at Wilson's desk and pulled out his note book.

"Um. I think we have a problem."

Wilson looked up at him from the desk, "What is that?"

Nelson stopped what she was doing and turned to pay attention.

"Well I spoke to the super at Murphy's place and he described the girlfriend as a blonde about five three and pretty with a first name of Susan. No last name that he could remember. She only came by on weekends."

Wilson was getting a bad feeling already.

"So I went the bank to see if anyone there remembered her and came up blank. They remember she came in and opened an account but they never saw her in the bank again. The video tapes are saved for thirty days. They don't know exactly what day she came in but it was over a month ago so her image and date stamp time are gone. They mentioned that Murphy had been a different man since he met her. Before he met her he was an introvert but after he was outwardly happy."

"Okay you and Nelson go through his apartment with fine toothed comb. She must have left something there that will help us find her."

A thought was forming in the back of Wilson's brain that wasn't helping him concentrate. He turned to the Big Board and noticed the bullpen clock read half past noon. Morning was over and no accidents reported. It was going to be a long day.

At two fifteen Nelson and Anthony came back into the bull pen empty handed.

Anthony started, "His apartment was void of anything that indicated a woman had been there except for a couple of blonde hairs we found in the bedroom. We dropped them off to Garcia and the Techs at the Lab. I know the super said she was only there on weekends but there should have been more evidence of a woman spending the night. I make more mess in one hour than she did in two days."

"But the problem is we don't know how much cleaning up Murphy did during the week." Nelson said.

Wilson was staring at them saying nothing verbally but the thought that was bothering him before was back and they saw it on his face.

"What is it?" Nelson asked.

"Nelson if your boyfriend had just died from a strange illness wouldn't you want to know that you were not infected by the same disease?" He could see the wheels turning in their heads and continued. "She and the super found him on Monday. Officer Campbell said the super wanted to know if it was contagious but she hasn't come forward to ask questions about her boyfriend's death. If she can't be found then she is either dead or she does not want to be found."

"Oh no," said Nelson.

"Oh yes," replied Wilson. "I'll call Caswell right now."

"This is Chief Caswell."

Wilson shook his head at the greeting. Caswell knew it was Wilson calling but he continued the charade.

"Chief we have some new information that we thought we should pass on to you."

Nelson considered what the Mayor had said about Wilson and politics and she smiled.

His conversation with Caswell was dramatically diplomatic.

"I am listening."

"The girlfriend of the first victim Tom Murphy is missing. It is possible that she is the killer."

"Possible or likely?"

"I would lean towards likely."

"Because you are sure she isn't another victim and that makes her disappearance suspicious."

"Yes sir."

"Well you know the statics on female serial killers doesn't back up your hunch."

"Yes sir I understand what you mean. But this seems to be in the upper percentile due to the intelligence of the accidents."

"You do realize that you just used the word intelligence in a death of a man stupid enough to be run down in a stampede."

"Yes sir. I just wanted to say that a woman might be involved because we have been assuming it was a man up to now."

"Anything else?"

"She is blonde about five three and might be named Susan."

"That narrows it down to a few hundred people in Kelby."

"Sorry but that is all we have at this time."

"Well call me when you have something a little more concrete."

"Yes sir."

Click

Wilson wondered if in some way Chief Caswell and Captain Stone were related. They both have an edge that defies the logic of their popularity. How they achieved their success seem to mystify Wilson because he believed that lobbying and bull shitting were negative attributes and not positive virtues.

CHAPTER 11

AT SIX O'CLOCK Anthony came back to the bullpen with pizza. Wilson wasn't hungry yet, he was leaning back in his chair thinking. Mayor Gregory and Deborah Webster were home and safe still guarded by a patrolman and the rest of the town of Kelby was oblivious to the killer amongst them. The Mayor and Chief Caswell had decided that mass panic was not needed so only those in the picture were advised of the connection to the first two deaths.

The feeling of helplessness was grating on Wilson. Had they thwarted the killer's next attempt? Was Wilson's assumption of a two day turnaround incorrect? So many questions were going through his head. Was there even going to be another death or had the killer had their fill. Maybe they had only pushed the killer to wait in the wings but how much time had they bought by doing so. The killer had waited over two years to start the accidents. Why? What was the trigger that started this spree? They were missing key pieces to the difficult puzzle. It couldn't be a disgruntled employee because no one was fired and no one from Kelby was on the short list of research scientists for the lab.

A two year delay suggested that the killer was otherwise engaged. Did that mean they were in jail? Murphy met his new girlfriend just over a month ago. How many women were released from prison at that time? There were probably too many to count. They munched on the pizza and batted ideas back and forth. Considering the lack of information available any idea might have some validity.

"What if she is a paid assassin from another big research company trying to slow them down?" asked Anthony.

"But Murphy wasn't a part of the lab. If they wanted to slow them down they could just torch the lab at night."

"Yeah. I suppose so."

"If the killer is a she, it must be a very strong motive," said Nelson. "Like Caswell said there are few women serial killer and this one is focused on the lab."

"Okay so what is that these people did to piss her off?"

"Maybe the lab was supposed to be built in her town and she was going to get the contract to build it like Melissa did. Then it got pulled out for some reason and she lost out and went off the deep end."

"That has some merit."

Wilson said to Nelson, "Call the Mayor and ask how they got the lab."

Nelson called the Mayor's number.

"Good evening Detective Nelson. Do you have good news?"

"No sir not yet. But I need some information."

"Anything I can do to help you just ask,"

"How did Kelby get the research lab?"

"Well it was something of a stroke of luck. Dr. Brennan had been looking for a while at places to build and one day he came across our website with the invitation to open your business in Kelby. When he inquired about support from the Governor he got a green light to pursue financial support and then we found a property for the site and the rest as they say is history."

"So there wasn't another city bidding for the lab."

"Not that I am aware of. It certainly wasn't a negotiation point in the process."

"Okay thanks."

"Is that all?"

"Yes sir, for now."

"Okay. Goodnight Detective."

Click

It was past eight and time was running out; Wilson wondered if he had over reacted. There was definitely a killer but would they strike again. Logic says yes, but in what time frame. In less than four hours he may be forced to drop the case. A mystery woman may be the killer and they can't even find her. If she isn't finished then the rest of the people on the list were still in danger. Wilson hated the feeling of being helpless. He made a call with his cell phone.

"Hi," she said cheerfully.

"Hi back."

"Is everything okay?"

"I just needed to hear your voice."

"The case not going well."

"Not really. It may over soon. We only have until midnight to find the killer and we aren't even close to a solid lead."

"Take a deep breath and clear your mind. Pretend you are on the golf course and relax it will help you concentrate."

He smiled, "You always see a way to calm me down."

"You allow me to reach you."

"Well, not always."

She laughed, "No not always."

"Thanks I needed a pick me up."

"Oh that was not a real pick me up. That is just to remind you where you can go to get a real pick me up," she giggled.

"Thanks. I hope to take you up on that tomorrow."

"Anytime sailor."

"Bye."

"Bye."

It was nine p.m.

*   *   *

Chief Caswell had waited long enough; it was time to call it a day. The Kelby people that the Chicago detective had anticipated were potential targets of accidents were all home and safe and the Mayor and Deborah Webster were on police patrol watch until midnight. Caryn Olson the Mayor's assistant was also home and safe. He laughed. Everyone in City Hall knew that the name assistant was a spurious name for lover. Gregory wasn't fooling anyone and probably not even his own wife. If he was going to have an accident Caswell thought, it would be more likely that his wife would cause it. The notion that a killer is stalking some of the residents of Kelby was far-fetched to him. This was his town and no big city detective was going to come in here and chase a ghost. He said goodnight to the nightshift desk sergeant and headed out for a coffee before making the trek home. Jill's Coffee Bar not only served a very good cup of coffee but it was also free. He pulled his cruiser into the half full parking lot and then walked inside to pick up his coffee. Jill had started getting his coffee ready when she saw him park his vehicle. He smiled at her as he walked to the counter. If he was going to have an affair, Jill would be his choice. She had a lustrous body and a great smile and when she said "Hi Chief" her voice was melodic and soothing. Yep, she would be his first choice. He said hi and grabbed his coffee off the counter, turned around and slammed right into a woman with her head down going through her purse. His coffee flew out of his hands barely missing the girl and then exploding when it hit the floor.

"Oh my god I am so sorry," she apologized.

The pretty brunette diffused Caswell's ire with her remorseful look.

"That's okay it's only coffee," he said.

"Please let me get you another one," she said.

Jill spoke up, "No need it was just an accident." She made him another. The brunette had moved around the Chief and put her purse on the counter.

"I am so glad it didn't go all over your nice uniform."

"Nope not a drop," said the Chief as he looked down at his pant legs.

"I am so relieved," she said smiling. "I would have paid for the dry cleaning."

"No problem ma'am."

Her purse fell of the counter and spilled open on the floor.

"Oops," she said.

This one is a real klutz the Chief thought to himself as he bent over to pick up some of the items that had rolled to his feet.

When he handed them to her she handed him his new coffee.

"Thanks," he said.

She smiled and nodded as he walked away.

The Chief checked the time; nine twenty. The drive home from Jill's Coffee Bar was only twenty minutes but it gave him ample time to think and enjoy his cup of coffee. He sipped on his coffee as he drove and considered that he must be tired tonight or maybe it was just all the phone calls with that detective, feeling like this he would be glad to hit the hay when he arrived home. He sipped more coffee hoping to recharge his batteries but it wasn't helping. He turned down the county road to his house as his chest started burning. He was sure it wasn't heartburn, and it was getting hard to breathe. He tried to focus his brain, must get home. His body tightened and he stepped on the gas. His vision was getting blurry and his cruiser left the dirt road but before he could regain control of the vehicle it slammed into a tree and without his seat belt on the Chief became a projectile, barely stopped by the windshield.

CHAPTER 12

NO ONE HAD left the bullpen and yet the quiet was disturbing. There was barely an hour left in the day. Wilson tried to accept that the deadline that he had originally anticipated was going to pass without incident. On one hand it would mean that no accident happened to anyone, but on the other hand it would mean that Captain Stone would stop this investigation. The best case scenario would be if there was an accident attempt but it was stopped by the patrolman watching the Mayor or Webster; and even better if the killer was caught outright. That would give Wilson the peace of mind that his presumption had saved a life. The big problem for Wilson was that he believed the killer was too smart to make an attempt in full view or in proximity of a policeman watching. It seemed to Wilson that the clock ticked louder as each minute went by, time drawing closer to midnight, and then his cell phone rang. He jumped and his hand was actually shaking when he picked up the phone. Nelson and Anthony watched in surprise.

"Wilson here."

"Detective Wilson, this is Assistant Police Chief Joe Driscoll calling from Kelby."

His heart sank. He knew that the only reason for the phone call was that someone had been in a planned accident. He had hoped for a better outcome but that was not to be. What he wasn't expecting was who had been involved.

"Sir, there has been an accident." Unlike his boss Driscoll was showing Wilson respect. "I am afraid it was Chief Caswell."

"What?" Wilson was as floored by the news as was Nelson and Anthony. A policeman, especially Chief Caswell was the last person Wilson anticipated to be a target.

"Yes sir. It was a car accident on his way home. He didn't survive."

"Are you in charge now?"

"Yes sir. On a temporary emergency basis. I would appreciate any help you can give me. I believed your theory even if the Chief didn't."

"We are on our way. Don't let anyone near the body until we get there, not even the coroner."

"Yes sir. Thank you."

"Thank you for calling Chief. We will be there soon."

"Grab an evidence kit and met us out front." Wilson said to Detective Anthony.

Nelson retrieved a couple of colas from the vending machine and followed Wilson downstairs to the parking lot. The trip to Kelby took almost an hour but they didn't feel the need to talk. Wilson followed Driscoll's direction to the county road where several vehicles with flashing lights were parked at the scene of the accident.

New Police Chief Driscoll greeted them as they got out of the SUV. He had trimmed dark hair and a friendly face and unlike the slightly out of shape Chief Caswell, Driscoll looked like he just walked off a college football team. He walked them to the crashed cruiser.

The cruiser had struck a tree head on and the Chief was thrown through the windshield most likely killing him instantly.

"He didn't call in after he should have been home. When I called his cell there was no answer. A patrol car drove out to the house to check and found his car here. I would say that it looks like he fell asleep at the wheel but as this is Chief Caswell I suspect that is not the case."

"What makes you so sure Chief?" asked Anthony.

"He picks up a coffee each day on the way home no matter what time of day it is."

Wilson looked inside the vehicle for the coffee cup and saw it on the floor of the passenger side.

"Bag that cup." Anthony retrieved it and sealed it in an evidence bag.

Wilson asked Driscoll, "Where does he pick up his coffee?"

"From Jill's, it's a coffee shop in town."

Wilson looked around and then said, "We need to go there now."

"Okay follow me," said Chief Driscoll.

Fifteen minutes later they pulled into the coffee shop parking lot and went inside.

Jill the owner, was cleaning up getting ready to close down for the night. One couple was still nursing their coffees making eyes at each other. Jill paused her wiping down a table when she saw Driscoll walk in with the detectives. She had seen enough cops to recognize that the plain clothed people with Driscoll were also police. When Driscoll stopped halfway down the counter she left her cleaning rag on the table and walked towards them. Something wasn't kosher.

"Hi Jill. These are Detectives Wilson, Nelson and Anthony from Chicago."

She just nodded waiting for more information.

"There has been an accident. Chief Caswell is dead."

She put her hand over her mouth and sat down on a chair. Despite his gruff exterior Jill never experienced anything but the nice side of Chief Caswell.

"These detectives have some questions for you," said Driscoll.

"He was just here getting his coffee," she said.

"What time was that," said Detective Anthony with his note pad out.

"Um, about a quarter past nine."

"Is that a normal time for him to come in."

"No, he was all over the board time wise but he always came by before he went home."

"Always?" Added Wilson.

"He might miss once in a while but he was my most regular customer. Well non-customer really because I never made him pay for his coffee."

"Did anything happen out of the ordinary tonight when he came in for his coffee?"

"Not really I saw him pull up and I had it ready for him when he came in. He didn't usually stay and chat much."

"And that was it. He left right away."

"Oh no. I forgot. He bumped into someone on his way out and he dropped his coffee. I had to make him another one."

Nelson asked, "Can you describe the person he bumped into?"

"It was a woman; she was very apologetic, offered to buy him another coffee. She even said she would have paid for his dry cleaning."

"Describe her physically please."

"Uh, short brown hair, pretty. Five-three."

"How sure are you about the height?"

She pointed to the colored height measuring strip beside the doors.

"Okay then what did she say?"

"I don't know I left his coffee on the counter and went to serve another customer over there." She pointed to a table against the wall.

"And then the Chief left?"

"Ah no. She dropped her purse on the floor and the Chief helped her pick up her stuff that had fallen out and then he left."

"Is there anything else you can think of?" asked Nelson.

"No that was it."

"Okay thank you Jill," Driscoll said.

When they were back at the vehicles Driscoll asked if it had helped.

"Oh yes," said Wilson. "We already knew the woman is about five-three."

Driscoll showed a surprised look.

"She had blonde hair before but that's not difficult to change," said Nelson.

"She knew he picked up a coffee every day. That fits with our idea that she is a local person. Then she bumped into the Chief. That is a classic pick pocket move. In this case she wanted to make him get a new coffee. She dropped her purse another distraction probably so she could spike his coffee."

"Spike his coffee?" queried Driscoll.

"You said the Chief wouldn't have fallen asleep so chances are the coffee cup will show us some drugs that did it to him."

"Wow. I suspected there was more to this but I had no idea it would be this complex."

"I am afraid so but killing the Chief even rattled us so don't feel bad."

"Where do we go from here?"

"Well the pattern is two days. We have forty-eight hours to find out who our mystery woman is. Tomorrow we will sit down and go over everything with you."

"Great. Thank you," Driscoll said.

CHAPTER 13

THE TEXT MESSAGE was very clear. *8 am – Stone.* Captain Stone was looking for his update and this time Lieutenant Gary Trentini was in attendance. Wilson was hoping this would be a better discussion than the last one they had but he didn't want to be disappointed so he prepared for the worst.

"Okay Wilson what the hell happened last night." Stone started.

"We thought the Mayor of Kelby or the President of the Chamber of Commerce was the next target."

"Instead it was the Chief of Police. Sounds like you were slightly off target there." He yelled across the desk.

"We tried to warn Chief Caswell but he got a little uptight when we suggested that we could help. I was surprised that he agreed to put patrol cars out for the Mayor and Ms. Webster."

"Well it makes us look bad when we can't find a killer after three murders."

"She is a very smart killer sir."

"You are sure it is a she." Stone said unenthusiastically.

"We are now sir."

"Hmm. Who do you have on it?"

"I have Nelson and Anthony and Assistant Police Chief Driscoll in Kelby." Lieutenant Trentini just listened and watched Wilson.

"How is the relationship with Driscoll?"

"Very good so far sir. He wants our help."

"Good. We don't need a political war as well. When do you expect to find this woman?"

"I am hoping that Driscoll knows Kelby well enough to help us narrow it down. We are sure she is from Kelby so we hope someone there knows her."

"And you think you have another two days before she strikes again?"

"Yes sir."

"Goddam Wilson can't you find an easy case once in a while."

"She will slip up sir."

"You better hope so. We can't afford to look like idiots to the press. Keep us posted and if you need any evidence rushed through just use my name."

"Yes sir."

Wilson left the Captain's office and headed back to the bullpen. Next on the agenda was a trip back to Kelby to brief Chief Driscoll. Nelson and Anthony were waiting for him when he came into the bullpen.

He looked at Anthony, "I need you to do some grunt work today."

"Whatever you need."

"We know she drives a white car. I will get better description for you from the security guard. I need you to find white cars with a woman owner in her thirties and the name Susan."

"Okay. That should keep me busy for a while," Anthony chuckled.

"If you find anything even close call me right away. We only have forty eight hours to find her."

"Got it."

Wilson turned to Nelson, "Let's go."

Wilson drove as fast as allowed at least by police standards. They first went to the guard house of the research lab to talk with Smitty. He smiled when they pulled up.

"Good morning Detectives."

"Morning Smitty. We need you to describe the white car you saw parked on the road last week. Be as accurate as you can."

"Well it was white, a bit dirty though. Smaller car. I couldn't see if it was a two door or four door. It had a bumper sticker on the driver's side, blue and red. No idea what it said though?"

"That helps Smitty."

"Anytime guys."

At ten a.m. they pulled into a visitor parking spot in front of the Kelby Police Department. The desk sergeant called Driscoll as soon as they walked in the door.

"Good morning detectives. He'll be right with you."

Nelson looked at Wilson. Her face conveyed surprise at the change of attitude in the last twenty four hours.

Reading her mind Wilson said, "I was thinking the same thing."

New Police Chief Joe Driscoll came down the hallway and greeted them with a firm handshake.

"I have the investigation room set up for us. Our best people will be sitting in with us. Right this way," he said as he walked down the hall to an open door.

When they were in the room Chief Driscoll closed the door and called attention.

"This is Detective-Sergeant Wilson and Detective Nelson from Chicago PD."

In the chairs were six uniformed officers. They all nodded acknowledgment.

"As you are aware we are coordinating with them on the investigation of Dr. Brennan and Chief Caswell's deaths. Detective Wilson head the investigation. Everyone here will go through me. Detective Wilson will brief us now."

"Gentleman. First let me convey my condolence for your loss. It is never a good day when we lose a brother." There were nods and confirmations from the gathering.

"Now here is what we know. We are looking for a woman about five-three with short brown hair but might have a shoulder length blonde wig."

Nelson gave him a peculiar look. They had not yet seen the hair analysis from the blonde hairs in the apartment but Wilson had decided to include it whether or not it was wig hair.

"She is a very smart and angry woman. She might be named Susan but we can't confirm that. We believe she drives a white car with a bumper sticker on the driver's side of the rear bumper. She knows the town of Kelby so she either lives here now or did live here previously and she may have moved back recently. We need to look at new arrivals in Kelby over the past three to six months and see if they lived here before."

The group was carefully writing down their notes.

"She appears to be in her thirties so if you are in your thirties you might have gone to high school with her."

A hand went up in the front row.

"Yes," said Wilson pointing at the officer.

"Some women look facially younger than their age and at five three she might pass for a younger woman."

"Good point. So don't leave out any potential lead. Follow up and be absolutely sure. And remember if you think it is her call for back up immediately. We don't know if she is armed but it would seem likely."

Wilson wrote down the target list on the board in the same order as the Big Board back in the bullpen but this time with three names crossed out.

"This list is from most likely to least likely target. She has killed three people and she may still be after more. If she is then either Mayor Gregory or Deborah Webster are most likely the next target and we have thirty seven hours left."

Another hand rose. Wilson pointed.

"What happens if she can't get to a target in that time frame?"

"We don't know. We haven't stopped her yet."

Wilson turned and taped the ribbon cutting ceremony photograph to the board. "Something about this picture set her off two years after it was taken. Any thoughts about it are welcome. It is possible, in fact very likely, that those of you who were raised here already know her. Something connects her to this picture. She is angry at these people and we need to know why. We are less than an hour away so report anything you think is relevant to Chief Driscoll. Don't dismiss it until you have confirmed it. Thank you for your time and good luck."

The six officers packed up their things and left the room.

Driscoll spoke first. "That was good. It is always good to hear a presentation from someone they can't tune out."

"They tuned out Chief Caswell?" Wilson asked.

"Most times. We will keep two officers with the Mayor and with Webster. One will be inside and the other one on the street."

"That's good. I think we should talk to Olson too."

"Yes, I think that would be a good idea. She is at the Mayor's office this morning getting caught up after all the meetings this week."

Chief Driscoll drove the detectives in the large black and white Kelby Police Department SUV. The drive was only ten minutes to City Hall from the police station.

They found Caryn Olson at her desk. She was only moderately surprised to see them thinking they were her to see the Mayor.

"You remember Detective Wilson and Detective Nelson?" said Driscoll.

"Yes of course, but the Mayor is in a meeting."

"We are here to see you Ms. Olson."

"Oh, okay."

"In light of Chief Caswell's death we were wondering if you could take some time off and visit someone out of state."

"Um. Well I guess I could. I will check to see when I can get away."

"You will need to leave today," Nelson said firmly.

"That soon."

"We can't take any more chances. You need to go as soon as possible."

"Okay."

"Where are you going to go?" asked Nelson.

"My mom lives over in Fort Wayne."

"That's good," said Wilson. "Detective Nelson will go with you to help you pack and do not call anyone to tell them you are leaving."

"No one? Really?"

"Yes really. We have no idea who the killer is and they might be masquerading as your friend. So tell no one. When you get there call Chief Driscoll, no one else."

"Yes detective." This time she replied with nervousness in her voice and Wilson realized that she finally grasped the seriousness of the situation.

"Bring Detective Nelson to the police station when you are ready to leave."

Nelson and Olson left the building while eyes watched them over top of the cubicle walls.

Wilson and Driscoll stood on the sidewalk and looked up and down the main street.

"How long have you lived here?" Wilson asked.

"Three years."

"Hopefully some of your officers who grew up here will think of something that will give us a lead."

They drove back to the police station and waited for Nelson.

"Do you really think she will kill again?" asked Driscoll

"I am afraid so. She has a well-focused anger and that may end badly."

"How so?"

"If we get in her way she may lose that focus and instead of a controlled game plan she may let out all her anger at once."

"And what happens then?"

"We call it suicide by cop."

"This is the first murder case I've experienced and I think there was only one other one in Kelby years ago so we are learning as we go."

"It's not a fun learning process and rarely satisfying. Half of the killers we've put away were just stupid. They committed an emotional act that they will regret for the rest of their lives."

"What about the other half?"

"They are either evil or sick and don't regret killing their victims after they are caught."

"Why did you choose to be a homicide detective?" Driscoll asked.

Wilson frowned. "Don't get me wrong. I do take pride in putting killers away. I have to believe that each time I do I have potentially saved the next victim on their list."

"Someone is walking around alive whose life could have been snuffed out too soon."

"Exactly."

"I am quite happy with the odd Saturday night bar fight, a domestic dispute involving too much booze and a couple of petty thefts."

"Well hopefully when this is all over that's what you will go back to."

Olson's car pulled up to the building dropping off Detective Nelson.

Wilson turned and shook hands with Driscoll.

"Keep in touch. Call me about anything that comes up no matter how small."

"I will."

CHAPTER 14

THEY GRABBED BURGERS and fries on the way back to the bullpen. There were now just thirty five hours left in the new deadline. Anthony was still hard at it, going through list after list of white cars looking for a lead, trying to find a needle in a haystack. They all stopped to eat and think. Normally finding a killer after the first forty-eight hours could take weeks or months or even years. They have less than two days to not only find the killer but prevent the next murder.

"The good news is that the two potential targets are protected. The bad news is we have no idea what she will do because they are."

"Do you think she will wait for a chance or go after one of them anyway?"

"If I knew that we could lay a trap for her. She has been very careful so far so I don't expect her to give up and go home."

"Especially if she is still intent on killing more people in the picture," said Nelson.

Wilson said, "That is the question we need the answer to." He looked at Anthony "Any luck?"

"I have gone through hundreds and there are two possible hits on my list so far," said Anthony.

"Susan Marie Hanson drives a white two door and lives just outside of Chicago. And Susan Yanamadala also drives a white two door compact and lives near Kelby."

"Okay. Nelson, check out the Hanson car for a bumper sticker. Anthony, you keep looking and I'll call Driscoll and have him check on the other car."

Anthony gave Nelson the address of the Hanson vehicle and she tore out of the bullpen. Anthony handed the address of the other car to Wilson.

"Chief Driscoll speaking."

"Wilson here Chief. I have lead I need you to check out."

"Absolutely."

"We found a woman named Susan Yanamadala who owns a white two door and she lives on county road fourteen. We need to check her car for that blue and red bumper sticker."

"I will have a patrol car go right now. It's not far. I will call you back as soon as we have confirmation."

"Thanks Chief."

Twenty minutes later Nelson called in.

"There is no bumper sticker on this car," she reported.

"Okay come on back."

By the time Nelson had returned Chief Driscoll had called in to say the same thing about his lead. Two down and no new leads from Anthony yet.

"Okay let's give Sarah Garcia a call and find out how that coffee cup analysis is coming."

"On it," replied Nelson as she called.

"Sarah Garcia."

"Hi Sarah. Detective Nelson here."

"Wow. Are you planning on becoming a psychic anytime soon?"

"No why?"

"I was just handed the file for that coffee cup Detective Anthony dropped off last night."

"Great. We are all here. I am putting you on speaker."

"Okay, whoever did this was good. This coffee was laced with GHB."

"The date rape drug," Wilson asked.

"Yes. But it is clinically used for narcolepsy and cataplexy."

Wilson asked, "We know what narcolepsy is but what's cataplexy?"

"It is a rare muscle disease that causes the muscles to lose their tone in spasms."

Nelson asked, "And the GHB knocked him out?"

"Oh it probably did more than that. The dose was double what you would see in a rape case."

"Would that be because of his size?"

"That could be a reason or maybe they didn't want to take a chance on how much or how little he would drink on the way home. The coffee was a triple-triple so it hid the added flavour of the drug."

"What did you mean when you said *probably did more than that*?"

"He might have had a heart attack before he passed out. With that level of the drug in the coffee he wasn't drugged to just fall asleep. Fred will be able to tell you more."

"Thanks Garcia."

"Sorry it was under these circumstances."

"Us too."

Click.

"Let's go see if Fred completed the autopsy before he finished work this morning."

"If not maybe Cindy can answer some questions for us," said Nelson.

"Hope so," he replied and for the first time this week he walked to the elevator and not the stairs with Nelson in tow.

Ten minutes later they reached the basement of the M.E. Building and found Cindy Matheson at a table looking at a stiff but she waved them inside.

"Come on in. This is not contagious just a drowning," she said of the corpse that looked more like someone sleeping. "I am guessing you want to see the file of Police Chief Caswell."

"All done?"

"Indeed. Fred stayed until all the reports were finished," she said as she peeled off her gloves and picked up the file folder of the work desk. "Shall I read or do you want to peruse."

"You read and we'll ask questions," Wilson answered.

"Okay then. Well technically COD was a heart attack brought on by a lethal ingestion of Sodium Oxybate. The accident would have killed him also but it was a fraction late. He was probably having breathing problems and then the heart attack hit so even if he missed the tree he was already a goner."

"We had the coffee cup liquid analyzed by Garcia and she emphasized that might have happened."

"They really made sure of the outcome. There is a chance that half that amount would have had the same result. His heart was not in the best of shape. Lots of scar tissue and plaque in his arteries. Undoubtedly he had mini attacks before, perhaps brushed them off as heartburn or angina and most likely ate an aspirin and survived."

Wilson pondered, "So the killer probably didn't know about his heart problems but she knew he took his coffee extra sweet. Thanks Cindy."

On the way back to the bullpen Nelson said, "Knowing about how he drinks his coffee adds more fuel to your idea that she is local to Kelby."

"True," he replied "But she is either walking around like a ghost or is she someone that no one knows. How can she get so close to everyone without them seeing her?"

"I am sure she will be more noticeable now."

"Except that even if she didn't think we knew about her before yesterday she has to know we know about her now and that should make her more careful."

"If she doesn't make a mistake how do we find her?"

"She has already made mistakes." Wilson paused. "We just have to find them."

"But if she quits now she might get away."

"She isn't finished but I think we might have changed her pattern. The Chief was in the back row. She may have gone after him because we covered the Mayor and Webster."

"So do you think she will go after the front row again?"

"Probably not while the Chief is covering them. She seems to be picking them off when they are alone."

They arrived back at the bullpen in time to get an update from Anthony on white cars.

"I found three more," Anthony said as he waved the paper. "These are all in Chicago."

"Okay you take one, give one to Detective Nelson and the other one to Officer Campbell. That way we can check all three at the same time."

"I will call Chief Driscoll and see how their investigation is going."

A minute later he was on his own. He reached for his cell phone to call Chief Driscoll when he noticed that he had an email from the FBI. It was from Special Agent in Charge Mark Giordano. That could only be about David Bay, the murderer in the case that he solved with the help of the FBI. David Bay was sent to the Durning Institute and Hospital, specializing in treatment for the mentally unwell. He was undergoing observation and treatment for Dissociative Identity Disorder while in confinement for two murders. Wilson opened the email to see what the news was. Giordano was emailing Wilson to inform him that Bay was being released from the hospital after six months of treatment. He was being transferred to the Statesville Correction Center to serve out the rest of his sentence. This was good news for the FBI who had to wait until Bay passed the psychiatric evaluation before they could move forward on the industrial espionage charges against two drug companies that had bought the documents that Bay had stolen. Giordano thanked him again.

Wilson forwarded the email to Nelson and picked up his cell phone.

"Chief Driscoll."

"Hi Chief. Wilson here."

"We have some info for you. Chief Caswell was drugged with GHB. He died from a heart before the accident happened."

"That confirms our thoughts."

"Yes. Any luck with the new residents."

"No I am afraid not. So far none of the women drive white cars."

"We are looking at three more white cars here in the Chicago area but I'm not holding my breath."

"The service for Chief Caswell is going to be two p.m. on Sunday," Driscoll said.

"That is going to be interesting."

"I agree. Will you be in attendance?"

"Yes of course. Nelson and I will be there," Wilson confirmed. "We have been discussing the possibility that protecting the Mayor and Webster steered the killer towards Chief Caswell."

"That would mean she skipped over Olson."

"Yes. So either she was never a target or the Chief was already a planned hit."

"Maybe prominence in Kelby is part of the answer."

"Well that makes the Mayor the most prominent and then Webster."

"I think with everyone at the service on Sunday that she may postpone her apparent schedule of every two days."

"I hope so. It would give us another twenty four hours to look for her."

"Maybe we will catch a break soon."

"Good night Detective."

"Good Night Chief."

Detectives Nelson and Anthony returned to the bullpen within minutes of each other. Both of their vehicles had clean bumpers. Officer Campbell called in shortly after that with the same result. Wilson told them about the service the next day for Chief Caswell. Nelson would go with him to the funeral and Anthony would continue to look for white cars. He told them to go home.

"What about you?" Nelson probed.

"I have a few things to check on first. I will see you in the morning."

"Good night."

He picked up his cell phone and called Jennifer.

When her phone rang and she saw his cell number she smiled.

"Hi," she answered with a soft, hopeful voice.

"Hi Jen," he replied.

"Is this good news? Your case is over."

"No but we are at a slight standstill. I have to go to a policeman's funeral Sunday."

"Oh dear."

"I was hoping you were up for some company tonight."

"Yes, I am. Come over whenever you can."

"Okay. I'll be about an hour."

"I will leave the driveway lights on," she said smiling.

Wilson was happy to have some semblance of normality waiting for him tonight. If left to his own devices he might never surface during a case like this but he learned that too much focus becomes obsessive and that leads to errors in judgement and the best way to catch a smart criminal is to make fewer mistakes than they do. Wilson turned to his computer and opened the email he had received from Special Agent Giordano and after reading it again he had a thought. He hit reply and began typing.

CHAPTER 15

WAKING UP SUNDAY morning in a strange bed was at first concerning to Ryan but the smell of fresh brewed coffee and the sound of a woman singing softly somewhere was calming. He was right where he wanted to be, at least for the moment. He had a big day ahead but right now all he wanted to see was Jennifer's smile. She was stirring his coffee as he came into the kitchen. She turned and smiled as he had hoped.

"I was going to bring this to you in bed," she said.

He reached out and hugged her close. He loved how she felt in his arms. She became a little girl when they hugged and kissed. Romance with her was easy and natural not like anyone else he had been with. She treated him like a man not like a cop and her soothing voice let him drop his guard and brought out his softer side.

"I know but I have to get going soon."

She showed him her pouty face looking like a child not getting what she wanted. Her girls were with their father this weekend so it was a good opportunity for Jennifer and Ryan to have some alone time. He laughed and kissed her. They sat down and sipped their coffee.

"I will be back tonight," Ryan said almost as a peace offering.

"What about the funeral?"

"I will be late but I will call you."

Back at his condo he showered and changed into his black suit for the funeral in Kelby. When he arrived at the bullpen just before eleven he checked his emails to see if anything had happened. Wilson had received an answer to his question and he smiled. If the killer made a mistake today he would be ready for her. As soon as Detective Nelson arrived at the station they climbed into Wilson's SUV and headed to Kelby. They grabbed lunch to go on the way and drove straight to the Kelby Police Department to meet with Chief Driscoll who informed them of the funeral itinerary. They would attend church ceremony first and then go to the cemetery.

"The procession will lead from the church to the cemetery in the northeast section of Kelby. It will take twenty minutes. We still have the Mayor under protection."

"What about Webster?"

"She was going to stay home but all the officers and patrolman want to be at the cemetery so to keep her protected she will ride in the limousine with the Mayor."

"The question is, assuming they are the next targets, will that will make it more difficult for our killer to make a move on them, or will it be easier because they are together."

"She would be foolish to make a move with the entire Kelby Police department at the funeral."

"Yes and she does not seem to be foolish just angry." Wilson looked at Driscoll. "Let her try something today and see where it gets her."

Wilson's smile made Driscoll wonder if he was implying that he knew something that the killer didn't. If he did know something that the killer didn't know then Driscoll felt he was as much in the dark. His cell phone rang and he gave an affirmation by nodding his head. It was time to go.

The three of them rode in the big Kelby Police Department SUV. When they left the church to form the procession, they drove directly in front of the hearse. They followed the three motorcycle patrolmen to the cemetery. The limousine behind the hearse carried Chief Caswell's family and the limousine behind that carried the Mayor and other delegates including Deborah Webster. Numerous police cruisers followed the limousines and then the general public vehicles came at the end. Fortunately for all on hand the day was clear, not a rain cloud in the sky.

Chief Driscoll and Detectives Wilson and Nelson kept their eyes peeled for a white car even though logic dictated that the white car was not going to show up here. If there was any chance of the killer showing up logic would dictate that she would be pretending to be somebody else. Wilson secretly hoped that she would show herself in any form. That would be a mistake she would regret. After several short good bye speeches and the last sermon from the minister Chief Caswell's casket was lowered into the ground.

Slowly vehicles began leaving the cemetery. There wasn't a single thing about the funeral that seemed at of place. It might have been a false alarm. When they arrived back at the Kelby Police Department there was a man in a black unmarked car waiting for them. He was wearing a black suit so he may have been one of the people at the funeral. The man got out of his car when they parked and waited for them to exit the SUV before walking towards them. Chief Driscoll did not recognize the man and that made him nervous and he put his right hand on his gun holster. Nelson watched him carefully at first and then noticed the concern on Chief Driscoll's face but before she could say anything the man in the black suit spoke up.

"Detective Wilson," he said walking straight towards him.

Wilson did not seem as concerned as Nelson and the Chief about this man.

"Yes," replied

"For you sir," he said as he reached out with something in his hand and Driscoll reached for his gun. Nelson reached across and put her hand on Chief Driscoll's arm. She had realized that the man was FBI.

"Special Agent Giordano asked me to give this to you."

Wilson took the item from him and said, "Thank you."

The man turned around got back in his car and left promptly.

Wilson flipped the item in the air and Nelson and Driscoll saw that it was a USB key. He tossed it at Driscoll.

"A little present for us and hopefully a surprise for the killer."

"I don't understand."

"I called in a small favour last night. On that USB are pictures of all the women that attended the cemetery today. The FBI has very special people who can take very good pictures. We need to go through them with your team of officers and see if there is anyone they don't recognize."

"Wow, okay I will call in the squad."

"I am sorry I didn't tell you earlier but I wasn't sure he was even here. I didn't see him at the cemetery."

"I didn't see him either," said Nelson. "He is good."

When the investigation squad had assembled in the boardroom Chief Driscoll projected the pictures onto the big white wallboard for everyone to see. One by one the pictures were confirmed as residents by someone in the room. An hour later the pictures were finished and there was no mystery woman left to identify. She hadn't gone to the funeral as herself or in disguise. Wilson's hunch had not paid off.

Wilson said, "Thank you for your time gentleman." His voice was cordial but Nelson knew he was pissed that the killer had not made a mistake by showing herself.

Driscoll noticed the mood change as well and said, "I think it was a good idea."

"Yes but the road to hell is paved with good ideas," replied Wilson.

"I think that is good intentions," said Nelson.

Wilson shrugged his shoulders, "I know I was rephrasing."

"You can't be right all the time," Nelson added.

"Why not!" He said smirking.

They all laughed and the tension of not finding a picture of the killer dissipated.

"Okay what now?" asked Driscoll.

"That is a very good question Chief. If she wasn't watching the funeral where was she? She has controlled her anger and let it out at very specific times. Her game plan is still a mystery. Maybe she is finished but I just don't feel she is."

"If she knows we are watching maybe she will wait longer if there is another target in her sights," said Driscoll.

"I hope she does because the longer she waits the more time we have to find that car and then her. In the meantime we have to go back over everything she did and see if we can figure out where she made a mistake."

"Okay we'll keep a close eye on everyone here and maybe review the pictures again. Who knows it might trigger something," said Driscoll.

"Let me know if you find anything that makes you think twice."

"Will do."

When they arrived back at the bullpen it was almost six p.m. Detective Anthony had found two more white cars driven by a woman named Susan but again neither had bumper stickers so the needle in the haystack was not rising to the surface.

They ordered in Italian sandwiches staying away from the pizza this time.

"Let's go back to the beginning," said Wilson.

"Murphy's death?" asked Anthony.

"No further back to the day she started all this."

Nelson said, "You mean when she entered the bank to open the account and meet Murphy."

"Yes. But think about it. She waited for the day that Murphy was covering for his assistant manager so she would be able to meet him without interference."

"Yes," exclaimed Nelson. "That means she was stalking him long before that day."

"She had to have been and whatever reason she started all this in motion happened before that. She dated him for a month and stalked him before that so something happened about two months ago that spirited her to start the murders."

"Maybe something happened at the lab back then?" said Anthony.

"I don't think so. I do think something about the lab is the key but we can't find a link between her and the lab. She didn't work there."

"Considering that she gets around it would seem likely that she isn't working right now."

"But she must have a source of income or money in the bank."

"She took almost two months to plan and kill Murphy and then manages to kill her next two victims in two days."

Wilson interjected, "Overlapping reconnaissance."

"So she was watching all three of them at the same time," said Anthony.

"Was she watching three or four?"

"Wow she is good."

"And we have to be better. Somehow we have to get one step ahead of her."

"I wonder if anything happened in Kelby two months ago that would shed any light on this," Nelson queried.

"Let's find out," said Wilson as he dialed Chief Driscoll.

"Chief Driscoll," he answered.

"Hi Chief. Wilson here. I have a quick question for you. Did anything significant happen in Kelby about two to three months ago?"

"I really can't think of anything off the top of my head but I will ask around and see what may have caused any ripples."

"Great. Still all quiet there?"

"Yep, no news is good news," said Driscoll.

"Okay. I will check in later." Wilson ended the call.

Nelson said, "So she had all the murders planned out and for Caswell to be on Friday night."

"Yes. But she couldn't have known exactly when his funeral would be so that was why she wasn't there. She already had other plans."

"Like what?"

"I don't know yet but we only have a few hours left."

"Well she certainly wasn't going to try anything with everyone watching."

"No she wasn't was she. So where was her focus this time?"

They didn't have to wait long to find out. A moment later Wilson cell phone rang. It was Chief Driscoll with some news.

"Hi Chief, you found something out already," Wilson asked.

"No I am afraid I have other news. She burned down the research lab."

"I am putting you on speaker Chief."

"Hello?"

"Yes we are here Chief, what happened?"

"We are not sure of the exact details but it appears the weekend security guard went to the bathroom and shortly after he returned to the gate house the lab went up in flames. It had just gotten dark. The Fire Marshall said it must have been some high octane accelerant. The place was totally blaze by the time the guard ran the fifty yards back to the house. The Fire Marshall thinks the chemicals inside may have made the fire burn faster."

"Wow, so that was what she was up to. I knew the lab was a connection to her but for her to burn it down means she must have really hated it."

"Luckily no one was there. The arson expert will have a report for me as soon as he can but I don't think we need it to confirm that it was her."

"Didn't the security company put up cameras around the house after the death of Dr. Brennan?"

"Yes they did; several as a matter of fact. Their facility is in Chicago much closer to you than here. I can call them and advise them you want to view the images from tonight."

"That would be great. Maybe we will get lucky and catch a glimpse of her."

"Good luck. I am on my way to the research lab or what is left of it."

Chief Driscoll gave Wilson the phone number for the security company head office and then called them himself to advise them of the fire and to tell them to expect a call from the Chicago PD. Ten minutes later Nelson called the security company and they gave her a password so the she could log onto their website and watch the evening videotapes on line. Once Nelson had logged in they sat around her computer and watched the security video. There were six cameras but Wilson suspected that only the one facing the field where they had previously found the footprints and the one above the entrance doors would provide any images.

"Nothing on the cameras facing south and west," Nelson said.

"What about the one facing the barn and the one facing the field?"

Nelson brought them up on monitor and fast forwarded the video from the one facing the field.

"There!" Wilson shouted.

"Can you play both of them at the same time in real time?"

"Yes."

She played the videos and a figure all in black came into view carry two satchels. After placing the satchels down near the door the figure disappeared out of view in the direction of the barns. A few minutes later the figure was back carrying two plastic drums of what was probably gas for the tractors. The video taken from the top of the door did not show a view of the face of the person. The figure disappeared again for a few minutes and then it lit what appeared to be some kind of fuse on the ground. Suddenly flames came into view and then the cameras went black.

They slumped back down in their chairs sitting around Nelson's desk. The killer had avoided detection again. They saw her but not enough to identify her. She had snuck onto the property and boldly walked past the cameras to burn the research lab. She was driven and smart and it looked to Wilson that he was going to have to pull a rabbit out of his hat if he was going to catch her off guard. It was almost midnight.

"That's it for today. Let's try to think of ways we can get ahead of her. Thanks guys. Goodnight."

He called Jennifer to tell her he was on his way.

CHAPTER 16

RYAN WOKE WITH the thought of another forty eight hour window staring him and his team in the face, but that thought was pleasantly disrupted by Jennifer bringing him coffee in bed.

"There, I trapped you," she said to Ryan as he reached out and took the mug from her.

"This is the nicest trap I have ever been in," he replied while watching her smile.

Jennifer giggled, "Well the girls are back tonight after school so enjoy it while you can."

He and Jennifer had been seeing each other for over six months and sometimes they would all go to lunch or a movie but Ryan did not stay over when Jennifer's twin daughters were home. He was sure the girls knew that he and their mother were involved intimately but it was never brought up in conversation. He sat up and sipped his coffee while Jennifer talked about her upcoming day. She has an engagement announcement photo shoot with and an anxious mother in law to deal with.

"It sounds like you are going to be busy," he concluded.

"Yes and no. The photo shoot this morning will be hectic but editing the pictures requires a little patience and a fair amount of time."

"That sounds like my week only I don't know how much time I can use up."

"I know you probably don't want to hear this but I do worry about you when you throw yourself into your cases," Jennifer said.

She was right he didn't want her worrying about him, "I am having lunch with Jim today."

"Good," she said. "I am sure he will keep you grounded and give you some perspective."

"Yes he always does, doesn't he?"

She smiled and tilted her head. Ryan looked at the clock. He wished he could stay and talk longer but it was just past seven and he had to get going.

"I'll call you later," was his announcement that it was time for him to go. He headed back to his condo for a quick change into a blue suit and then straight to the bullpen.

When Wilson arrived in the bullpen Detective Anthony was already there with coffee and pile of unhealthy looking donuts. Wilson was sure there was enough sugar on them to attract ants from a mile away and as expected Nelson turned her nose up at the donuts when she arrived. They each grabbed a coffee and Wilson began a brainstorm session about the past week.

"Okay she chose Murphy first and Brennan second and the Chief third. Why in that order?"

"Well maybe because Murphy was far enough away from Kelby that she thought he wouldn't be linked to Brennan right away giving her more time to sneak up on Chief Caswell." Anthony chipped in.

"Good point," said Wilson. "But she underestimated Fred."

"And us," said Nelson "I don't think she thought we would be this close this fast."

"I agree and I like your optimism, but getting close to her isn't a thought that has crossed my mind. She had a well-conceived plan and when we threw roadblocks in her way she adapted and that is scary."

"True but better a burn down than a murder."

"Absolutely, but can we stop her from burning down the whole town of Kelby?"

"Well maybe not. But at least we have her changing her game plan so as you said she might make a mistake."

Wilson's cell phone rang, it was Chief Driscoll.

"Wilson here."

"Good morning Detective Wilson. I have some early news on the fire."

"Good."

"The fire inspector said it burned too hot to be just gasoline from the equipment shed. He thinks it had a booster like toluene."

"I see."

"It doesn't burn as fast as gasoline but it boosts the temperature making the fire an inferno. Not sure if that helps us much."

"Everything we learn helps us somehow Chief. Our job is to figure out how."

"That is all that we have right now other than what you have seen on the video tapes."

"That wasn't much. She was covered up in black."

"While that does disappoint me it doesn't surprise me."

"I agree. We are going over everything here to see if we come up with anything new."

"Let's hope it is productive," said the Chief.

Click.

Wilson continued, "So again why Murphy?"

"I don't understand what you mean," said Anthony.

"I mean, she went out with him for a month then killed him and then two days later she killed Brennan. She could have killed Brennan any day she wanted."

"Of course," said Nelson. "Murphy was the prime target and she wanted him to number one."

"Bingo! That is a clue. Now what does it tell us."

"That it was important to her that he was first so it was personal."

"Yes, and cold calculated too."

"Hell hath no fury like a woman's scorn," added Anthony.

"That would be a motive to kill Murphy but not the others."

"Yes. It is unlikely that they all spurned her at some point especially Brennan."

"So it is personal but not intimate personal," Nelson said.

"Is she exacting revenge for something that is not a boy-girl thing," Anthony queried.

"Yes. So what could cause a woman to go postal?"

They both turned and looked at Nelson.

"What? Am I supposed to know everything just because she is a woman?"

They both laughed.

"No, but tell us what would make you go off the rails and not PMS because that would be short term and less resolute."

"Hmm," Nelson was thinking out loud. "Betrayal can come in many forms."

"Like?"

"A broken promise."

"But what could have these people promised her?"

"Are we sure it was not a job?" Anthony asked.

"If it was only a job then Brennan would have been the only target. Neither Murphy nor Chief Caswell would have been in the picture."

"Burning down the research lab was directed to stop them working. Maybe they are using her data without giving her recognition."

Wilson countered, "Perhaps but again why Chief Caswell. We need to know what his connection was to the lab."

Anthony mused, "I wonder if there was any warnings sent to some of the people in the picture."

"What kind of warning?"

"Maybe a letter that was more pleading than warning."

"We need to go through Brennan's place for that. Anything at the lab is gone."

Wilson picked up his cell phone and called Chief Driscoll.

"Hi Chief. I have a little job for you."

"Good. We aren't finding anything under the stones we are turning over here."

"I need you to dig up everything about the lab that involved Chief Caswell."

"That I can do."

"We need to know everything that he was involved with no matter how small. Also I need you to go through Brennan's place and look for any letters sent to him about the lab. They might have even been sent as an email. There might have been some kind of cryptic warning sent to him."

"Okay. I'll get back to you as soon as I have something."

"Thanks Chief."

Click.

"Anthony you go back to Murphy's place and take look for an actual letter or anything resembling that and Nelson, pick up Murphy's laptop from evidence and take it over to Digby."

Ross Digby was a computer guru whose services Wilson would occasionally require.

Wilson added, "Let's see if he can hack into it. Maybe he can find an email or other information about the research lab."

When Anthony and Nelson both nodded their confirmation and left, Wilson called Professor Maltby to find out where they were meeting for lunch. Jim Maltby was a coffee connoisseur and they often met at unique cafes throughout the city.

"Hi Jim."

"I hope you aren't calling to cancel our lunch?" he inquired.

Ryan laughed, "No, just checking to see where we are meeting."

"Well I was thinking that I will to pick you up at the station house since we are going just down the street. See you in twenty minutes."

"Great I'll meet you out front."

Wilson stood and on the sidewalk still pondering his case as Jim Maltby drove up.

They drove only about two blocks and then parked in the public parking before walking one more block to get to coffee shop Jim had chosen for today's lunch. On the way to the coffee shop Ryan briefed Jim on the current case. Today they were sampling Spanish coffee, in particular a version called Café Bombon, which was espresso and sweet condensed milk combined in layers, looking similar to a shooter. They both ordered the egg salad sandwich to go with it.

After a sip of his coffee Jim said, "She does seem like a focused, intelligent person."

"Too focused for my liking," said Ryan.

"Yes I understand. No luck finding her yet?"

"Not yet but we have more than a few people looking."

"She reminds me of a raptor."

"She hasn't killed with her own hands yet."

"I was thinking more of the bird definition not the dinosaur although they do have similar traits. Hawks and owls are classified as raptors, they watch from afar, strike and then retreat."

"Yes she does that."

"A raptor won't strike until it is ready. It can be very patient waiting for just the right moment."

"So if we keep guarding the Mayor and the Chamber of Commerce woman she won't strike."

"Won't is a definitive word, might not, would be more accurate."

"But for how long."

"Precisely. She may wait for you to make a mistake or she may decide to remove the protection herself."

"You think she might take out the policemen watching them?"

"If she is that driven then it is likely to happen if she sees an opening. Or maybe she makes the opening herself."

"That is not good."

Jim sipped a bit of coffee and said, "Well then you need to be proactive instead of reactive."

"Easy to say but how."

"If you are reasonably sure the Mayor is her next target, tempt her into the open by offering him up. Figuratively, not literally."

"Make her think we aren't covering the Mayor so she will try something."

"Yes."

"Dangerous," replied Ryan.

"She is more dangerous right now because you don't know what she is thinking."

"Tell me about it. She is driving us crazy. She has ties to the lab but we can't find what they are."

"Yet," Jim added.

Ryan smiled, "Okay, yet."

"Do you remember a few years ago that woman who killed her boyfriend out of jealousy because she thought he was fooling around with his secretary."

"Yes."

"But he was really taking dancing lessons to impress her."

"Yes," Ryan replied slowly wondering where Jim was going with this line of thought.

"Well maybe your lab killer is really taking dancing lessons."

"Huh?'

"Perhaps the lab is not the real focus of her attention."

"Great," Ryan said. "Care to e-*lab*-orate for me. Pun intended."

Jim chuckled, "You need to get inside her head to do that."

They finished lunch and Jim drove Ryan back to the station.

"You always leave me with something to think about," Ryan said getting out of the car.

"Hopefully that will kindle some ideas for you," Jim replied waving goodbye

When Wilson returned to the bullpen Nelson was still out but Anthony was back eating a leftover donut. "My wife has me on such a tight diet I never see dessert at home."

Wilson wanted to laugh but decided to just pretend to show him sympathy for his plight.

"I'm afraid his place was lacking in paperwork. He must have done all his work on his laptop. There was only one bill, but he had a shredder full of paper."

"Maybe Nelson is having better luck at with Digby and the laptop."

No sooner had he said her name than she walked into the room and the look on her face was promising. In her hand were a few pages of print outs. She marched up to Wilson and handed him the pages.

"We didn't find threatening letters but we found email love letters, from a Susan Scott."

"Great work. Now let's find out all about her. Anthony check with DMV on her name. Nelson check for any Scott's with a sheet. I'll call Chief Driscoll with the news."

The Chief answered on the fourth ring.

"Chief Driscoll."

"Chief! We have a name. She calls herself Susan Scott," exclaimed Wilson. "We are running that name through the DMV right now."

"Gosh that is great news. I'll check with our staff about that name. However nothing came up about letters at Brennan's place. I'm still looking for the link between Chief Caswell and the Genesis Research Lab."

"I'm keeping my fingers crossed that she used her real name but I will reserve my excitement until we actually find her. Let me know if anything happens at your end."

"We will. Good luck with her name."

"Thanks."

By the time he hung up Anthony had found a Susan Scott but she drove a brown car and she was over fifty years old

Wilson had an idea, "Ask Dixon to check her credit card records in case it is a case of identity theft."

"Good call. Be right back."

Wilson mulled over Professor Maltby's curious suggestions in his head. How can the lab be the focus of her attention and yet not be?

Nelson brought nothing back with her this time.

"Nothing under that name in the books," she said.

"I am not all that surprised. Anthony has gone to see Dixon to do a credit check on a woman matching that name in case it was identity theft."

Nelson raised her eye brows, "That could be a real possibility."

"It would certainly help her to stay under the radar but it could also lead us right to her depending on what she purchased."

Anthony came back later with a slightly dejected look on his face. The lead was a dead end. There were no new phony credit cards issued under the name of Susan Scott and no unusual purchases on her existing ones. Wilson was not surprised. It was not logical that someone who had taken the trouble to execute such elaborate murders would make a simple mistake but then stranger things have happened.

"Okay back to square one. There were no strange warning letters found. What does that tell us?"

"She wasn't interested in warning anyone."

"Why not?"

"Because she was angry and wanted revenge and she was no longer interested in anything they had to say."

"Yes, but what could connect them all if it wasn't the lab?"

"I don't understand?" said Anthony.

"Chief Driscoll has found no link between Chief Caswell and the lab. I can understand why he might have been in the picture but if that is his only connection to the lab why was he killed. He must have done something that pissed her off that has nothing to do with the lab."

They both looked at him absorbing what he had said but said nothing back.

"A rash is a symptom of a histamine reaction. You see the rash and put cream on it but the cause is inside the body. The lab is her rash but the cause is inside her head."

"So building the lab didn't set her off because it has been over two years," said Nelson. "Something happened between then and now that set her off."

"Exactly. We need to find what that was and who in that picture is connected to it."

Anthony said, "So burning the lab down was just for fun."

"Yes, if she still plans to do more damage to people."

Nelson said, "What if there are people she is after that weren't in the picture."

"Holy crap. You mean absentees," said Anthony.

Wilson called Chief Driscoll right away.

"Hi Chief," Wilson spoke with an urgency, "I have another task for you. Can you please find out if anyone who was supposed to be in the picture was not there the day the Genesis Research Lab cutting ribbon picture was taken."

"Sure thing"

"It might be a dead end but we don't want to take any chances."

"I agree Detective."

Click.

"Okay next."

"Next?"

"What can these people have in common that is separate from the lab?"

Wilson wrote the names of the people on their list across the top of the Big Board and underneath he printed their job title.

"What links these people that would not apply to the lab?"

"Maybe money."

"That links some of them, the bank, the construction company, the insurance company, and a research scientist who started the process but not a police chief or a mayor."

"Or the president of the local Chamber of Commerce either."

Anthony said, "What would drive a woman to kill for revenge?"

"The death of a child might do it," answered Nelson.

Anthony said, "That would be another needle in a haystack for us to look for."

Wilson chipped in, "Yes, it's a long shot but let's not leave it out of the equation just yet. We have money and death now what else."

"There is jealousy but I don't see how that will fit here."

"No it probably doesn't but what if the motive is not singular but plural."

"You mean like money and something else."

"That could explain why we can't connect the motive for the deaths to each other." "If there is one motive for some of them and another for others how are we going to find it?"

"We need her to show us her true colours. A dual motive means she is truly dangerous."

Wilson picked up the phone and called Dr. Devlin the shrink that Wilson and some of the Chicago PD leaned on for advice. His timing was perfect because the doctor had just returned from a court hearing and was not with a client.

He answered his phone on the second ring, "Dr. Devlin."

"Hey Doc we are sitting here in the bullpen and came up with a question that perhaps you can help us with." Wilson gave him a brief rundown of the crimes.

"Your case sounds like someone with acute mental distress. It affects the way they think and feel. It can be caused by a chemical imbalance in the brain or a significant stressful experience in some cases causing a brief depression and then a rage. They can't understand why everyone didn't see the problem the way they did so they attach resentment to them. In your case they are trying to resolve the problem by acting out their rage."

"And what might trigger this?"

"Well there are many possibilities. Each person will be impacted differently by a stressful situation. A loss of a job or a death in the family is an example. Whatever it is, it is a loss that has significance to the person reacting. They might honestly believe that when they have finished they will have resolved the situation and life will go back to normal the way it was before the trigger event."

"Well that is not going to happen."

"No. Sometimes they come back to that realization before they have finished and if they do then they may have either a complete breakdown and are committed or they become so remorseful that they commit suicide or worse go postal. You know how that plays out."

"Yes. We don't want it to go that far."

"It all depends on the person's state of mind. Like coma patients there is no precise way of knowing what will trigger then out of their fugue. I hope that was useful."

"Hopefully it will be when we find her. Thanks Doc."

Click

"Okay. Nelson, let's go with your idea. Check with the M.E. office for child deaths in the past 6 months to see if anything connects to Kelby. If that was her trigger it should be hard to hide from it."

The bullpen phone rang and Wilson answered.

"Detective Wilson"

"It's Fred."

Wilson looked at his watch. It was four-thirty pm. "You are in early?"

"No I am still at home but I wanted to share some news with you right away. The chemical analysis on the water that killed Murphy is in, and my suspicion was right. It is not city tap water."

"What is it?"

"Well I can't be exact but it is likely pond or lake water."

"From where?"

Fred laughed, "I am a Medical Examiner not a Limnologist."

"A what?" Wilson exclaimed.

"That's a person who studies lakes and ponds. But even they can't tell you which lake it was from. You need to find a suspect lake and then test the water."

"Another needle in my haystacks."

"Yes, pretty much. Sorry."

"No it is good information. We might need it later."

"Cheers."

Click.

Wilson looked over at Anthony who was still exploring the data base looking for white cars connected to someone named Susan. Everything he thought of was a needle in a haystack. The only way to speed things up was to burn down the haystack. Needles don't burn. The problem was he had too many haystacks, for now he would leave things as they are and hope for a break.

CHAPTER 17

NELSON WAS PICKING up breakfast for everyone and bringing it back to the bullpen. Everyone included Officer Andy Campbell, who was transferred to the team from his night shift, with the blessing of Captain Stone, for the rest of this case. Nelson arrived just in time to hear an update from Kelby. Chief Driscoll checked in with the team and Wilson put him on speaker phone.

"Well I wish I had new information that was more positive. We have not found any new women in Kelby who we cannot verify as real residents. Unfortunately that does not mean she is not here."

"True. She could be hiding in plain sight. Like with a relative who would be oblivious to any connection," added Nelson.

Chief Driscoll continued, "Also we have found no connection between Chief Caswell and the Research Lab. Perhaps he was just there at that moment and was looking for some good PR for his next term."

Wilson chipped in, "He may have been in that picture by his own design but the killer had a beef with him. And if it wasn't connected to the lab could it have been an arrest?"

"I will have to double check our records but I don't remember anyone having a run in with the Chief while I have been here. Especially not a woman."

"Maybe she didn't have a run in with the Chief. Perhaps it was a relative of hers who did. Did anyone have an accident or die while in custody?"

"Gawd no," replied Driscoll. "The Chief could be bombastic but never out of line."

"Okay. Remember we need to look at any idea no matter how strange it may sound. If we don't figure out her motivation we might not find her."

"Understood," said Driscoll. "We checked every white vehicle in Kelby and any driving on Highway 88 and so far none have a bumper sticker."

"That's not too surprising. She isn't likely to be driving around in it now. If she thinks we are on to her she would have hid it somewhere and picked up new wheels."

"Yes. That sounds logical," Driscoll replied. "We'll keep looking just in case and on the other thing you asked me to check on there was technically one missing person from the picture. According to the Mayor everyone was there who was supposed to be, plus the Chief, except for the Deputy Mayor, Andrew Spencer. He was supposed to be in attendance for the picture taking but had to stay at city hall to attend a planning meeting.

"Where is he now?"

"Most likely in his office at city hall."

"He might be on her list."

"I will advise him and assign an officer to shadow him."

"Good."

"One more thing Detective, only one of our officers went to high school here in Kelby but he doesn't remember any specific girls that stood out as potential perps."

"Okay. It was a long shot. We need some spaghetti to stick to the wall."

"Pardon me!" said a confused Chief Driscoll.

"It is and old adage Chief. If you throw enough cooked spaghetti at a wall eventually some of it will stick. We need some leads to stick to the wall."

"Oh, I never heard that one before. Not really a pasta guy but I like that."

Nelson chipped in, "We have been looking into baby deaths in the event that might have been her stressor but again there were no connections to Kelby or Chicago."

"No we haven't had any baby deaths here. Knock on wood. Something like that I would have remembered," replied Driscoll.

"Okay," said Wilson. "We are back to square one. The key is Chief Caswell. Whatever the reason she had him on her hit list will lead us to her. I know I have asked already but Chief we need you to go back to Chief Caswell and check back a year before the lab was built for any connection no matter how small."

"Okay I will put one of my guys on it right away."

"One more thing Chief. Are there any lakes or ponds around Kelby?"

"Well we don't have a lake nearby as it is largely farm land but there is a pond south of route 64 that people fish in. There isn't much in it mostly catfish."

"That might be what we are looking for although if it is that close to Kelby I am not sure it will help much."

"Well. Good luck today Detectives."

"You too Chief and remember call about anything that looks like a lead."

"I will and hopefully next time we will be discussing a good lead," the Chief signed off.

As soon as he hung up the phone Wilson turned to Nelson.

"Bring up the internet map site of Kelby and see if that pond is on it."

They all moved behind Nelson as she searched on her computer for the map displaying Kelby. There was a small dark spot just south of Route 64, east of Golden road.

"There it is." Nelson pointed at the screen.

"Please send that to Andy's cell phone." He turned to Officer Campbell.

"Andy I need you to find that pond and get a water sample to the M.E. as soon as possible."

"Got it."

"And Andy. Low key. No speeding. And just in case keep an eye out for a white car."

"Absolutely!"

Anthony asked, "If this is the water supply why did you say it might not help us?"

"We are reasonably sure that she is from Kelby. Using a water supply from Kelby only confirms what we suspect. It doesn't hurt but it doesn't provide any new clues to who she is."

"Oh yeah."

Wilson walked over to The Big Board and flipped over a sheet. "Okay back to square one," he said and then he wrote *Loss* at the top of the page.

"Let's list all the losses that might be a trigger." They shouted them out at random and Wilson wrote them down.

LOSS

— Death in family
— Divorce
— Fired from job
— Bankruptcy

"Any of those could be a trigger for a psychotic break," said Nelson. "But I think we can rule out bankruptcy since she had money to invest in Murphy's bank."

"Yeah that's true," added Anthony.

Wilson crossed out ~~Bankruptcy~~.

"She could have been fired from her job since she seems to have plenty of free time right now," Anthony said.

"Good point" Wilson put a check mark behind – Fired from job √.

"If you combine that with a divorce then she would be very motivated but how would that connect to the lab?"

"Good question. Or is she single?"

"What if she got a divorce and left her job with a retirement package."

"Very possible. It explains her independence but again what would her divorce have to do with the lab."

Anthony and Nelson went silent at that thought.

Wilson broke the silence. "We looked at baby deaths thinking she might have been a mother. What if it was her mother that died instead? That could send someone into acute depression and it isn't a big leap from there to a mental break down."

"But depression and mental break down wouldn't leave her with the sharp wits required to do what she has done so far."

Anthony said, "So in place of depression, something pushed her into rage."

"That fits," said Wilson pointing at the list. "One of these by themselves might equal depression but all three at once would be a big stressor. Would that be big enough to switch her emotions to rage?"

Nelson sighed, "Oh my. Can you imagine having to deal with all three of those at the same time?"

"And here is the kicker. If she had been bankrupt she might have gone a totally different direction."

"Like suicide."

"Yes."

"Well how are we going to find out where she worked and got divorced if we don't know her name?" Anthony asked.

"Well, believe it or not, we have something almost as good."

Nelson and Anthony looked at each other with confusion and then turned to Wilson for clarification.

"We are now reasonably sure that someone's death was part of the trigger. Right!"

The both nodded waiting for more clarity.

"And . . ." Wilson paused for effect. "We are also reasonably sure that the death has to have a personal connection to the killer."

They nodded again still waiting for Wilson to give them the final piece to the puzzle.

"And that means that we are almost certain that someone who died in Kelby in the past year is the connection between our killer and the picture of the opening of the lab."

"And it might be a relative!" Anthony shouted.

"Give that man a cigar," said Wilson.

Anthony beamed a smile but Nelson sat back in her chair and pondered what was discussed.

She added, "And since Chief Driscoll has been in Kelby for the past three years he should know what we are looking for."

"Give that girl a cigar too."

Nelson frowned at Wilson.

Wilson called Chief Driscoll's cell.

"Chief Driscoll," he answered.

"Chief we have some news," replied Wilson.

"Good news?"

"In a manner of speaking. We might have been off base about the baby death but we think we were in the right ballpark. We believe our killer lost a family member in the past year."

"And how does that help us," Driscoll inquired.

"We are reasonably sure that is was a relative that lived in and died in Kelby."

"Really. That is a good lead."

"Yes, one less haystack to look through."

"Do we know if it was male or female?"

"We are not sure of the gender. You'll need to check anyone who passed away in the past year and who had any connection to the lab, no matter how small."

"Terrific. We will get right on that."

"Thanks Chief."

Click.

Wilson looked at the Big Board and then back at everyone.

"We need to get inside her head. We need to think like her to figure out what her next move will be."

"You mean because we have guarded all her targets?"

"Exactly. Up until now she has had her way and attacked when her targets were alone."

"Do you think she will wait for an opening or change her pattern?"

"If we keep her potential targets guarded she will either have to give it up or adapt a new plan."

"From the tone of your voice you don't sound like you expect her to stop," Nelson said.

"No I don't. As Dr. Devlin alluded, she may not have an off switch and she is very smart, so we need to adapt a new plan before she does."

"Let's hope she doesn't have any sniper training," Anthony scoffed before adding, "Do you think she would hire a shooter?"

"So far she has been hands on so I don't expect that to change. She wants to exact the damage herself. She wants her pound of flesh."

"What else can she use for weapons."

"Right now her mind is her best weapon. Look at how she killed three people. If they had been killed at random intervals they might have passed through the system as accidents."

"It seems like she has planned this all out to every detail," said Anthony.

"Oh no!" moaned Nelson.

"What? What is it?" asked Wilson.

"What if she planned everything out? Including us guarding the people she hasn't attacked yet. Could she be that smart?"

"Perhaps. She has shown great ingenuity so far. So we have to be even more calculating."

"How would she get at guarded targets?"

"Good question. One way is take out the place and not just the person using a bomb but I don't think she will do that.

"Because she wants to do it herself."

"Yes."

"She has used personal contact as her method to kill her first three victims. She won't be able to that anymore unless she can make herself invisible."

"Well she has done a good job of that so far," remarked Anthony.

"Not quite. She simply made herself look like someone other than herself and since we didn't know anything about her she could walk right by us before and we would never have known. She knows that her encounter with Chief Caswell was witnessed so she knows we know her height, weight, and sex."

As he finished his last sentence Officer Campbell returned to the bullpen.

"All done. Gave the sample to Cindy," he said referring to his trip to Kelby to retrieve a pond water sample.

"Great thanks Andy," Wilson replied and then a moment later. "Damn!"

"What? Andy asked.

"I just realized we missed another haystack."

Wilson quickly picked up the phone and called Chief Driscoll on his cell.

The Chief answered, "Driscoll here."

"Chief I just had a thought. Now that we have a rough description can you check all the hotels and motels in your area for a woman that would have paid in cash, not by credit card? And ask them about a white car."

"Of course. I will get my guys on it right away."

"Let me know if anything pops up. Remember she is dangerous. We'll check the Chicago area."

"Good luck Detectives."

Click

Officer Campbell stood up before Wilson could speak. "I'm on it."

"Get a couple of patrolmen to help you out."

"Don't worry my nightshift guys love a challenge," Campbell smiled as he headed downstairs.

CHAPTER 18

THE LACK OF leads made it seem that time was dragging but in fact it was passing normally. They were unable to stop looking at the clock on the wall above the door to the bullpen and each time they did the anxiousness crept in. It had been two hours since they had last spoken to Chief Driscoll. They had not expected anything back from Officer Campbell yet either, but the missing link to the killer loomed in their thoughts. Was the killer somehow going to keep up her two day schedule even with all the targets guarded? Did they really have all the targets guarded or was there one they hadn't thought of yet? Their pizza lunch was resting heavy in their stomachs, as if not digesting at all.

Wilson's cell phone ring snapped them all to attention.

"Wilson," he answered quickly.

"Driscoll here." Not Chief Driscoll this time. There was a distinct sense of urgency in his voice. "I think we have something."

"Let me put you on speaker Chief," Wilson replied. "Go ahead."

"Okay. I found someone that might be a lead. Sorry, not might, is a lead." He was talking faster than he had on previous phone calls. Looks from the faces of Anthony and Nelson indicated they noticed it too. "Four months ago a fellow by the name of Robert Doyle passed away after being admitted to the hospital here. There is a lot to discuss but the first point is, he was the former owner of the farm where the lab was built."

All three detectives had gaped mouths as they understood the importance of this new information.

Wilson was the first to speak, "That's fantastic. Better than I would have hoped for."

"Well you are going to really enjoy the rest then," replied Driscoll. "He had several health issues which lead to him going into the hospital for the last time but one of them was that he was suffering from cataplexy and was being treated with a drug called sodium oxybate and it is almost identical to GHB."

"Holy crap." yelled Anthony. "That's what was used to kill Chief Caswell."

"My reaction was similar detective," said Driscoll.

Wilson could not quite imagine the restrained Chief Driscoll acting the same as the often exuberant Detective Anthony.

"That's a great lead Chief."

"Well I'm not finished. There's still more," said Driscoll.

Sometimes it rains and sometimes it pours, you never know.

"His wife died over 10 years ago. That was when his health issues seem to have started but he has a son that still lives and works in Kelby."

"We're on our way Chief."

"I will have him picked up and brought in."

"Great. See you shortly."

Click.

With their adrenaline pumping the three detectives emptied the bullpen and a minute later they were in Wilson's SUV on the way to Kelby. The trip to Kelby took five minutes less than the last time but it felt longer to the detectives. Anticipation has a way of making time drag and even with the speedier pace Wilson drove it did not change the feeling.

Chief Driscoll was waiting for them in the lobby of the Kelby Police Department. The excitement of this break in the case had him edgy as well. They said their usual greetings and then Driscoll lead them to the observation room beside the investigation room where Frank Doyle was sitting in a chair behind a metal table.

He was wearing jeans and a red checkered work shirt over a white V-neck tee shirt.

At first sight, through the two-way mirror, he was very normal and unassuming looking but the detectives didn't take their eyes off of him for a second. All kinds of thoughts were going through Wilson's mind about this man's possible connection to the murders.

"I have another surprise for you," said Chief Driscoll.

Wilson blinked at Driscoll without replying. His mind was on Frank Doyle. Chief Driscoll pointed to a clear zip locked plastic bag on a table behind them and they all turn and stared at it. Nelson was the first to react.

"Are you kidding me," she said as she reached for the plastic bag.

Wilson looked back at Doyle one more time before joining Nelson in the inspection of the bag.

"These are Caprinas." Nelson said as she turned them over to look at the soles. "With mud in the treads and look they're size nines!"

Wilson smiled at her excitement as she appraised the shoes.

She was almost shouting in her zeal. "These are the boots that made the footprints at the farm near the fence line. The mud in the treads will confirm it."

Wilson turned to Driscoll, "How did you find them?"

"He works at the lumber yard on the west side of town. We went to his work to pick him up and when he went to his car to throw in his lunch pail, there on the floor were these shoes. They were in an unlocked car and in plain sight. But we asked if we could look at them and he said yes."

"Wow," said Anthony. "Talk about good luck, or good timing."

"Yes. Timing is everything. I heard Andre Agassi say that in a commercial," Chief Driscoll countered.

Nelson said, "We'll take them to the Techs and have the mud compared with the sample we gave them. I don't think there is any doubt that they are a match to the footprints near the fence."

"You don't seem quite as excited as the rest of us," Chief Driscoll said to Wilson.

"There is a Mickey Gilley song that says, *the girls all get prettier at closing time.* I remember meeting a girl in dark bar one night and she gave me her number. Next day when I met her for lunch she wasn't quite as pretty as I had remembered. Low lights and alcohol can do that to you and so can an adrenaline rush."

"So you are saying we should not get the cart before the horse."

"Precisely." Wilson turned to Nelson. "Let's go talk to Mr. Doyle."

Nelson and Wilson entered the investigation room and said hello to Frank Doyle while Detective Anthony and Chief Driscoll watched through the glass and listened on the speaker.

"We appreciate your help in our investigation Mr. Doyle."

"You can call me Frank."

"Okay. Frank it is."

"You understand we are coordinating with Chief Driscoll on the murders."

"Well I do now. I didn't before."

"Before?"

"Before Chief Driscoll came and asked me to come in and answer some questions about my dad."

"I'm sorry to hear that you lost your father."

"Thanks."

"Your father owned the farm that the lab was built on."

"Yep. Grew up there. We had chickens, sheep, pigs, cows and two ponies."

"Two ponies?" asked Nelson.

"Yeah, one for me and one for my sister."

"You have a sister?"

"Yes."

"Is she older than you?"

"Yes,"

"What is your sister's name?"

"Louise."

Wilson frowned. He had anticipated the name Susan.

"Why did your father sell the farm?"

"He didn't sell it?"

"What?"

"I thought you knew?"

"Knew what?"

"About what happened to the farm?"

"Frank we don't know anything about the farm so fill us in about everything would you."

"Sure," he said shifting in his seat. "Well after Mom died Dad got sick. Lots of strange things were happening to him. Doctors were always changing their minds about what was wrong with him. One minute it was Lyme disease and the next it was some neural virus and the next it was Parkinson's. What they needed was a guy like House to solve Dad's illness."

"That must have been awful," said Nelson.

"It was. To pay the medical bills Dad had to do one of those reverse mortgages with the bank."

"Which bank?"

"The insurance company hooked us up with a bank. First Chicago something."

"The First Chicago Savings and Loan Bank?"

"Yes that is it."

Wilson and Nelson looked at each other. Tom Murphy's bank. This was the beginning. They now had a timeline.

"What was the name of the insurance company?"

"I can't remember but they were the owners. Their names are the company name. They were in Chicago too. I don't think there were any insurance guys in Kelby when Dad bought the farm."

"Was the insurance company called Rothenberg and Snyder?"

"Yeah I think that was it.

Nelson turned and looked at the glass.

"Oh crap." Anthony muttered in the other room.

"What's wrong" asked Chief Driscoll.

"The insurance guy Taylor refused protection. He is in Chicago right now without anyone watching him."

Anthony pulled out his cell phone and called Officer Campbell.

"Campbell," he answered.

"Anthony here. I need you to get a hold of Ernie Taylor right away."

He filled Campbell in on the news and then gave him the phone number and address.

"Don't take no for an answer and then go over to his office and stand guard until we get back."

"Got it" Campbell replied.

Anthony texted Nelson's cell phone. "Sent Campbell to see Taylor."

She turned and nodded after seeing the message.

"Why did the insurance company suggest a reverse mortgage to your father?" Wilson brought up to Doyle.

"The insurance coverage was all used up after a few years. The doctor's bills were piling up so they came up with a bank that would help us. I don't know what we would have done if that hadn't happened."

"Then what happened?"

"Well my sister was gone by then. She went away to school to study Biology. She's like a scientist. The money for her school and the ongoing bills ate up all the mortgage money and we had to move off the farm. They sent us a notice that we had to move."

"An eviction notice?"

"Yes. I got a job and an apartment in town."

"Where is your sister now?"

"I don't know. I haven't heard from her in a few years. She got married. I don't think she liked me much. I wasn't as smart as her."

"But you looked after your father."

"Mostly. Louise sent money each month."

"How did she send you the money?"

"Through Western Union."

"So you never knew where she lived?"

"No. She would phone Dad sometimes."

"What happened after your father died?"

"What do you mean?"

"Well, the funeral?"

"Louise had him cremated. She paid for it. She has Dad's ashes."

"Anything else you can think of to tell us?"

"Like what?"

"Anything that you think will help us."

"Sorry I don't know any more than what I just told you."

"What about your hiking shoes?"

"What about them?"

"Do you always keep them in your car?"

"Yeah. I like to hike sometimes and they are the best for all terrain. If I'm driving and a see something I want to explore I just put them on and go hiking."

"Do you often go hiking on the old farm?"

"No, the letter said it would be trespassing. That's what it said."

"You mean the eviction letter?"

"Yes."

"So you haven't gone back at all."

"Nope."

"Not even for a nostalgic visit."

"No way. Chief Caswell was very clear about trespassing."

"Chief Caswell told you not to trespass."

"Yes."

"When did you tell you that?"

"The day he said we had to leave. He brought us the letter."

"Chief Caswell asked your dad to sign the eviction notice saying you would leave that day," asked Wilson.

"Yes sir. He said we had to leave right away. He said he had given us plenty of time."

Wilson turned and stared at the glass.

Chief Driscoll left the observation room and returned a few minutes later with a file in his hand.

"Okay Frank let's take a break. Do you want a pop?"

"Yes please. Diet cola please."

"Okay. And see if you think of anything else about the farm."

"Okay."

Wilson and Nelson left the room. One the officers brought Frank a pop a few minutes later.

"Well. What do you think of that?" asked Wilson to the other three in the observation room.

"It seems like he's telling the truth," responded Anthony.

"I concur," said Driscoll as he handed the file to Wilson.

Wilson opened the file folder and read. It was a copy of the eviction notice.

At the bottom was the signature of Chief Caswell and one of Robert Doyle.

Wilson handed the file to Nelson. She and Anthony read it together. When they were finished they looked up. That was the connection between the killer and Chief Caswell. Wilson watched Frank Doyle sipping his cola. He shook his head and looked down at the floor.

"What is it?" asked Chief Driscoll.

"Does he appear smart enough to plan these murders with a female partner?"

Anthony said, "Not exactly."

"He loved his father but he isn't angry and he obeys the 'no trespassing.'"

"He can't remember any specifics like the name of the bank or the insurance company," said Nelson.

"And he keeps his hiking boots in his unlocked car. I wonder how many people knew that," Wilson added.

Wilson turned to Chief Driscoll. "See what I mean. He isn't as pretty now as he was when you found his shoes."

"What should we do?"

"Well let's see if he knows anything else that might help us after he finishes his pop."

"Wait a minute," Wilson said. "Let me see that file again." Nelson handed the file folder to Wilson.

He reread the file and then dropped his arms to his side and took a deep breath.

"What is it?" asked a concerned Nelson.

"Check the dates."

She looked at the dates and did a double take with her mouth open.

"What is it?" asked Anthony and Driscoll simultaneously.

"The eviction letter was a thirty day notice from the court but Robert Doyle had signed the letter two days before the final eviction date. He was evicted two days early."

Chief Driscoll looked at the letter again. Now it was his turn to sigh in disdain.

The detectives looked at him waiting for him to look up.

"Chief Caswell went on vacation to Punta Cana the day after the eviction."

Now they knew the reason behind the two days between the murders.

"So he rushed Doyle through the eviction because he had a vacation booked."

"I never knew about this."

"Well our killer knew."

"Doyle must have complied with the eviction without filing a complaint."

"Perhaps, Chief Caswell was intimidating. It fits with Frank's reaction to him about the trespassing."

"Yes, the Chief could be intimidating to those who respected authority."

Detective Anthony's cell phone went off surprising them.

"Anthony," he answered and listened for a moment.

"What!" Pause.

"When?"

"How the fuck . . ." He slumped into a chair staring at the other three with his mouth open like he couldn't talk.

"Okay, okay. We'll be there shortly."

Click.

"Ernie Taylor didn't answer his phone and when Campbell got to the insurance office he was at the bottom of the stairs. The M.E. says a broken neck from the fall. I walked up those stairs. That is a long fall."

"Or a short push," said Wilson.

"That answers some questions," added Nelson.

"Like what detective?" asked Chief Driscoll.

"For starters she is sticking to her two day schedule. We debated this today thinking that if we had all the targets guarded she might wait for an opening. She is staying one step ahead of us."

Wilson chimed in, "And now we know that Frank has nothing to do with any of this. She was setting him up as a patsy or maybe just a distraction for us."

"She probably took his boots to misdirect us. She knew we wouldn't be able to tell on the video if it was woman or a man starting the fire at the lab."

"She might have been waiting for you to pick him up so she could head to Chicago."

Anthony said, "She is rubbing it in our faces now. She thinks she is smarter than us."

"Well. So far she is. Scientists are pretty smart," said Wilson.

"You think it's his sister?" ask Chief Driscoll.

"Well Chief she fits all the criteria; means, motive and method," Wilson replied. "And since we don't have any other suspects yet until we can eliminate her as a suspect she is our focus now. Dig up everything you can on her and fill me in later."

"As soon as I have something I will call you," replied Chief Driscoll.

The detectives left Kelby for the drive back to Chicago with more on their plate than when they arrived.

CHAPTER 19

THE M.E. AND the CI Techs didn't find any sign of foul play in the death of Ernie Taylor. It appeared that he had fallen down the stairs of his second floor office and broken his neck in the process. But did he fall by accident or was he pushed. It was the perfect murder, if it was murder and as far as Wilson was concerned it was murder. It was far too much of a coincidence that another person in the photo could have died by accident on one of the days they were expecting an attack.

Standing at the top of the narrow stairs the detectives looked down where the body had laid when they arrived. Detective Anthony, having been here before, checked the doors of the hallway and found one that was open just a few feet from the top of the stairs.

"If she hid in here and gave him a good shove once he was on the stairs he wouldn't have had a chance." He looked at the door handle closely.

"We won't find any fingerprints; she is too smart for that."

"But how would she know when he was going to leave?" questioned Nelson.

Wilson looked down the hallway to Taylor's office and said, "Maybe she had checked his routine and knew what time he was leaving each day."

"I think I have an idea how she did it." Anthony said. "There is no access for handicapped people here. If someone who was handicapped called him about a meeting he would have to come to them."

"Of course," Wilson said. "She could have arranged a meeting with him by phone explaining that is was a handicapped claim and then waited in there for him to leave. Good thinking Anthony. If she waited until he was already on the stairs she probably wouldn't have had to push him very hard to get to get him tumbling and therefore there will be no bruising on his back in the pattern of someone hands."

"Wow. She gets scarier every day," said Nelson.

"At least we have a day to find her," added Anthony.

"Nelson, drop off the shoes to Garcia for comparison and meet us back at the bullpen."

The first thing Wilson did when he, Campbell and Anthony arrived back at the bullpen was flip the sheet of paper on the Big Board and write KILLER at the top of the new page. And then underneath he wrote.

— Scientist
— Sister
— Snapped

He stopped, put down the marker and sat on the edge of a desk, arms folded, staring at the board. Officer Campbell and Detective Anthony sat either side of him. They were all staring at it when Nelson arrived. She joined them in this team staring. They now knew why the killer was using a two day time frame and why Chief Caswell was a target. Regrettably they also knew why Ernie Taylor was a target when they had previously thought he was not.

The death of Dr. Brennan was a small mystery as the lab was not involved with the eviction of Mr. Doyle from his farm. Perhaps his being on the farm and feeding the cattle that had belonged to her father was enough for the killer. Or as Dr. Devlin had suggested maybe she believed that if she eliminated the lab then in her mind the farm would miraculously revert back to her father. Not knowing what was going through her mind was a major hindrance to stopping her from attacking her next victim. They had guessed wrong twice; first with Chief Caswell and now with Ernie Taylor. After having assigned Officer Campbell to the investigation team Captain Stone will not be happy to hear about the latest murder. But as far as the investigation was concerned Taylor was as far off the chart as you can get and he had refused protection.

Wilson's cell rang and he knew who it was right away.

"Chief?"

"Yes Detective. I have some information for you."

"I am putting you on speaker Chief."

"It turns out that Frank Doyle's sister is named Susan Louise Doyle. Her mother called her by Louise, after her grandmother, and everyone else just followed."

Wilson went to the Big Board and wrote the name under *Killer*.

"She went to Indiana State University and got her degree in Neuroscience. That was ten years ago. That makes her thirty-five now. Her Illinois driver's licence lists her at 5' 3" with blonde hair with hazel eyes."

The blonde hairs they found in Murphy's bedroom were her real hair. And evidence to use later.

"After she got her B.Sc. degree she moved out of state. We haven't been able to find out where she went after that."

Wilson spoke up. "That's great Chief. We can follow up on that from here."

"Any leads from the new murder?"

"No Chief. So far she has been very skilled at leaving little evidence behind."

"This is like something out of a James Bond movie."

"Chief we can't take any more chances with her. Everyone connected to the farm needs to be watched and that includes Frank Doyle."

"You think he is in danger?"

"He was there when the eviction took place and from the sound of their relationship she didn't have much time for her brother before she snapped. Now who knows what she is thinking about him."

"I'll keep him here where we can keep an eye on him."

"Good. What about the deputy Mayor? The one who wasn't there when the picture was taken."

"We asked him to move in with Deborah Webster the president of the Chamber of Commerce. That way we can watch two of them at the same time."

"That should slow down Doyle's plans."

"Have you heard from Olson?"

"Yes, she said she is safely stashed in the basement of her mother's house. I have two men covering the Mayor and his wife and two men covering the Deputy Mayor and Ms. Webster. If anyone attempts to approach those houses we will be ready. Everyone else are far out of town and fairly well hidden."

"Okay Good. Everyone is covered," Wilson said. "Now let's see if we can find Susan Louise Doyle before the next forty-eight hours is over."

Chief Driscoll said his good-bye.

Click.

Wilson turned to his team, "We need to track down her movements. Anthony, give Indiana State another call and get more info on her and then have Dixon do his thing with it. Maybe he can get us caught up."

Detective Anthony nodded his head and then disappeared through the bullpen doors without a word.

"Andy, keep on the hotel trail looking for that car. I doubt she is still driving it around so if she has new wheels it has to be sitting in a parking lot somewhere."

In the same manner as Detective Anthony, Campbell nodded and left.

Wilson turned to the big board leaving Nelson looking at him as if waiting for him to give her instructions. Nelson's cell phone rang. Sara Garcia.

"Yes," she said and then listened.

"No."

"Okay." Listening again.

"Thanks Garcia."

Click.

"The boots are a print match and the soil is a match to the sample we gave them off our shoes after taking the pictures by the fence," Nelson said to Wilson.

"It confirms our speculation that she used her brother's boots to mislead us," Wilson said. "I doubt there is any chance of recovering DNA by now but . . ."

"But what?" Nelson asked him.

He held up his index finger while he pulled out his cell phone and called.

"Chief?"

"Detective? Some news?" Driscoll replied.

Wilson updated him on the boots while looking directly at Nelson.

"I need your guys to check Doyle's car for finger prints on the back doors. If she lifted the boots at night and wasn't wearing gloves, even if she wiped the doors down, she might have missed a spot in the dark."

Nelson smiled and nodded.

"Good idea. We will do it right now before it gets dark."

Good-byes.

Click.

Nelson cell phone rang again. It was Campbell.

"Yes. Okay. Thanks Andy."

Click.

"That was Campbell. On his way out he stopped by to see Cindy about the water sample from the pond in Kelby. It wasn't a match."

"No surprise there. Other than her brother's boots I doubt she would have used anything local. Too easy to trace."

"True."

Wilson turned to the Big Board again. He flipped the pages over going back to the first page with list of the names of the people in the newspaper photo.

1 — Tom Murphy
2 — Dr. Emmet Brennan
3 — Mayor Gregory
4 — Deborah Webster
5 — Caryn Olson
6 — Chief Caswell
7 — Melissa Green
8 — Ernie Taylor
9 — Kathleen Shearer
10 — Alex Chung
11 — Ivar Ericson
12 — Aaron Goldstein
13 — Gil Ackermann
14 — Mayor of Chicago
15 — Governor of Illinois

After looking at the board for a few minutes he said, "Of course."

"What?"

"It was reconnaissance."

"How do you mean?"

"She didn't kill Murphy until she was ready to start that's why it was thirty days. And that was how she was able to kill Taylor so easily. She had being following him as well as everyone else. She waited until she knew everyone's movements before she started. Hell, she might have even got more info from Murphy in their pillow talks."

"Which means?"

"She was going to wait for all of them to be somewhere alone and she knew where that would be for each one of them."

"We were too late for Taylor but we have the others protected so she can't get at them," said Nelson.

"Do we really? How can we be sure?" Wilson countered. There was tension in his voice. "We need to find out what she knows about the rest of them. She knows the moment when they will be alone each day. We have to talk to them tomorrow. We have to go through their daily routines and find out when they become vulnerable."

"Sounds like a good idea."

"Go find Anthony and the two of you go home get some sleep. We need to be sharp an early meeting tomorrow."

"What about you?" she inquired.

"I'll call Andy and tell him the same." He smiled at her. "I have a dinner date with three beautiful young ladies tonight."

She knew that meant it was pizza night at his girlfriend's house and her two daughters would be joining them. She was both happy and jealous at the same time. Detective Anthony also had family to go home to but she would be eating alone and calling her mom. Her mom would sometimes worry about her too much and while that was draining some days it was better than being alone with no one who cares about your day's troubles. Sometimes she wished it was that elusive boyfriend who she would be calling to talk about her day and plan a weekend date with. She was firm believer in fate and that you are where you are because your actions have put you there but after two bad relationships she had decided that this alone time was needed. The question was how long she would be alone. The answer was yet to come.

CHAPTER 20

THE IDEA OF having the breakfast choice decided upon by Detective Anthony's taste of morning cuisine was enough for Wilson to suggest that he would supply breakfast for the morning powwow. Knowing the strict diet that his wife had him on at home Anthony would have brought the sweetest doughnuts he could find. An eight o'clock meeting, instead of seven thirty, with breakfast provided was a small reward for a hard week of work. When Nelson arrived at seven-fifty she was surprised to see the other three already there and burrowing into the breakfast wraps that Wilson had brought in for them.

Wilson had updated Officer Campbell and Detective Anthony on the agenda of the meeting before Nelson had arrived. Everyone would have their assignments today and he didn't want there to be any misunderstanding about the importance of following up on any lead they stumble upon. They could not afford to let anything drop through the cracks if they were to find the killer before she could kill again. They now had less than forty hours to accomplish their task.

"Andy you keep on that missing car. Call anyone you can think of that might be able to help find it." For some reason Wilson tended to call

Officer Campbell by his first name and yet it had nothing to do with their personal relationship considering that they rarely saw each other outside of work.

"Anthony, you follow up with Dixon on the school information and keep us posted. Nelson and I are going back to Kelby to re-interview the remaining potential targets in case we missed something. Our killer seems to know when everyone would be alone and we need to know that also. In fact we need to know everything we can about her today. No detail is too small and email to everyone at the same time."

"Now I have to go update Captain Stone."

Heads nodded and silently two of them moved out of the bullpen. He looked at Nelson.

"I'll be back shortly and then we will go."

Captain Stone's office door was open and Lieutenant Trentini was sitting in a chair to the right. Neither of the men appeared to be in a good mood but Wilson hoped it was not because of the case his team was working on.

"What do you have for us Wilson?"

"Well sir there was another victim last night here in Chicago."

"I thought you said she was after people in Kelby?"

'Yes sir but this one, the insurance agent for the Lab has an office here. He fell down a flight of stairs but we are reasonably sure he pushed."

"And no one saw this happen?"

"No sir, he was leaving for a meeting and we think she staged it."

"So she is keeping to her schedule."

"Yes sir."

Trentini said, "Do you need anything else to help in your investigation?"

"Not at the moment. I think everyone is giving their full attention to the case."

"Well if you do, just ask and don't let anyone slow you down. If you run into any roadblocks call me and I will straighten it out for you," said Trentini.

"That's great. Thank you."

"Find us that killer Wilson," Stone said encouragingly.

Wilson turned and left reflecting on how cooperative his superiors were being. They were keenly interested in Wilson's team catching the killer and yet they were keeping their distance for the time being. The political undertones were obvious. If he failed then it was his team that will take the brunt of the culpability but if he succeeds then the department, and his superiors, who supported him in his efforts will share in the credit.

A quick stop for a coffee to go and then Wilson and Nelson headed west on Dwight D. Eisenhower Expressway to the Ronald Reagan Memorial Highway. The previous trips to Kelby were reactive but this time it was a proactive trip. They were still playing catch up with the killer but now they had leads and a game plan and for the first time since they started Wilson felt that they might be gaining control of the situation.

Forty five minutes later Wilson pulled his SUV into one of the visitor parking spots at the Kelby Police Department and from there they were driven by Chief Driscoll to the lumber yard where Frank Doyle worked. They met him in the lunchroom on his break.

"Good morning Frank."

"Nothing good about it," he mumbled back.

"Tough night?"

"Sleeping on a cot isn't very comfortable."

"Well we'll see if your bed can be brought down for you. Hopefully it won't be much longer but it is important for your safety."

"Yeah so you say."

"When are you alone Frank?"

He looked at Wilson confused by the question. "I'm always alone. I don't have a girlfriend."

"So other than at work you are alone. What about friends and hobbies?"

"I play online poker but I am alone then. Don't have many friends that I hang with."

"Well that's a problem for you then."

"Why's that?"

"The killer is waiting for her victims to be alone. That means you are at severe risk and we can't protect you outside of here."

Doyle said, "Sounds like she is on tilt."

"Yes it does. So you are going to have to stay at the police station when you are not working."

"Geez."

"Sorry, but we need to keep you alive."

Nelson waited until they had left the lunch room to ask Wilson what tilt meant.

"It's a poker term for a player that has lost their composure after losing a big hand. They will bet with anything trying to win a hand. They usually lose all their money or tournaments chips if they don't recover quickly."

"Interesting comparison."

Nelson's cell phone chirped indicating that she had an email. Wilson had put his cell phone on vibrate.

When they were back in Chief Driscoll's Police truck Nelson opened the email.

She read it out loud to Wilson and Driscoll who were sitting in the front seats. "It's from Detective Anthony. Susan Louise Doyle graduated from Indiana State with a Bachelor of Science degree in Neuroscience. The university didn't know where she went but Dixon tracked her to Kansas State where she has been working as a research lab technician in their Neuroscience department. She quit about two months ago and didn't leave a forwarding address. They don't know why she quit but apparently it had nothing to do with her job. She was well liked there. She is married to a John Roger Fisher of Winnfield Kansas."

"That is great information isn't it," Driscoll asked of the two detectives. Wilson smiled and Driscoll noticed. Their hard work was beginning to show some rewards. Every time they learned something about her they were a step closer to finding her.

Nelson replied, "Yes it is Chief."

"Tell Anthony and Dixon 'Good work." Wilson clicked the buckle on his seat belt. "Let's go visit with the Mayor now."

The drive to City Hall much like all driving in Kelby was without a slowdown for road construction work or congestion of traffic. Unlike the profuse traffic of a Chicago rush hour the streets of Kelby were a pleasure to drive on and the fact that driving to any destination in Kelby was never more than twenty minutes was an added benefit.

The receptionist at City Hall was expecting them and called the Mayor as soon as they entered the building and then greeted them.

"Right this way please," she said as she directed them to the Mayor's office.

"Mr. Mayor," Chief Driscoll said as he nodded towards the man behind the large antique wooden desk. The Mayor's office was medium in size, hardly as pretentious as some of the big city mayor offices.

"Well detectives what can I do for you this time?"

Nelson updated the Mayor in on the new information, "Sir we need to go over some daily details with you. We are trying to determine at what time each of the potential targets would be alone during the day."

The Mayor studied the detectives, "Well I can sum that up for you very quickly. I am never alone."

"We understand that sir but we are looking for loop holes in your schedule that might leave you unaccompanied by anyone."

"At the risk of repeating myself; except in this office," he motioned to a door on the right side of the office, "and in my private washroom I am never alone, ever."

"So there isn't a time during the daily routine that you go anywhere alone?"

"Detective Nelson there isn't a time in most months where I am left alone to do something, except as I stated, here in this office. I am currently escorted to and from work by an officer and my wife is with me at home so no, I am never alone."

"That's good. We need to cover all the bases. We are trying to determine who would be her primary target on Thursday."

"I understand and I appreciate your diligence but I can assure you that she will not be able to attack me without someone else present and I have no intention of giving her that opportunity."

"Thank you Mr. Mayor."

They said their good-byes and walked slowly back to the front lobby. Wilson was curiously quiet and both Nelson and Driscoll had noticed this. He stopped in the lobby as if deep in thought. Nelson and Driscoll stopped and turned to face him.

"Hmmm," Wilson murmured.

"What is it?"

"The Mayor is front and center in the picture right beside the first victim, Dr. Brennan. If she is waiting to pick her spots as we have just surmised then it fits that she hasn't tried to attack the Mayor yet. But if he is never alone and she knows that then how is she planning to attack him."

"Maybe she will be very patient," said Driscoll.

"Maybe," Wilson said. "Or maybe she has something special planned for him. If so, then what is it? And when?"

Nelson said, "If she is going to attack the Mayor even if he is with someone then she either is changing her plan or it was part of her plan all along."

"Precisely, and that is a scary wrinkle," said Wilson.

He was not feeling as confident now as he had felt before the meeting. Not knowing how or when she was planning on attacking the Mayor made him nervous. Intangibles and variables leave too many openings for mistakes and a mistake by the detectives could have serious repercussions. Meaning someone's death.

They left City Hall and climbed back into Driscoll's truck. It was time for lunch and review of the two interviews. Driscoll took them to a greasy spoon on the main street. A clubhouse, a tuna melt and an order of quesadilla were the required food intake.

"Detective," Chief Driscoll said to Wilson after swallowing the first bite of his clubhouse sandwich. "Do you mind if I ask you a difficult question?"

"Fire away," responded Wilson as he inhaled another slice of the quesadilla.

"Interesting choice of words considering my question. I was wondering if you had ever shot anyone."

Nibbling on her tuna melt Nelson looked at Wilson. In the year they had been together she hadn't asked him this question even though she had wanted to do so. She knew Wilson had fired his gun and there were consequences because of it.

"Well I know that most cops have never pulled their gun out in all their years on the force. The ones that have retired without having to pull the trigger while on a call have always said how happy they were to have never been in that situation. I however won't be one of them. I fired my gun the first week I was on the street." Wilson took another bite of his quesadilla while Nelson and Driscoll waited patiently for him to continue.

"I saw three people that appeared to be in the middle of a drug buy on a street corner. I had no idea what type of drugs they were selling or even if it was drugs. It just looked like it was a buy. Before they saw me I called it in. I was a half a block away when they noticed me. I was supposed to observe and wait for back up to arrive. They took off in three different directions."

Nelson and Chief Driscoll were on the edge of their seats. Wilson took another bite of his quesadilla wiped his mouth with a napkin and continued.

"I decided to follow the one that I thought was the dealer. He had a bit of a lead on me and when he went around the corner I followed. I turned the corner and saw him running into a side street and when I reached it and looked into the side street he just disappeared. I stopped running and walked, carefully checking back doors of the stores for an open door. There was truck alley about half way down the street. I assumed he must have gone down it. I should have stopped there and waited for back up but I was a bit bull headed back then. I had no fear of right or wrong so I entered the alley. It was dark and the person I was chasing was dressed in black so I listened for noise and watched for movement. Nothing. I took a few slow steps down the alley and then stopped. There still wasn't any noise or movement. At that point I should have backed up and waited at the street for the back-up to arrive and I was just about to do that when I heard a scraping noise. I unclipped my holster, looked down the alley and concentrated on listening. I heard heavy breathing. There was a dumpster on the right maybe fifteen yards ahead. I was fairly sure he was behind it. I decided to calmly talk him out. He wasn't very receptive so I moved closer keeping the dumpster between us. I could hear him moving now so I told him not to try and run. I told him I was a track star in college. I guess he believed me because he decided to make a stand rather than run. I heard the scuffling sound again. It was him getting to his feet. I thought he was giving himself up. I already had visions of grandeur about the arrest. A shadow stepped from behind the dumpster. I couldn't tell the age. I started to step forward when his arm came up and I saw a flash. I dove to the ground and heard a whizzing noise go past my right ear. I guess he thought since I went down that he hit me because he didn't shoot again. I rolled over and pulled my gun out exactly as we had been trained to do. In the prone position I pointed my gun and fired. It was too dark to tell but he was turning to run. I hit him in the back of the left thigh. He screamed and fell and his gun bounced across the alley. I told him not to move and I kicked his gun further away from him. I was about to call it in when the back-up arrived. My first arrest and I had shot the perp."

Nelson and Driscoll had been like children listening to their favourite bedtime story. Their faces had been frozen in anticipation of the outcome of the story. It was one thing to see this acted out on a TV cop show but to hear a real life experience from someone that you know was adrenaline-charging.

"I thought everything was going to be okay but little did I know how much I had pissed off Captain Stone. He kept me on desk duty for two more weeks after the review board cleared the shooting. Ignoring protocol, when the circumstances didn't warrant it, did not sit well with him. He rode me for the next couple of years and to this day I cringe when he calls me to his office."

CHAPTER 21

WITH LUNCH OVER with they were on their way to the next interview with Deborah Webster at the Chamber of Commerce. It was just a five minute drive away. Nelson's phone vibrated. It was an email from Officer Campbell. She read it to herself first and then repeated it to Wilson and Driscoll.

"They found the white car. A state trooper, one of Campbell's contacts, found it in a hotel parking lot in Davenport, Iowa about three hours away. The bumper sticker is blue and red as described by the security guard. It's a Kansas Jayhawk logo. It has Kansas plates. It has been there for several days according to the hotel manager. Campbell is on his way there to verify in person. He will send pictures."

Wilson nodded his head but not in acceptance of the information but rather that it made him feel better that they were closing in on her. The car would surely lead them to her, or would it. Wilson knew that many times in the past investigations leads haven't always given you everything that you want from them. The fact that the car has been abandoned means she has acquired new wheels and could have been driving around Kelby in total anonymity.

"Chief," Wilson said, "Have your men watch out for rental cars and any cars with out of state plates."

"Good idea."

Even though they had a time frame pushing them Wilson knew he had to be patient with his team and with new leads. Jumping to conclusions was a mistake they could not afford. Now was not the time to overlook an important detail due to excitement. Neither the conversation with Frank Doyle or the Mayor had provided them with any insights but Wilson's experience led him to believe that sooner or later something would shed light on the day's task of finding out how she knows when her potential targets will be alone. In the back of his mind Wilson was burying a concern that he didn't want to address just yet. What if she was changing her method for attacking the rest of the people in Kelby? What if there would be no more attacks of people when they were alone. Was she smart enough to have preplanned to change gears halfway through her rampage? Were they on a wild goose chase today looking for the next situation where one of the people would be alone? All these questions bothered Wilson but due diligence was required before addressing them.

The Chamber of Commerce building was in the middle of a row of store fronts on 4th Street. It was considerably newer than City Hall but it was already in the process of getting a face lift. The original red brick store fronts were being replaced with a softer brown brick and a beige fascia. Newly detailed bay windows on the second floor apartments were topped with reddish cone turrets giving the street a castle effect. Only the red bricked, square shaped bank on the corner ruined the outcome. A candle store sat to the left of The Chamber of Commerce and a women's boutique took up the spot on the right side. On the glass door a sign hanging from a string and a small suction cup read 'Welcome'. When the three of them were inside the reception buzzed the president of the Kelby Chamber of Commerce to let her know that they were there.

Deborah Webster was a striking red head and although not really tall her three inch heels elevated her from five-six to five-nine giving the illusion of a tall women. As the President of the Chamber of Commerce she had a hand in new business development in Kelby and one of those new businesses she helped bring to Kelby was the Genesis Research Lab built on the vacated Doyle farm. That put her in the picture and most likely now in the sights of Susan Doyle. Webster was not lacking in self-confidence and that probably helps her in the execution of her duties.

"So to what do I owe the pleasure of your visit?"

Wilson took the lead this time, "We are double checking everyone's schedule to see if there are any gaps we have overlooked."

"Well you have the Deputy Mayor staying with me and the officers guarding us I don't see how there can be any gaps."

Wilson nodded, "Yes it may seem that you are well covered but we don't want to take any chances. If you review you daily schedule is there any time when you are ever on your own?"

Webster skipped through a week of her datebook and then looked up. Her face showed vulnerability previously not displayed. She rested her chin in her hand her and sighed.

"I have lunch with my mother every Thursday at one o'clock. She lives at the Kelby Retirement Home at the north end of town. She has a bad hip and uses a wheel chair to get around. I never miss that lunch. They serve tuna melt sandwiches and my mother hates tuna. They would make her another sandwich but sitting there smelling the tuna would put her off the rest of the day so I take her out."

Wilson sighed. There it was; an opening for Doyle. Thursday was the next potential target date and it was a reasonable assumption that Doyle expected Webster to keep her dinner date with her mother.

"That was very helpful. It makes everything clear now." Wilson was almost ecstatic knowing that they were now one step ahead of the killer but he didn't dare show it. "You would normally drive there alone?"

"Yes. Do you think I will have to cancel my visit on Thursday? I could take her shopping on Saturday instead."

"I am not sure just yet. We need to think about it." Wilson turned to look at Nelson who interpreted his look that she should say something.

"If you leave here with a police escort that might disrupt her plans," Nelson said. "I wonder if she is expecting you to get away this one time."

"My car is in the back parking lot so it would be easy for me to leave without the officer knowing."

"Yes it would, wouldn't it," mused Wilson. Nelson knew that tone of voice from Wilson meant he was thinking of something that he had not yet revealed to her.

"You think she should go alone to lunch on Thursday and see if it draws out Doyle?"

Wilson smiled at Nelson, "Sort of."

"Won't I be in danger," said Webster in a concerned tone.

"Not at all," Wilson replied. Nelson was beginning to grasp where Wilson's was going.

"You will be safe and sound having lunch with your mother right here in your office."

'What? How?"

"We will bring your mother here."

That confused Nelson; she hadn't considered that as a part of the plan.

"But how does that help you if I am not alone driving to the home?"

"Oh you will be." Webster was totally confused by this but Nelson nodded that she now understood the plan.

"Detective Nelson with a wig and high heels would pass as you getting into your car in the back parking lot."

"Oh, wow. Do you think so?"

"If Doyle is waiting for you to leave for lunch on Thursday she won't be close enough that she would be able to see your face clearly."

"How can you be sure Detective Nelson will fool her?"

"Well there is an automatic brain response to visual stimuli. Our minds sometimes formulate thoughts for us that are not necessarily correct. When you are expecting to see an image of someone and the image appears we accept it because we expected it. Subtle differences are not readily noticed because once the brain has accepted the image and it moves on to the next task. When Doyle sees Detective Nelson dressed as you, walk to your car, her thoughts will already be on getting into position to follow you and therefore she won't notice any small differences."

"Wow."

Wilson was doodling on his note pad. "At the same time that Detective Nelson gets into your car your mother will be leaving leave the home to come here. Doyle can't be in two places at the same time so she will never see your mother."

Chief Driscoll, quiet until now, spoke, "I will arrange the van to pick up your mother."

She could down her in the parking there and be miles away before anyone noticed."

That image sent a chill through the bullpen and there was a brief silence before Wilson spoke.

"That means we will need more support at the home. Nelson you will need to wear a jacket tomorrow to hide some protection. That blue suit should work," said Wilson.

"I'm glad you are so up on my wardrobe," Nelson laughed nervously. She knew why he had made that suggestion and she was glad to hear his comment about extra protection but the thought of walking around with a bulls-eye on her chest was less than agreeable even if it was only a short walk across a parking lot."

Wilson picked up the desk phone and called Chief Driscoll to update him in on all the news relating to Susan Doyle. He also brought him up to date on the theory of the attack on Webster at the home on Thursday.

"Chief we will need a couple of eyes near the Chamber of Commerce looking for anyone looking suspicious and a couple more near the retirement home. They should be in plain clothes, no uniforms. We can't be sure that the attack will be tried there but we need to be ready in any case. We will also need to look out for any rental cars or cars with out of state plates parked near the home."

"I will have that arranged."

"We will meet you at your office around ten o'clock."

"I will have everyone ready to be briefed. I sent the prints we lifted off the door handle of Frank Doyle's car to your tech people as you requested."

"Thanks," said Wilson. "Hopefully we can match them to the ones we lifted from Murphy's apartment and connect her to his death also. We'll see you in the morning Chief."

Wilson hung up and stared at the phone for a moment. Was this plan going to work or was this all going to end badly.

"Okay everyone be back here at eight in the morning for a briefing before we head to Kelby."

CHAPTER 22

PEERING OUT FROM his seventh floor condo Wilson viewed the Thursday morning weather as favorable, overcast skies but no sign of rain. A rainy day would have made the conditions particularly difficult for the officers looking for a vehicle or a suspicious person. Being able to act as naturally as possible is a big benefit when carrying out a stake-out, or when doing covert work. Standing outside in the rain even under an umbrella is far less subtle and more noticeable to someone who is looking for signs of a tail. A short visit last night with his girlfriend Jennifer had temporarily eased his mind about today's activities but now dressed and ready to leave for the precinct the worries were creeping back into his thoughts. Susan Doyle was a calculating vindictive killer with multiple targets on her list. It doesn't get much more difficult than that, when it comes to doing detective work and finding her. Having Nelson pretend to be Webster seemed like a good idea at the time but now the thought of placing her in the killer sights was churning Wilson's stomach. Everything would be fine, if they could find Doyle before Nelson leaves the home to get back into Webster's car, but if they don't what then. Would he flinch and pull the plug and stop Nelson or risk her life as she walked across the parking lot. If Doyle has any inkling that they are looking for her she would know for sure if they aborted the deception. All these thoughts turned his usual pleasant drive to the precinct into an irritation but once inside the bullpen he started to feel control coming back to him.

Nelson was already there adjusting the buttons on her navy suit jacket.

Underneath her jacket was a lightweight bullet-proof vest. Her navy suit was one she had bought herself after she had dropped some of her weight two years ago. She had gone on to lose even more weight later so the bullet-proof vest was barely noticeable when she did up one button. When Wilson saw her, with the vest on, his nervousness lessened and the tightness in his chest dissipated. One deep breath and he was able to smile again. He turned away just as Officer Campbell and Detective Anthony walked in with coffee and donuts. Anthony was grinning like a cat; anticipating delving into his donuts. Eating donuts at work was one of the little secrets that he kept from his wife. For the past year his wife has had him on a very healthy diet due to his high blood pressure but once a week he manages to bring donuts, his number one vice, into the bullpen.

"Andy you go with Anthony in his car. When we get to Kelby Chief Driscoll will have a car for you to drive. The fewer out of town vehicles used the better. Nelson will ride with me. The bomb squad will do a dog walk through the parking lot around Webster's car to be sure there is nothing attached to it. I doubt there will be anything for them to find especially as she is being guarded but as her ex-husband is a welder and we have no idea what she learned from him I think it is better to be sure."

"When we get there we'll drive the route in both vehicles at exactly the speed limit to get a feel for the time and then stop at the home before heading back to the Kelby Police Department to meet with Chief Driscoll and his troops."

We will turn right on 4th Street straight past the Chamber of Commerce building and then right on Sycamore Street heading north past the hospital and then left on Meadow Lane to the home. The whole trip should take no more than ten minutes so I don't expect any interruptions from another vehicle. Watch for anything that looks out of the ordinary. Okay let's roll."

Forty-five minutes later they were stopped at the corner of 4th Street and Main. Both cars turned right and then a few blocks later right again onto Sycamore. The first part of Sycamore was residential housing until they passed a small park, and then after the high school it opened up to a surprisingly large mall, that encompassed both sides of the street for two blocks. Two more blocks and the hospital came into view. They turned left at the next street, and a minute later pulled into the parking lot of the retirement home.

They all got out their vehicles and looked around the parking lot.

"This is a really good spot for a home," said Anthony. "The hospital is two blocks away and the dentist and rehab facility are at the end of the street."

"I thought that the route was very open," said Officer Campbell. "Not really suitable for a surprise attack."

"I agree," said Nelson. A second later she wished she had replied differently. She had agreed to several comments the last two days.

Wilson was facing them but not looking at them. He was looking past them at the trees and bushes behind the home. When they noticed his unreceptive face they turned around to see what he was looking at. All four of them were now staring at the trees. The treeline behind the home stretched for a couple of hundred yards. It was an ample expanse for an archer to hide. The entrance to the visitor parking lot was at least fifty yards from the tree line at the back of the home. Wilson wondered just how good of an archer was Susan Doyle.

Wilson turned to Nelson, "Remind me to make sure we talk about the trees with Chief Driscoll. The only place you will be exposed is in the Chamber of Commerce parking lot and here. If she is going to hide in those trees to shoot you we can make the angle of the shot more difficult for her." He pointed to the front of the building. "If you park at the front corner you will be walking from the door to the car at a forty-five degree angle away from the trees. That will only give her about ten seconds to shoot but by that time we should already have her."

"I certainly hope so," said Nelson thinking that she has never been shot at, let alone been hit, while wearing a bullet-proof vest and that it would be an arrow not a bullet didn't make her feel any better about the situation.

They climbed in the two vehicles and headed for the Kelby Police Department. When they arrived Wilson noticed that there were twice the numbers of personal vehicles in the parking lot as any other visit.

An officer was waiting for them and directed them to the large conference room where the six-man Kelby Police Task Force was seated. They were wearing their own clothes; one in a suit, the rest in casual attire. The suit was Chief Driscoll. The officers guarding the Mayor, the Deputy Mayor and Deborah Webster would still be in uniform. These officers, the task force, were the only ones who were aware of today's covert plan. The fewer people that knew about the plan the better, as far as Wilson was concerned. Once inside the conference room Nelson removed her jacket and the bullet-proof vest underneath it revealing a simple white cotton blouse.

Wilson gave a brief update to the troops to get them up to speed.

"We are going to need a distraction when the dogs sniff Ms. Webster's car. If Doyle was watching to see Webster leave the building at lunchtime, she might be watching the parking lot all morning so I was thinking that if we could get a fire truck to drive down 4th street at eleven o'clock that might be enough of a distraction for the sniffer dogs to walk around her car."

Wilson looked at Chief Driscoll who was already dialing his cell phone. A minute later he disconnected and nodded to Wilson. "It is all set. They will keep the siren on for about two minutes as they drive past."

"Good. We are going to be looking for any cars and or people on the other side of the trees behind the retirement home. We are assuming that she will be using a bow and arrow to shoot at Webster, well Nelson."

Again he looked at Chief Driscoll. "We will also need an ambulance to arrive at the retirement home as Nelson walks to the car. It should look like an emergency call with short siren. I will call you from the lobby when Nelson is ready to leave the home. If Doyle is in the trees waiting for her chance to get Webster in her sights it might distract her enough that she misses her target. I am going to park in the first spot closest to the road and then move my truck just before Nelson arrives. The distance from the trees to where the car will be parked is over fifty yards. She will need to be a very good shot to hit her target from there, especially if there is any wind today."

Chief Driscoll was on his cell phone talking to the paramedics about the visit to the home. Wilson looked at the clock it was ten-fifty. Ten minutes to go for the bomb-sniffing dog to start.

Chief Driscoll ended his call. "All set. They will wait for my call in the parking lot of the dental clinic at the end of the street."

The room went quiet as they all watched the minutes tick by on the clock on the wall.

Wilson's phone rang and a couple of the officers jumped in their seats. Waiting to hear about a possible bomb must have made them edgy.

"Detective Wilson," he answered.

"Mac here sir." Mac was short for MacFarlane. Barney MacFarlane was a short, stout, red-headed Scotsman who had been with the bomb squad for the past ten years. His Scottish brogue was legendary around the Chicago P.D. "All's well. Y'ur guud to go. I looked and there was nothing under the car. And Missie didn't even stop once so her nose didn't pick up any residue."

"Great, thanks Mac." He disconnected. "The car is clean."

The officer's faces displayed their relief.

He continued, "The two officers with eyes on the Chamber of Commerce building will need to watch for any cars pulling out to follow Nelson in Webster's car. If nothing happens scoot up to the bush and help monitor any activity there but one of you stay in the car in case there is a chase. The other two officers there will already be on foot. There can't be too many ways she will approach the bush with a vehicle but there are several foot paths and one paved bicycle path. The farm land to the west doesn't offer much cover so she would be seen if she walked through the field. The subdivision to the north has a cul-de-sac and a dead end, ending at the trees. It would be a good spot for her to enter but again her vehicle would be exposed.

One of you should approach from the county road on the west side in case she is using the farm as an entry. The other one needs to check the two dead ends and enter the woods from there. If the farm is clear drive to the mini mall on the east side and check all the cars there. There is a footpath that goes behind the building, follow it into the woods. If she is carrying a compound bow it will be difficult to conceal. Stop any people you see walking through the woods and ask them if they have seen anyone carrying a long bag or case and then tell them to calmly leave the woods. If she is up in a tree she won't be able to get away right after she shoots. If she is on the ground hiding behind a tree you might be able to see her from a path, if not, be careful entering the trees she may hear you approaching her. Remember we only want to see her first and then we can all close in. You should only need to search about fifty yards of that tree line at the back of the home. Anything outside of that distance and she won't have the right sight line for the target we are giving her so concentrate on the area of the woods closest to the parking lot."

Wilson looked up at the clock. It was almost noon. "One more thing gentleman; put your cell phones on vibrate, and good luck."

"Chief you ride with me. That way we communicate quickly to everyone. We will drop Nelson off at the Chamber of Commerce on our way."

One of the officers handed Officer Campbell the keys to his vehicle.

"Andy, park as close to the corner as you can and then you can mosey up and down the street like a shopper, until Nelson sends you a text to say she is leaving."

"Anthony, you park in the back and come into the building like an employee. When Nelson is ready to leave, you go first and walk real slow so she can leave the parking lot before you, without it looking like you were waiting for her."

"Works for me."

"And remember, report anything that looks suspicious. Okay. Let's roll."

Wilson stopped his white SUV directly in front of the Chamber of Commerce front doors and Nelson walked inside. With her navy jacket, red wig and bullet proof vest inside her large plastic shopping bag she looked like any other shopper on the street. Once inside Deborah Webster's office she would redress, put on make-up and high heels and transform herself into a different person. When she leaves the office impersonating Deborah Webster the real Webster will stay behind closed doors and only Webster's mother who will arrive soon for lunch will know she is still there.

Wilson and Chief Driscoll arrived at the home just as Webster's mother was being helped into the van for her trip to have lunch with her daughter. He received a text from Anthony, 'five', meaning they were five minutes away. Minutes later Nelson arrived, looking remarkably different than earlier. She parked in the empty parking spot waiting for her. Officer Campbell had been driving in front of Nelson and he pulled into the parking lot of the dental clinic to await the arrival of the paramedics. Detective Anthony, who had been following Nelson, parked in the min-mall. He got out of his car and looked around. If Doyle was scoping out this area for one of her attacks maybe someone saw her. He went into the corner store and bought some gum.

"Have you had a woman customer lately, attractive, about five-three, blonde hair," he asked the clerk.

"Maybe half a dozen," the clerk replied.

Well it was worth a shot thought Anthony. It was half past one and Nelson would be leaving the home soon.

In the foyer of the retirement home Nelson was as nervous as one could be waiting to take her walk across the parking lot to Webster's car. Wilson and Driscoll had no news. No one had been seen walking in the woods, and the three officers had not seen anyone in the trees near the back of the home. Wilson was almost as nervous as Nelson. In detective work, no news is not always good news.

"Time to go," said Wilson as he called Officer Campbell to tell him to send the paramedics in exactly thirty seconds. Twenty seconds later Nelson exited through the front doors with Wilson close behind. Half way to the car Nelson heard the paramedic ambulance siren and her muscles tightened in the anticipation of feeling the punch of an arrow hitting her body. Wilson walked towards his SUV five cars away from Webster's car. It was Wilson's hope that the ambulance siren along with his presence in the parking lot would be enough of a distraction that Doyle would either miss her target, or abort her attack. The seconds ticked away practically in slow motion but incredibly when Wilson reached his SUV Nelson was safely in her car.

Feelings of relief were quickly replaced with a moment of frustration. What had happened? Had the attack been aborted? Was Doyle still in the woods?

Officer Campbell had followed the ambulance to the home and now came running into the parking lot only to see Nelson in the car and Wilson standing beside his SUV.

He stopped dead in his tracks on the pavement. Confused he looked back and forth from the trees to Nelson.

Wilson held out his hands, "Nothing."

Chief Driscoll came into view with his cell phone to his ear. He was talking to one of his officers on the other side of the woods. "No one has left the woods," he said. "They have the area covered."

The three of them looked at the woods. Were they wrong? Detective Anthony pulled his vehicle into the parking lot as Nelson got out of Webster's car.

Wilson turned to Chief Driscoll. "Call your man at the Chamber of Commerce to make sure Webster is still there."

A few minutes later the officer confirmed that Deborah Webster was still in her office with her mother. The five of them stood in the middle of parking lot, almost making a circle. Instead of them making Doyle miss her mark she had made them miss her. How could they have been so wrong? If they were wrong what was her target today? Everyone was protected. None of this made sense. Wilson's shoulders began to droop. He fought hard to keep from getting angry. In his younger days this situation would have had him cursing and yelling but he had learned from playing golf and poker that emotional anger was a negative force that disrupted the mind and body. This new found control was almost his personal version of Zen.

Nelson was still shaking her head. Anthony was standing with his hands on his hips trying to comprehend the scene. The only one of them who didn't seem rattled was Officer Campbell. He stood tall, almost at attention observing everyone, waiting for his next instructions.

Wilson's mind was jumping from thought to thought almost too fast to process. They needed to focus on other possibilities, but what? Did they really have everyone guarded?

"Chief, call the Mayor and make sure he and the Deputy Mayor are still protected and double their protection."

Another minute went by and when the Chief ended his call he confirmed that everyone was safe and well protected.

Wilson paced up and down the sidewalk in front of the retirement home. He was mumbling and biting his lip. Finally he stopped pacing and threw up his hands before letting them drop to his sides in defeat. He didn't know what to do next. Despite his internal mantra he was as frustrated as he could remember.

"This is a bad beat," he said to no one in particular.

Nelson asked, "What does bad beat mean?"

Wilson let out a long sigh, "It's when you have the best possible hand with one card to go and the last card gives your opponent a better hand.

The problem here is that we don't even get to see her hand. She's keeping us guessing."

Chief Driscoll's cell phone rang and he quickly answered while the others listened intently to the one-sided conversation.

"Yes."

"What happened?"

"And she's okay?"

"Don't touch them. We'll be there shortly."

Click.

CHAPTER 23

CHIEF DRISCOLL LOOKED at the faces of eagerness staring at him. "The Mayor's wife received a couriered envelope."

Their expressions had not changed.

He continued, "Nothing to worry about, it was not a letter bomb. But I am guessing that it was from Susan Doyle. She received some pictures."

Anthony said, "What kind of pictures?"

"Apparently dirty pictures of her husband and another woman."

Wilson, Nelson and Driscoll climbed into the SUV and the others followed in their vehicles. When they arrived a Kelby police cruiser was parked in front of the Mayor's house with an officer still behind the wheel. They were only three blocks from the Chamber of Commerce building.

"Andy, make sure that Webster's mother gets back to the home safely and then meet us back at the police station."

The Mayor's home was a two-story, double-peaked, red brick house with white trimming and a balcony between the garage and the main section of the house. The front door was in the middle of the porch and the balcony kept a chair on the porch dry when it rained. It was newer and considerably less ostentatious than the older, borderline mansions on their street, but still quite a large home for a couple with no children.

Chief Driscoll led them up the steps to the Mayor's front door. The officer inside opened it before they knocked and showed them into the front room. The wine colored room was large with a grey stone fire place on the far wall. White cornice adorned the seams where the wall and ceiling met. Two ample couches and a knitting chair took up most of the space. A glass top coffee table sat between the couches.

The Mayor's wife was nowhere to be seen. On the coffee table were the tri-colored courier envelope and the pictures.

"How did it go down," the Chief asked his officer.

"Well, the doorbell rang and when I opened it there was a courier in his uniform and the delivery truck parked in front of the house. He said Mrs. Gregory had to sign for the envelope so I called her to the door and she did. She was confused about the delivery. She said she wasn't expecting anything. She took the envelope into the front room and opened it on the coffee table. As soon as she saw the pictures she clamped a hand over her mouth but she still let out a small shriek. Then she started crying. I stepped forward to see if she was okay and I saw one of the pictures. She looked up at me almost scared and then ran upstairs. That's when I called you Chief."

Nelson said, "I'll go and see if she is okay." Wilson nodded his approval.

"We need to talk to the courier," said Wilson. He looked at the officer. "Go with Detective Anthony and bring that courier back here."

They both replied "Yes sir," at the same time and left immediately.

Wilson looked at the pictures without touching them. He moved them around the table using his pen. There were six – eight by ten color photos of the Mayor having sex with a young woman. Chief Driscoll chose not to look at the photos. The sexual contact was enough to cause any spouse distress but these photos were particularly graphic. Adding to the situation was that there was leather paraphernalia and outfits often associated with BDSM sex. The Mayor and the woman were in a woman's bedroom most likely belonging to the woman in the photo. It appeared the pictures were taken from outside the room through a window. When Wilson looked at the last photo in the pile the woman's face was visible. Nelson had been correct. The Mayor was having an illicit affair with his attractive female assistant, Caryn Olson.

Wilson went out to his SUV to get an evidence bag and returned to put the photos and envelope inside. If there were any finger-prints on the photos he wanted them preserved. He signed and sealed the evidence bag as Detective Anthony and the Kelby officer returned with the courier driver and his hand held scanner.

Wilson had once sent a package with a birthday gift inside by a courier. It was supposed to go to a golf buddy in Wisconsin and even though the address was written on the outside of the package a courier scanned in the wrong bar code information and it was shipped to someone in California. He never found out what happened but he hoped whoever it was delivered to enjoyed the exploding golf ball. That was the last time Wilson ever used a courier for personal deliveries.

"This is Alex the courier driver," said Anthony.

"Where did you get the envelope?"

"It was in my route bin when I got to the depot."

"Who sent the envelope to Mrs. Gregory?"

The courier pressed a button on his scanner and after a beep he read off a name.

"Harpo Yerfniw. Must be a European name."

Wilson grabbed the scanner from the courier and read the name himself to confirm what he had heard. "Shit."

He handed the scanner back to the courier.

Anthony asked, "Do you think it's a private eye?"

"No," Wilson shook his head. "It's backwards for Oprah Winfrey."

"Oh yeah," said the courier snickered.

"So you have no idea who sent the envelope?"

"No sir. They could have dropped it off at any of the dozens of drop off boxes or depots."

"Okay. I guess that's all for now."

"Um sir?"

Wilson looked at the courier, "What is it?"

"Did you want to know about the other one?"

Wilson was astonished, "Other one? What other one?

"The other envelope sir. They sent two envelopes."

"Did you deliver the other envelope?"

"Yes sir."

"When?"

"Right after I left here."

"To who?"

"To the editor of the Kelby Journal."

"And did he have to sign for it also."

"Yes sir."

"Maybe he hasn't opened it yet," said Anthony.

"No sir. He opened it right away."

Chief Driscoll let out a sigh that everyone heard.

The police officer drove the courier back to his truck.

Nelson came back down the stairs and Wilson filled her in on the latest news.

"So this was her real target," said Nelson. "We couldn't have done anything to stop her today."

"Like a smart bomb," added Anthony.

"Yes. She killed both the Mayor's marriage and his career at the same time and he doesn't even know yet."

"I am going to go and tell the Mayor in person," said Chief Driscoll. "Despite his indiscretion this is not something he should be told about by a newspaper reporter."

Wilson nodded in agreement.

"I suppose my men won't be needed to guard the Mayor anymore."

"No I don't think so now," replied Wilson looking out the front room window to the street.

"I'll see you back at the police station when you're finished."

"Okay," said Wilson.

When the Chief was gone Wilson said, "We forgot how smart she is. Revenge can take many forms. '*Take advantage of the enemy's unpreparedness, travel by unexpected routes and strike him where he has taken no precautions.*' It's from The Art of War."

Nelson reflected, "She has scored a double hit with this one. The Mayor will never get re-elected and he will be divorced. Mrs. Gregory has already called her lawyer."

Anthony said, "Olson will never get her job back either."

"She may not want to come back at all now."

"Doyle had almost four months to plan everything out and no one was aware that she was right there watching them. It would have been like she was invisible to them."

Nelson said, "That would explain how she knows so much about everyone. But now we have no idea what her attack plan is. Are Webster and Spencer still potential targets or was this the coup de grace?"

"I don't know but it doesn't feel like it."

"This must have been a satisfying day for her, sitting around doing nothing and yet her plan still went forward and if she knew anything about our plan she must be ecstatic. Do you think she might have been watching us?"

"I don't think levity plays a part in any of this. Dr. Devlin said people suffering from this type of breakdown are focussed only on their goal. She would have to be an outright psychopath to take pride in her deception."

The front door bell rang and Nelson answered it. The woman standing sideways on the porch appeared nervous and for a split second Nelson was too. This could not be Susan Doyle, could it? She was the right age but wrong hair color but since Nelson had been a red-head earlier today that didn't matter. Her right hand went instinctively to her hip where her gun was holstered.

"Are you Detective Nelson?"

"Yes I am," she said as her fingers unclasped her holster clip.

"Maggie said to ask for you. I'm Carmen. Carmen Abate. Maggie is my best friend. She called me about the pictures."

Nelson took a breath, "Please come in. Mrs. Gregory is upstairs."

"She said you were very kind to her considering the circumstances. Thank you. She needed someone to be there for her. I am so glad she wasn't alone."

Nelson watched the woman walk up the stairs. She couldn't begin to imagine what Mrs. Gregory was going through. Nelson's bad break ups seemed pale compared to this. It was different breaking up with a boyfriend no matter what the issue was. The remnants might be a bag of clothes to return, but with marriage the fallout includes friends, relatives and memories as well as communal property. It would be a long night for the Gregory's.

"Well," said Wilson. "I believe that is our cue to leave."

They closed the front door quietly behind them.

Everyone on the task force had returned to the Kelby Police Department by the time that Nelson and Wilson arrived. Wilson filled the Chief in on the Mrs. Gregory's guest.

"It is good that Carmen is there," the Chief replied. "Mayor Gregory was surprised but not shocked. It didn't seem like he expected the affair to stay a secret forever." Wilson noticed that the Chief did not refer to the other issue in the pictures.

"They rarely do Chief," said Wilson reflecting on the number of domestic disturbances he had witnessed over the years.

"I am not sure he will be welcomed at home tonight. I suggested that he get a room and go see is wife in the morning. I am sure he will take care of letting Ms. Olson know what has happened."

"It seems strange to say that today was a small victory. The attack was on paper, no one was killed," said Wilson. "I wish I could say definitively that she is finished but my gut says no."

"I agree. The day's result is disappointing but not tragic. Where do we go from here?"

"That's a very good question Chief. Does she have something spiteful to use against Webster and Spencer or is she going to go back to the physical attacks."

"I just had a thought Detective. Deputy Mayor Spencer was not in the newspaper picture about the lab opening."

"Correct."

"And now he will most likely replace Mayor Gregory as interim Mayor until an official election process."

"Your point being," Wilson inquired.

"Well she had to know that would happen. Maybe he was never a target and she wants him to be the new Mayor."

Wilson considered the Chief insight, "Interesting. Or does she want to give him a short-lived peek at his potential future before she pulls the rug out from under his feet."

"I must admit that sounds more like something she might do. Perhaps I am too much of an optimist."

"Don't ever stop being an optimist Chief; just temper it with the odd objective assessment every now and then."

"Good advice. Thanks."

"We're going to head back to Chicago and keep looking for her. It would be helpful if we knew what she was driving now."

"We will keep everyone on staff looking for women and cars they don't recognize."

"I just wish we had a better inkling to who was really on her hit list. We wasted a lot of time and effort today on an idea that actually had merit. We really can't afford to be that far off the mark again if she isn't finished yet. The next time might be her time to take a stand. We can only hope, as Dr. Devlin explained, that her brain might switch back on and she will give up, but I am not going hold my breath."

"No we must remain on our toes," said Chief Driscoll.

"I think she will give us a clear sign when she is finished but you might be onto something about Spencer though. His not being in that picture might actually mean he is out of the picture."

"For his sake I certainly hope so."

"In her state of mind I don't see her doing anything that would be deliberately helpful to anyone. I think it is just a case of pure luck for Spencer. He may just be the right guy in the right place at the right time."

"Well at least we now have some time to think about. Drive careful," said Chief Driscoll.

The four of them headed back to Chicago in the two vehicles. Wilson considered Chief Driscoll's demeanor and wondered how badly he would get chewed up in the big city. He liked the Chief. He had a level head on his shoulders. Maybe Wilson was wrong; maybe the Chief could adapt to big city life but that would be a debate for another day.

Back in the bullpen they sat down at the desks. Nelson sat in her chair but Anthony and Campbell sat on top of a desk. Wilson flipped to a clean page on the Big Board and wrote '*Coup de Grace*' at the top. Nelson smiled. He was using her expression. Underneath he listed three names.

Webster
Spencer
Frank

He turned to them.

"Does anyone think that Webster is not a target?"

No confirmation from the trio indicated they still felt that Webster was on Doyle's hit list. The only thing in Webster's favor was that no women have been targeted yet but could have been because Olson was only a bit player in her master plan and Melissa Green was inaccessible.

Nelson said, "Mr. Spencer has suddenly become Mr. Lucky. I don't think she deliberately arranged for Spencer to be in line for a promotion but if she manipulated it by accident maybe he isn't in her sights."

"I think you might be right. If he was on the hit list she probably would have him ahead of the Mayor," said Anthony.

"Or she is giving him a false sense of security to make him more accessible later," offered Campbell.

"Good insight Andy. It could be either. That leaves her brother."

Nelson said, "I think if he is on her list that he would be the last one. It would be an obvious link to her and so far she has been very good at hiding but then killing your own brother seems beyond the realm of her wrath. Besides he isn't going anywhere and they can't watch him every second of the day so she won't be too concerned if he is actually one of her targets."

"So we are in agreement that Webster is a real target and that Spencer and the brother are maybes."

Heads nodded in agreement.

"She must know that we know about her now even though we pretended not to find her car. She might have even followed us back here from Kelby in her new vehicle."

"Judging from the photos of the Mayor I am guessing she has pictures of us too."

"Then she really knows who we are," added Campbell.

"Holy crap," said Anthony.

"I am going to park my SUV and get a rental car for a week."

Parking his white Blazer for a week was a painful thought to Wilson and the others knew it. His truck was his baby. He treated it better than any other vehicle he had ever owned. All the other cars and truck were just transportation but Wilson had a love affair with his Blazer. He had never been so comfortable driving any other vehicle before and from the first time he sat in the driver's seat he knew that he was going to buy it. Of course he let the salesman completely finish his spiel before pretending that he was going to leave the car showroom. The young salesman pleaded for him to reconsider and after a small negotiation he reduced the price to Wilson's satisfaction. But now the situation dictated the need for

Wilson to change vehicles. If they were successful in stopping Doyle from reaching her next target she might turn her sights on them and Wilson's white SUV would be easy for her to follow.

"I'll switch cars with my wife," said Anthony. "And park it down the block too."

Officer Campbell would be safe in his cruiser as he would look like any other cruiser and Nelson, as usual, would be riding with Wilson.

"She's most likely in some cheap motel somewhere staying below the radar. We need to find a way to draw her out into the open. So far it seems that it has been her that has been drawing us out in the open. So bring some new ideas in with you tomorrow. We need to figure out from what we know, how she intends on attacking Webster. I don't care how farfetched you think your ideas are, just write them down. Now get out of here and drive careful."

Wilson had no idea why he added that last bit, it just came out. Maybe Chief Driscoll was rubbing off on him.

CHAPTER 24

DETECTIVE ANTHONY PARKED his wife's car in the shopping mall two block away from the precinct. When he walked past the precinct parking lot he did not see Wilson's white Blazer and he wondered what he was using for wheels. Whatever it was it should provide some anonymity for a while. It was nice not to have to rush around this morning and he would have loved to have been bringing in donuts but Nelson had agreed to bring in the breakfast today and knowing her it would probably involve bagels. As soon as he exited the elevator he smelled the fresh baked goods that Nelson had brought in. It wasn't that he didn't like the smell of fresh bagels, his wife made them for breakfast sometimes too, but his addiction to donuts far exceeded any logic that his brain provided to him. To appease his craving he would dip his bagel into his triple-triple coffee. It was a small compromise but one that he had to live with.

Officer Campbell was already happily munching on his bagel. Nelson saw the look of apprehension on Anthony's face as he eyed the box of bagels and while there was temptation to make his unease linger she decided to quickly put him out of his misery. "I chose a blueberry-cinnamon bagel for you. It was the closest I could find that reminded me of a donut."

Anthony's face broke out in a smile.

Wilson was chewing on his first bite of his bagel and had already started a new page on the Big Board with the title, – 'WEBSTER'.

"Okay brainiacs let's get to work. We want a list of ways that Webster can be attacked."

The detective fired off their ideas as Wilson wrote them on the page.

"Drowning"

"Choke"

"Electrocute"

"Drug"

"Stab"

"Burn to death"

"Shot"

"Blown up"

"Poison"

"Car accident"

"Okay let's start at the top, drowning. We don't know if Webster showers or baths but for it to be an accidental bathroom drowning Doyle would need to get into the house unnoticed by Spencer or the officers. That doesn't seem likely."

"Are there any lakes nearby?"

"No just a pond north of the town," said Campbell.

"Since she hasn't expressed an interest in swimming this does not appear to be a good option."

Wilson drew a line through 'Drowning'.

"Choking would require her to be in close proximity to Webster and since she is being watched all day and night that seems unlikely," said Anthony.

Wilson drew a line through 'Choke'.

"To be able to electrocute her Doyle would also need to get into her house or inside the Chamber of Commerce so I think we can rule that out."

Wilson drew a line through 'Electrocute'.

"I guess the question with 'Drug' is would she use the same method twice. Something tells me no," said Nelson.

"I agree," said Anthony. "It seems that she will make each attack in a different manner."

"I also agree," said Wilson as he drew a line through 'Drug'.

"The other deaths were ruled accidental but we now know that they were coerced accidents," said Campbell.

"Okay so let's address that when we get to 'Car accident'," said Wilson. "I think we can all agree that stab, falls under the same issues, as drug and choke."

They all grunted their consent as Wilson drew a line through 'Stab'.

"To burn her to death Doyle could be anywhere when it happened," said Campbell.

"Yes."

"It could happen at the house or at the Chamber of Commerce building."

"Or even in her car," said Anthony.

"The car would definitely make it singular. If she burned the house down she might kill anyone else in it at the time and the same for the building."

"And to burn her to death in the car would mean the doors were locked somehow or she was unconscious which would require drugs," said Campbell.

"So an unlikely scenario," said Wilson.

"Yes," replied Nelson. "If you look at the four deaths it looks as if she wants her victims to be aware that their death is imminent. As if she wants them to be terrified before they die."

"That is a very good point. So we should look at deaths in which the victim is possibly aware they are going to die."

"I think so," confirmed Nelson.

Campbell and Anthony nodded agreement and they all looked at the list together.

"Shot could be gun or bow, and as smart as she appears I think she could arrange for them to be looking at directly at her."

"True."

"You know," said Campbell pausing as if thinking at loud. "If she is a good archer then she might be a decent shot with a rifle too."

"Good information. So we will leave that on the list but I think that we can cross out 'Blown up' as it doesn't meet the criteria."

Again, nods of confirmation from the other three.

"What is the difference between 'Drug' and 'Poison'," he asked.

"Not a lot," said Anthony.

"The method of dosage might be the same, ingestion, but poison could pass as an accidental death like anaphylactic shock."

"Then we need to find out if Webster is allergic to anything and make sure that she doesn't eat anything unusual."

"But to do that it would mean Doyle would have to have access to Webster's food," said Anthony.

Nelson said, "If Webster eats only food she has prepared herself it would eliminate that from happening."

Campbell added, "And it would be difficult to poison her at a restaurant unless Doyle worked there as a waitress or cook."

"Difficult yes, but I am not convinced it's impossible for Doyle," said Wilson.

"Well," said Anthony. "If she doesn't eat on the days we are expecting an attack she won't have anything to worry about."

Nelson glared at him and when Campbell laughed she glared at him too. If they knew how hard it was for her to lose the weight she lost they wouldn't be quite so flippant when it comes to women and their appetites. A man can put on ten pounds and no one even notices but ten pounds of added weight to a woman feels like fifty pounds. And if men had their self-esteem as intrinsically tied to their emotions like women there would be a lot more men at the gym and substantially fewer beer bellies.

"Hopefully we can avert any poison issues with some preparation but let's finish the list first. We ruled out car accident on her weekly lunch visit with her mother and she is watched on the drive to work and home so unless she goes on a drive somewhere different I think we can rule that out. Does anyone have any thoughts on that?"

Campbell spoke up first, "Based on our assumption that she is going to keep it as personal as possible I don't see a car accident happening unless she knows how to cut a brake line and then we are back to the percentage factor. A car accident in Kelby is highly unlikely to cause a death unless the person is run over."

"I would have to agree with that too," said Nelson.

"That leaves us with 'Shot' or 'Poison'," Wilson said. And after a moment of thought, "Anthony, call Webster and find out if she has any allergies and tell her our thoughts about eating."

"Andy, send out Doyle's driver licence picture to all the hotels and car rental places again. Maybe a part time employee or a full time one that wasn't working when we sent it out last time might see it and we could get lucky."

They took a break while Detective Anthony spoke to Deborah Webster and Officer Campbell sent out the picture again. Wilson sipped some coffee and finished the other half of his bagel while reviewing the Big Board.

"I was just thinking about Mrs. Gregory," said Nelson.

Wilson turned back to Nelson and said, "She's an anomaly."

"Yes, that is what I was thinking. If Mrs. Gregory is not on Doyle's list then she was collateral damage in the opposite way of the Deputy Mayor."

"And," Wilson probed.

"Well as you said she probably isn't interested in helping anyone and maybe she is oblivious to anything that happens to anyone related to her victims."

"That sounds like a real possibility and unfortunately a dangerous one."

Nelson nodded her head in silent agreement.

Detective Anthony hung up his desk phone and walked over to the Big Board where Nelson and Wilson were standing.

"Well Ms. Webster was very helpful. It seems that she has a small allergic issue. She is lactose intolerant. She says that she avoids eating out as much as possible because she has to do so for business meetings. She watches her diet carefully and cooks at home."

"Good. That should eliminate poison."

Big footsteps as Officer Campbell quickly crossed the bullpen back to the scrum.

"We got a hit," he said. "A night clerk at the Liverpool Motel thinks she was there last week. That motel is just ten minutes away from the Lab."

"Great. You and Anthony go talk to him."

"Nelson and I have a meeting to go to."

Nelson gave him a look that showed her surprise. She had no idea what meeting they had to go to but she was hoping that it wasn't in Captain Stone's office.

Wilson smirked at Nelson's reaction to his statement then took out his cell phone and made a call.

"Hey Jim. Are you up for some Spanish coffee?"

"Absolutely Ryan. Where ?"

"The *Oscuro Asado Café.*"

"Good choice. Is twenty minutes okay."

"We'll see you there."

"We?"

"I am bringing a colleague with me."

"A colleague. That makes it sound serious."

"It is. See you in twenty."

Click.

Nelson was smiling. She was excited to finally meet Professor Jim Maltby, Wilson's mentor. Maltby had been the best friend and colleague of Wilson's father. Since the death of his father two years ago Wilson had leaned heavily on Maltby for advice and friendship.

The Oscuro Asado Café was located on North Orleans just north of West Huron. A large red canopy covered most of the side walk in front of the café but the afternoon sun was already dipping underneath it and into the eyes of the squinting patrons when Wilson and Nelson arrived. Professor Maltby as per his custom had already picked out a table for them and waved as they approached.

"Jim this is Detective Nelson."

Jim Maltby reached out to shake hands with Nelson and she said, "Please call me Laura."

Nelson observed the Professor's six foot frame and shock of hair and agreed with Wilson's description that he looked surprising like the actor from the TV show – 'Cheers'.

"Laura it is," he replied tilting his head to the right. "Now let's sit shall we."

Professor Maltby was a coffee connoisseur and loved to meet with Ryan at different coffee shops and cafés around Chicago and now that Jim was retired he also preferred the outdoors to being inside in an office. As a professor of Humanology, people watching was one of the things Jim Maltby enjoyed the most. His studying of people; their inter actions with others and their habits, fears and breakthroughs, fascinated him. It was Jim's insights on why people do what they do that Ryan was seeking today.

They sat at a table near the door to the sidewalk patio. Jim liked this table as it allowed him to watch the face changes and mood of the waitress as she walked by them. The people in the furthest table from the door, could not see all the interaction the waitress would have with the other patrons, but Jim could take it all in from his seat.

"This must be serious for you to bring support."

Ryan filled Jim in on the new case.

"Wow. That is a doozie. Your Dr. Devlin is correct in his assessment. Most people would have fallen to pieces under that much stress but her husband's description of her, places her on a different level. I am not sure I can add much that will help. She is very complicated and yet controlled. It would be good to have more information from friends and family but that doesn't appear to be forthcoming."

"No it's not. No one she went to school with in Kelby has spoken to her in years and her colleagues in Kansas said she was nice but very private."

"Yes, that would fit the pattern of someone very smart who wanted to be in control of her life. They are either an obnoxious bully type always giving unwanted advice or very reserved. You really need to get inside her head but she has gone out of her way to prevent that."

Nelson eased into the conversation, "How can we pick at her brain?"

Jim smiled, "If you can't get inside her brain to know where her train is going then throw a switch on her track. Either it will derail her or it will bring her to you."

"You mean make her change her prepared plan."

"Yes. Remember she isn't a machine, she is human."

"Huh?" said Ryan.

"A machine will do only what it is designed to do but a human being, no matter how focussed on a task, can be distracted."

"But how do we get her attention?"

"You have alluded to the fact that you believe she knows about you by now."

"Yes. We think so."

"Then lead instead of following."

"We tried that and it didn't work."

"Ah but wasn't that was more of a trap than misdirection."

"Yes. What do we need to do?"

"Make her think you are doing something that you aren't. You have new vehicles and she may not know that. If you remove the police cars and replace them with personal vehicles she might believe that you think the Mayor was her last victim since there is nothing to show conclusively that he isn't."

Nelson said, "You think she might let her guard down if we appear to be absent."

"She probably won't drop her guard much but even a small amount might give you an edge. When a bull is chasing a matador, the Subalternos wave a red flag, to get the bull's attention. They run behind the Burladero, a protective wall, and when the bull looks back at the matador, he is gone. What do you have that you can wave as a red flag?"

"I don't know. But I would like to have a Burladero when I do. Saturday is her next day for an attack if she is going to continue."

"If?" Jim asked. "You don't sound sure."

"I am sure she will attack but the 'who' and the 'how' I don't know."

"And you are hoping for another non-violent attack."

"Yes."

"Hmm," the professor murmured.

"You don't agree."

"The dirt she had on the Mayor was quite dynamic. She hurt him in that way far more than if she had killed him. He will always be remembered for his indiscretions now. If she had killed him he might have been remembered as a martyr to her cause. I doubt there is some major secret being shared by the rest of the people that would satisfy her need for revenge."

"That was my concern also."

They sipped their coffees while Jim watched the waitress serving the collection of customers on the patio. Nelson was captivated at being a part of the meeting. She had always thought how great it would have been to have had an older sister to learn from rather than being the older sister to her siblings. The other twist to her life was that being a cop restricted her opportunities to have a best friend, someone with whom she lean on and commiserate with. Instead she called her mother every day, not out of guilt but because her mother wanted to know that she made it through each day alive. Her younger brothers and sisters were business people and mothers; nothing to give her mother worries but the daughter who was a cop was the one she needed to hear from to ease her mind and sleep well at night.

"The problem with waving a red flag at her," said Ryan, "is that how could we be sure she would notice it."

"That's true," said Nelson as she told Jim about the sting operation they tried to lure her out at the retirement home.

"I see. Well perhaps you need a less subtle but still curious method to lure her."

"Like?" asked Ryan.

"Do you remember when you were still in uniform on the street the department used a sting to make some needed arrests of some unsavoury characters?"

"You mean the free baseball tickets scam?"

"That's the one. All those criminals were so keen to get something for free that they dropped their guard and walked into your trap."

"I don't see Doyle wanting anything like free baseball tickets," said Nelson.

Jim chuckled, "No I don't suppose she would either. What I was making reference to was the ruse itself."

Ryan was trying to get to where Jim was leading him but the synaptic transmissions in his brain were not firing in the correct order and the picture was not forming in his mind.

"You knew that some of the criminals you were after would fall for the free tickets trick. What you need to know to catch Doyle off guard is what would she fall for?"

Ryan and Nelson looked at each other, sipped more coffee but said nothing.

"How is your coffee Laura?" Jim asked.

"It's very good. I am enjoying it."

"Were you expecting it to be good?"

"I don't know if expecting is the right word. I haven't had Spanish coffee in quite some time but I was hoping it would be as good as the last time.

"And is it?"

"Oh yes," she replied smiling.

Ryan knew Jim well enough to know that he was not talking about coffee at all. It was a metaphor, but for what?

"Okay," said Ryan to Jim. "Spill the beans."

Nelson looked at Ryan with confusion her face.

Jim let out another chuckle and smiled.

"What do you expect from Doyle?" Jim asked Ryan.

"That she will keep killing until she is finished or until she breaks down."

"And what does Doyle expect?"

Nelson said, "That she will be able to attack and kill without being caught."

"That is correct. And for that to be the result two things must happen. She must have access to her victim and she must be smart enough to get away."

"We know she is very smart but we have everyone covered so she has no access."

"No access as far as you know. After all she is very smart."

Wilson nodded, "Unfortunately she is."

"To say, no access, is an absolute term. Protecting the possible victims is theoretical. You can't be absolutely sure."

"No we can't but what more can we do if they won't leave."

"Tell me Laura, would you have been disappointed if you sat down for a Spanish coffee and the waitress said "Sorry there is no more.'"

"Yes I would have."

"And would you have gotten up and left?"

"Yes."

"But if she had said 'there is more in the kitchen but I can't get it' would you have tried to go into the kitchen and get it yourself?"

"Yes I would."

"And there is the difference between absolute solution and a possible theory."

Ryan was still not getting the idea that Jim was trying to explain. Nelson was equally stumped.

Jim watched their faces smiling, "Hiding your victims from Doyle is similar to the coffee in the kitchen, it is still available but a new plan is required to get it. The absolute answer would be there are no more victims."

"Yes, but that would be because she killed them," said Nelson.

"Do you like magic Laura?"

"Sometimes. But only if it is really good like Copperfield."

"So if someone made a body disappear on stage you would be amused but know it was a trick."

"Yes."

"And you would rack your brain trying to decipher the trick."

"Yes."

"Now if a body disappeared in real life you would know it was not a trick but rather an accident or possibly foul play."

"Correct."

Ryan was smiling. At last he knew what Jim was trying to say.

"And even if you hadn't seen the body disappear if enough people witnessed it you would believe it to be true."

"That sounds like a couple of disappearances we have investigated," said Nelson.

"And in those cases you believed they were missing and possibly dead because of the circumstances presented."

"Yes."

Ryan interrupted the conversation, "But before we rule anything out we investigate."

Jim was smiling. He didn't need to lead Ryan anymore but Laura was not quite there yet.

Nelson said, "Yes."

Ryan smiled at her. "How many times have family members told you that the missing person is not dead?"

"Quite a few."

Ryan continued, "And until they see a body they hound us to know how the investigation is going. But once a body is found they begin to accept it."

She was staring straight ahead thinking. Her eyes began darting from side to side. Ryan leaned back in his chair knowing she was about to see the picture clearly.

"Oh my god," she said as she turned to Ryan. "Of course. Pull a scam on her. Make Doyle think one of her targets has died and see what she does."

Nelson looked at Jim, "Do you always have conversations like this with him?"

"Most times. I don't like to give him an answer. It is much more rewarding if he comes to the solution on his own."

"So we take away her coffee," said Laura to Jim. "And she will want to be sure it is gone."

Ryan was almost giggling at the enthusiasm pouring out of Nelson. To see her finally excited about something was great. Instead of being in the dull atmosphere of the bullpen where she would tend to follow rather than lead, in the open air meeting today she formulated the answer herself with very little nudging.

"Well I can understand now why you brought your colleague. Sometimes two heads are better than one. Now all you two have to do is decide which one of the protected people will be the coffee."

"We still have to hope that we have the right people protected."

"There are always variables. You should talk to your Dr. Devlin about what this situation might do to her. She will drop her guard and become curious but you need to know what is going to happen inside her brain so that you can be prepared for whatever circumstances may arise."

Ryan stood up signaling that the meeting was over. "Thanks Jim. Now we have to get back."

"It was very nice to meet you Laura."

"It was my pleasure Jim," said Nelson shaking Jim's hand.

Ryan left a reasonable tip on the table and Jim smiled.

CHAPTER 25

THE BULL PEN was almost empty when Nelson and Wilson returned but there were a few messages waiting for them about possible sightings of Doyle at hotels. Anthony and Campbell were not back yet so Nelson decided to follow up on a couple of the messages. The first one turned out to be a false alarm. The son of the motel owner had talked his girlfriend into spending the night and because his father didn't know he thought it might have been Doyle.

Nelson hoped the second call had more promise. The Westway Motel just east of Veterans Tollway on Maple.

"Mr. Cranford?"

"Yep."

"This is Detective Nelson you called in about the photo."

'Oh yeah. Call me Eric."

"What can you tell me sir?"

"Ah well let's see. It was Saturday; err no, sorry it was Sunday. She came in for two nights. Good looking girl she was."

"What colour was her hair?"

"Her hair? Hmm some shade of brown."

"How long was it?"

"Short I guess. Not quite on her shoulders."

"What colour were her eyes?"

"Eyes? Wow not sure I got a good look at them. They weren't anything special like green or blue. I would have noticed something like that."

"And how tall?"

"Well about the same as me. I'm five-seven."

"I see."

That was too tall to be Doyle. Instead of making more notes Nelson began twirling her pen between her fingers. It was a trick she developed in college when she was bored with a lecture. Detective Anthony would watch her do it and try to imitate her but his fingers would not cooperate and he was constantly dropped his pen on the floor. Nelson needed to confirm her suspicions, so she asked Cranford another question.

"Did she have any tattoos or piercings?"

"Can't say about piercings other than her earrings. But she had one of those tats that all the girls are getting. You know the one they put on their back above their thong. I saw it when she bent over to pick up her bag."

According to her ex-husband, Susan Doyle did not have any tattoos.

"Thank you very much Mr. Cranford. We'll be in touch if we need you."

Click.

The real detective work. Lots of phone calls that generally lead to dead ends.

The elevator doors opened and Detective Anthony and Officer Campbell hastily entered the bullpen. Their urgent pace caught Nelson's attention as she sat her desk.

Detective Anthony pulled out his note book and flipped it open to his marker. Officer Campbell stood at his left side ready to add any details required.

Wilson sat on the corner of Nelson's desk facing them waiting to see what the excitement was about.

"Okay, so the reason that we had a call from the hotel today instead of earlier was because the sighting was made by the nightshift supervisor, Mr. Shiv Shankar. He was called in today to do a double shift and was in the office when the email alert showed up on their computer. He saw 'the woman in the photo' come in around midnight last Tuesday. She stayed for two nights. She fit the description exactly; short brown hair, blue eyes. She even put down her husband's car as her vehicle but gave a fake license plate number."

"Two nights and two days," said Nelson.

"Yes, it seems her two day schedule extends to accommodations as well as killing," said Wilson.

Anthony continued, "She paid cash and registered as Annie Mae Bullock from Brownsville, Tennessee."

Nelson shook her head and laughed. The three men looked at her puzzled by the reaction.

"I'm sorry it is not really funny when you think about what Doyle is doing."

"What is so funny about that name?" asked Anthony.

"*I left a good job in the city*," Nelson sang to them and watched for a reaction but they just shook their heads. "That's Tina Turner's real name."

"That's the second time she has done this. Perhaps she has done it each time. She is very innovative. Let's hope she is thinking innovative tomorrow instead of vindictive."

"Huh," said Anthony.

"I mean I hope she does something comparable to what she did to the Mayor rather than kill someone."

"Yeah, that would be better," he replied.

"I doubt that there will be very many actual sightings of Doyle."

"Why do you think that?" asked Officer Campbell.

"If she is smart enough to use fake names she will in all probability use disguises as well and we know she is a blonde so the brown hair might be a dye job. She might have even dyed her hair black by now or bought a wig."

"And if she buys colored contacts she could hide her blue eyes," added Nelson. "Or cover them with sunglasses."

"So she could look like a different woman every day," said Anthony.

Wilson said, "We are not going to worry about what she might look like checking into a motel. What we need to concern ourselves with is what she will look like in Kelby. We have an idea how to upset her plans and draw her out in the open."

"Really?" said Anthony.

"Yes. We are going to kill off one of her targets."

Detective Anthony's mouth dropped open in surprise but before he could say anything else Officer Campbell asked, "How?"

"I haven't ironed out all the details yet. We need to go to Kelby in the morning and talk with the people there. But first we need to talk to Dr. Devlin."

Wilson dialed the Doctor's number. His receptionist told Wilson that he will just be a minute. They watched Wilson's face as he waited for the doctor to come on line.

"Detective?" said Dr. Devlin.

"Hi Doc. We're here in the bullpen and I have some questions for you about our killer. I am putting you on speaker phone."

"Okay."

"We are going to turn the tables on her by eliminating one of her potential victims."

"Well that will distract her. But if she is as intelligent as her killings indicate then she will adapt a new plan to get at that person."

"Sorry Doc. When I said 'eliminate' I meant that we are going to kill off the person we think is next on her list."

A moment of silence.

"Detective I am assuming that you mean fake a death."

"Yes Doc. But we are going to do it so that Doyle really believes that person is dead. Beyond a shadow of a doubt."

"Interesting idea."

"And we need to know how she will react."

"Her reaction will be dependent on how important that person is on her list of priorities. If that person is next on her list her reaction will be stronger than if it was the last person on her list. Also, if the order of the deaths are tied into each other it will change her reaction."

Wilson said, "Explain that last sentence please."

"She might have a specific reason for the chronological order of the deaths. Until you catch her you most likely won't know if she had each attack scheduled for a reason. If you eliminate someone before she wanted them to die it might upset her final plans."

"That is what we want to know. How will she react?"

"There could be two reactions. It might be that it doesn't bother her that she didn't get to that person in time and she just continues on with her plan. On the other hand it might be the tipping point where she both has a breakdown and snaps out of her psychosis, or worse, she becomes even angrier and adds to her list. The second scenario would make her very volatile and more prone to making mistakes."

"Would she lash out in public?"

"Not right away but if she does get angry enough she will. And as she makes mistakes she will feel like she has lost control and has painted herself into a corner."

"But she won't react like that when she sees the funeral."

"No, attending the funeral to confirm the death she should still be in a semi-denial mood. Driving home afterward, when she has absorbed the information, is when the anger will build up until it reaches a crescendo."

"So she isn't going to go postal in a crowd during the funeral?"

"From everything you have told me about her I would say it is extremely unlikely. She is intelligent and will feel invisible at a funeral. Until she feels threatened she will have control of her emotions."

"That's what I was hoping you would say. Thanks Doc."

"Good luck Detectives."

Click.

Campbell and Anthony stared at Wilson waiting for him to continue with more information.

"Okay. We are going to try and throw Doyle off her game with a little bait and switch."

"That's great," said Anthony.

The complete plan wasn't entirely formulated in Wilson's mind but the rough idea was getting clearer by the minute.

"Andy, you are going to have to find us a car the same model as Webster's. The model year can be a year older or a year newer. The colour needs to be fairly close. Her car is brown so wine, red, or even black will work.

It doesn't need a motor that runs. Just as long as it has a good rear end, four wheels and can be towed to Kelby."

Officer Campbell was familiar with all the junkyards in the Chicago area so this was a task right up his alley. He was excited about being able to contribute constructively to the investigation. Up until now he didn't feel much more than a fifth wheel even if there was only four of them on the team.

"When we tow it to Kelby we should keep it covered until it is time."

"That can be easily arranged," said Campbell.

"Good."

"Anthony, go see Mac at the Bomb Squad and tell him we need a small explosion that will burn up a car as if it was caused by a collision."

"Wow, sure."

"And let him know the make and model."

Detective Anthony and Officer Campbell left the bullpen full of excitement about their new tasks.

Nelson watched them leave wondering what Wilson had up his sleeve for her.

"We are going to have to hide Webster's car."

"What about putting it in the impound yard."

"I thought of that but then visions of Doyle taking pictures of us made me rethink it. I don't want to be too obvious with our plan. I don't want there to be any chance of Doyle catching a drift of what we are doing. I am sure when we talk to Chief Driscoll he will know a good place we use to hide the car."

Nelson said, "What do you want me to do?"

"When we go to Kelby tomorrow I want you to stay with Webster in her house."

She was confused by the simplicity of the request, "Okay."

"I mean overnight. Spencer has a date so she will be left alone and I don't want her to do anything that will make her a target."

"Like walking by an open window."

"Exactly. She might not even realize what she is doing and I don't trust the officer's experience in a stake out situation. If Doyle can't get to her or to her brother maybe she will resort to another fire or something."

"I am still hoping for a paper threat," said Nelson.

"That would be better but what could it be? I don't think it is a big secret that Webster is *very* single. People in small towns might not talk about in public but I am sure behind closed doors Webster's sexuality is debated. It wouldn't have that big of an effect on her job if Doyle had pictures of Webster and another woman."

"True. Hopefully she has something on someone else."

*　　*　　*

On the other side of Chicago at the Plaza Hotel, Lisa Raines pulled her suitcase behind her to the front desk to check in. As soon as the clerk entered her name she said, "Welcome back Miss Raines."

"Thank you." Lisa Raines stayed at the Plaza twice a year for her business visits but this time a conference on new drug applications has made her return visit much sooner.

"We have reserved the same room for you as you had last month as per your request."

"That's great." Lisa is a creature of habit. She preferred to stay at the same hotels and in the same rooms as much as possible. It provided her with a modicum of normality on her travels.

"Can I get a wake-up call for six-thirty please?"

"Yes. I will book that for you."

"And can you book a dinner reservation for two in the restaurant at seven Saturday evening?"

"My pleasure," said the clerk.

Lisa Raines walked to the elevator content in the knowledge that her stay at the hotel would be as comfortable as always. She had a long day ahead of her tomorrow, full of meetings, demonstrations and endless conversations about drugs and territory sales. She will be looking forward to a nice dinner and drinks at the end of the day.

CHAPTER 26

A BOX OF donuts was sitting on Nelson's desk when she entered the bullpen on Saturday morning. She wasn't sure if she was more surprised by donuts on her desk, or that Detective Anthony was already at his desk at seven a.m. Wilson wanted everyone here by seven thirty.

She pretended not to notice, not wanting to give Anthony the satisfaction of knowing that he beat her to work and that he brought donuts in. She picked up the box of donuts and as she moved it to the side of her desk the lid popped open and inside she observed that only half of the box was donuts; the other half of the box was bagels. Nelson paused and then looked over at Detective Anthony and smiled.

"You're welcome," Anthony said grinning like a Cheshire cat.

Wilson and Officer Campbell arrived shortly after Nelson.

Nelson had brought her overnight bag with her as she would be riding with Wilson in his rental car. After they all had several swigs of coffee and a donut Wilson started.

"Andy, everything to do with the car is your job. Once you have found the doppelganger car call me. When it's time to start the plan in motion you will arrange to have it towed to the Kelby. The incendiary device will be set and detonated by Mac once the car is put into place. Nelson will be staying with Webster until this is over. I want to get through today before we set up our deception. She can't get at her brother as long as he is still staying in the Kelby Police Department for protection. An officer will shadow Spencer on his date tonight. He will be coming into Chicago. We don't expect he is a target but we'll keep a watch on him anyway."

"Anthony, call Chicago Medical School and tell them we need a female cadaver and that we need to pick it up Sunday morning."

The thought of a cadaver made Detective Anthony shudder; the sight of blood could almost make him pass out.

Wilson paused for a sip of coffee.

"We'll check with Chief Driscoll on the best locations for the accident. Remember only Chief Driscoll is in the loop on this. Don't let it slip out to anyone. No exceptions. When we do this we will need everyone in Kelby to believe that Webster is dead. That way Doyle can't do any snooping around Kelby and find out from someone in the know that it was all a trick."

"Sounds good," said Anthony.

"Okay people let's get to work."

Detectives Anthony and Nelson waited at the rear doors of the precinct building. Wilson had parked his rental car two blocks away in the same parking lot that Detective Anthony had used to park his wife's car. Wilson picked them up in a quick run through the police lot. If by any chance Doyle was here and watching them this morning she would not be able to see them leaving the back parking lot onto the side street in Wilson's rental car, a silver four door. Wilson picked this vehicle for its commonness in traffic as there are more silver colored cars on the road than any other colour. Every little edge they had over Doyle was a tool to be exploited until the war was over.

They arrived in Kelby an hour later. The usual forty-five minute drive had been extend to sixty minutes with a slight deviation to the previous route. In the event that Doyle was watching the main road into Kelby they would avoid it and enter and exit the town from the north and the south.

They had arranged to meet with Chief Driscoll at a Denny's in the mall near the retirement home. His big Police truck was in the parking lot when they arrived. Wilson chose a parking spot on the opposite side of the restaurant and they entered through the side doors. Chief Driscoll was already in a booth; they moved slowly towards him and he motioned for them to sit down.

A blonde waitress wrapped in a blue apron zoomed in on them. "What can I get you folks?"

"Just coffee for now thanks," the Chief replied.

She plunked down a carafe of coffee and a plate of creamers and sweeteners and left.

The Chief poured coffees for everyone. "This must be pretty important for us to meet out here on a Saturday morning."

"Chief we have been formulating a plan to draw Doyle out into the open."

The Chief poured some cream in his coffee and stirred slowly waiting for more information from Wilson. Bit by bit Wilson laid out the basics of their plan.

"It sounds very elaborate and plausible. How do I fit into the plan?"

"This is a lot to ask but we need to keep this between the four of us here and Webster. No one else can know that it is going to be a fake death."

"You're right that is a lot to ask. My men will not be happy about being kept in the dark."

"I understand that Chief. It isn't a trust issue. If it wasn't for the fact that they could become targets later I would probably include them."

"I don't understand," said Chief Driscoll.

"Dr. Devlin said that it is possible if she gets angry because she has lost one of her targets, she might add targets to her list. If she found out your officers were in on the plan they might become her new targets. I am prepared for Doyle to turn her sights on me and this team but I can't risk the lives of your officers."

"Well that puts a whole new spin on the picture doesn't it," said Chief Driscoll.

"I hoped you would agree with me on that."

"I do. What else do you need from me?"

"We need a place to hide Webster's car that no one would find out about. We had considered our impound yard in Chicago but since we believe Doyle may have been following us we don't want to give her any reason to get suspicious."

"Hmm. If you stored a car anyplace in town it would generate curiosity. But there is a place that might be just what you need. And it might be one of the last places Doyle would think of looking or be watching."

Now it was their turn to wait for Chief Driscoll to provide more information.

"Chief Caswell had a large work shed on his property. It's big enough for two vehicles. Mrs. Caswell has gone to her sisters for a while so there is no one there to see anything."

"That sounds perfect," said Wilson. He could feel little pieces of the plan coming together. "Now we have to address the issue of Deputy Mayor Spencer. He is living with Webster right now so he will know she is not dead. Either we let him in on the plan or we move him."

"I think," said Driscoll, "that if the idea is to limit the possibility of a leak then we should move him."

"I agree," said Nelson. Wilson and Driscoll looked around the table. All were in agreement; Spencer had to be moved. Now the question was to where? Should it be back to his condo, into a hotel room or to the safety of the police department? The consensus was that he should go back to his own dwelling. It would be far less suspicious than a hotel room or the police department and as the front door is the only possible public access it is not too difficult to monitor the comings and goings. Since the interior door to the lobby could not be opened without the residents help there was no need for another officer to be inside the building. The officer outside in the visitor's parking spaces had a clear view of front door and anyone who enters. If a woman resembling Doyle entered the building the officer watching could call Spencer and advise him not to open his door to anyone and wait until he confirmed that it was just a resident. Chief Driscoll would be the one to tell Spencer he could go back home today.

"The other item on our list is a good spot to stage the accident," said Wilson.

Chief Driscoll pursed his lips and looked upwards, thinking.

"Pacific Road runs parallel to one Webster takes to see her mother at the retirement home. It has a few good curves that might lead to an accident if you were going a bit fast."

"That might be perfect," Nelson said. "It's logical that she might take that route once in a while."

"Anthony, you go with the Chief and help move Spencer out of Webster's house. Chief, let the officer inside Webster's house know that he can leave when Nelson arrives as she will be the weekend body guard. Take the officer outside with you to watch Spencer's place."

Back to Anthony, "Once Spencer is settled in you and the Chief meet us back at Webster's. Nelson and I will take a drive up Pacific Road and find good spot for the accident."

They left the restaurant through different doors.

Wilson turned right at the lights and drove two blocks over to pick up Pacific Road. At first Wilson thought Chief Driscoll must have been mistaken about the route. Pacific Road was straight and lined with houses but eventually the houses stopped and the road began twisting through farm land. A mile from the turn off to the retirement home a sharp bend in the road was reinforced by a steep embankment. Wilson stopped the car and they got out to survey the area. At the bottom of the embankment before the farmer's fence was a brick covered culvert that a stream flowed into. On the other side of the culvert a few trees provided shade.

"This is it," said Wilson. He looked up and down Pacific Road wondering what the traffic will be like on Sunday morning. "This is where the accident will be."

"Call Anthony and see how they are doing?"

Nelson called Detective Anthony.

Wilson pulled out his cell phone and called Officer Campbell.

"Andy?"

"Yes sir."

Wilson looked at his phone. He thought he had broken Andy of his habit of calling him 'sir'. Wilson had reminded Campbell several months ago that 'sir' was what he called his late father, a professor at Southern Illinois.

"Can you meet me on Pacific Road just south of the cross road that leads to the retirement home in about one hour?"

"Yes I can."

"Good."

"I have found the car we need. The front end is smashed up but the rear is fine."

"Terrific. I will see later."

Click.

Wilson turned back to Nelson.

"They're leaving with Spencer right now," said Nelson.

"Okay let's go see Webster."

Ten minutes later they turned down Webster's street; no police car in front of the house.

"I'll drop you in front and then I'll park further down the street."

Wilson slowed down and stopped and Nelson got out of the car once again wearing the wig that made her look like Webster. She grabbed her bags off of the back seat and walked up the steps to the front door. On the drive here she had called Webster and told her to be ready for their arrival and the door opened as she reached for the handle. Nelson slipped inside without looking back at Wilson's car.

Wilson parked on the next block then waited several minutes before getting out of his car and walking back to Webster's house. He entered without knocking.

Nelson and Webster were sitting in the living room and he joined them.

Webster spoke up first, "I assume you are going to fill me in on the details now."

Wilson had not like Webster's attitude during this whole affair and today was no different.

"Yes we are. The basic premise is that you will stay inside for the next few days. We will fake your death and then have a funeral for you. Detective Nelson will be your body guard here in the house and after your fake death we will have your mother brought here to stay with you. It will look from the outside that she is here to be consoled and go through your things. That way she won't have to listen to all the people at the home consoling her over your fake death. You will be able to tell her all the details yourself. Nelson will monitor any visitors coming to the front door."

"Are you sure this will work?"

"It will definitely stop her from attacking you," Nelson assured her.

"Don't get me wrong I am happy that I am safe but I just don't see myself as someone she will be after."

"Everyone who had a prominent role in the start-up of the Genesis Research Lab is a target and you fit that category."

"All I was doing was promoting business development in Kelby. The Lab was just one of many projects."

"Well then it was your bad luck to have your picture taken with all the others at the ribbon cutting ceremony."

Webster shook her head and groaned, "Who said there is no such thing as bad publicity?"

A knock at the front door indicated Chief Driscoll and Detective Anthony had returned. Wilson let them in.

"Now I will need the keys to your car," Wilson said to Webster. Wilson could see the reluctance in Webster's effort to hand over her keys.

"Don't worry. We aren't going wreck it, just hide it."

Wilson handed the keys to Anthony, "Okay take it away and bring back the plates. I need to give them to Andy. I'll meet you at the restaurant we met at this morning."

Wilson left to meet with Officer Campbell on Pacific Road.

As he sat in his car, at the spot on Pacific Road where the fake accident would take place, Wilson wondered about Doyle's ability to watch her targets. She can't be in two or three places at the same time. How does she choose who she wants to watch. Does she have an accomplice in Kelby? That idea seemed almost impossible but Wilson was not willing to rule out anything at this time. His thoughts were interrupted when a police cruiser pulled up behind him.

"This is it Andy," said Wilson as he pointed down to the brick walled culvert. "The car needs to be face first against the culvert with the rear licence plate facing the road. It will look like she lost control on the bend and went over the side. Anthony has gone with Chief Driscoll to hide Webster's car in a shed on Chief Caswell's property. He is bringing her plates back with him. Put them on the decoy car so anyone looking at the accident will see it is her plates. With the explosion most of the car will be burned so a black and white picture in the newspaper showing her plates will do the job nicely."

"Mac will follow you out here and set the charges as soon as you have the car in place. We will need to move fast. There won't be much traffic on this road on a Sunday morning but we don't need any onlookers."

"Got it," said Campbell as he snapped a few pictures with his cell phone.

"We are meeting Anthony at a restaurant near the retirement home. You can follow me."

On the drive to the restaurant Wilson was feeling good about the day's activities. Things were moving in a positive direction. Instead of chasing Doyle around they were going to get a chance to trap her in her own game. He restrained most of his enthusiasm however noting that in golf and poker until the last card is played, or until the last putt is made, nothing is a sure thing.

CHAPTER 27

THEY ARRIVED AT the restaurant before Chief Driscoll and Detective Anthony. Wilson parked in the same spot as earlier. Officer Campbell parked in the furniture store parking lot next door and waited in his cruiser. It wasn't long before the Kelby Police truck carrying Chief Driscoll and Detective Anthony pulled into the parking lot. No time for coffee this time. They walked over to Wilson's car and exchanged greetings. Detective Anthony held the plates in his hand. They were concealed by being wrapped inside a newspaper. Officer Campbell walked across the median separating the parking lots and joined them. Detective Anthony handed him the package. Almost as if they were communicating telepathically they all returned to their vehicles without saying a word.

As Wilson pulled out of the parking lot with Anthony beside him he had an unnerving feeling. It seemed that all the pieces were falling into place. Everyone was well guarded and even though it was a day to be wary of one of Doyle's attacks it did not seem possible she could do it without being seen and stopped. For Wilson, not knowing what was going on in Doyle's head was the potential Achilles's heel of their plan. Chief Driscoll had arranged for an officer to be driving the route between

Webster's house and Spencer's condo all night ready to be back up. There was little left to do except wait but for Wilson waiting was the hardest part.

Two years earlier he had waited. His father was in the hospital in the last hours of life; it was being taken by cancer. When his father slipped into unconsciousness the doctors told him that it would be soon now, but incredibly, hours turned into days. His father's heart refused to stop. His will to live was strong. The doctors were baffled. The cancer was going to win eventually but Patrick James Wilson was going down fighting. It had been five days since he had any food or drink. The intravenous in his arm was just fluids. Wilson remembered sitting by his bed watching his father's chest heave and sigh sometimes stopping for a rest before kicking in again. You never know your true strength until you are faced with real adversity and every time his father took one more breath Wilson smiled at his father's strength in the face of his final adversity. It would take another day before his father drew in his final breath with Wilson still holding his hand.

He could recall other memories of their lives but nothing stands out as strong as the memory of the day he lost the most important person in his life. Perhaps that was why he had not allowed anyone to get close to him for the past two years. But with the help of his father's best friend and now his new mentor, Wilson had finally overcome his fears and had started seeing a wonderful woman named Jennifer. Now, when cases like this come up, it is Jennifer who is doing the waiting. Wilson's new fear was how long would she put up with the waiting.

Detective Anthony could hardly miss Wilson's very quiet mood but on the drive back to Chicago he chose not to address it.

Pulling into the shopping center parking lot two blocks from the precinct Wilson said, "Andy knows the exact location of the accident. Make sure that he and Mac are ready to go in the morning and then follow them out there. We will set the scene at eleven while everyone is at church. There will be very little chance of any traffic then. After Mac sets off the fire call Chief Driscoll and tell him it is done. I will be at the Kelby Police Department with the Chief. It will take the Kelby Fire Department seven minutes to get there and by that time half of the car will be burnt. The photographer from the Kelby Journal will get a picture of them dousing the flames. It will be obvious that no one could have survived the accident. Fred will be on special call and will verify the body is female but when Chief Driscoll announces that it is Webster's car and that she must have been on her way to see her mother at the home the Journal reporter will have all the facts he needs to write the tragic story of Webster's death."

Anthony flipped open his book and wrote Wilson's instructions down in his notes. Wilson's secret plan was the first time that Detective Anthony had ever been involved in a real undercover operation and he was captivated by all the details. Most of the lieutenants rarely let Anthony into their brain when he was working a case with them, but Wilson kept him in the loop and gave him a chance to demonstrate his capabilities.

Back in the bullpen they checked and double checked every detail. Everything was going to plan. The day had been uneventful and they were hoping for it to stay that way. It was six p.m. and no attempt had been made on the three possible targets in Kelby but there were six hours to go. For the next few hours they would follow up on the messages, of the supposed sightings of Doyle, in the hopes of a break.

Spencer got out of his shower as his phone rang. It was a Chicago number and he was fairly sure who was calling.

"Hello?"

"Andrew?" a female voice asked.

"Yes."

"It's Lisa."

"Hi," his face was beaming. "I was fairly certain it had to be you but I didn't recognize the phone number?"

"I am calling from my room in the hotel. I have a table booked for us at seven and I am hoping you won't be standing me up."

"Not a chance. I am just getting dressed now."

"Good. I will meet you in the lobby at seven and then we will go eat."

"Terrific. See you soon,"

"Looking forward to it," she said.

Click.

Andrew Spencer was euphoric. After all the stress of the past week finally there was some normality to his life. It was Saturday night and he had a date with a beautiful woman. Even the officer who would be watching him from a cruiser was not a deterrent to him tonight. With his favorite blue suit donned he left for his date at the Plaza Hotel, along with officer in tow.

After Spencer parked his car in the visitor's parking lot of the hotel he walked across the street to where the Kelby Police cruiser was parked. He knew the young officer that had been assigned to watch him.

"I am going to be inside for a while and with any luck I might not be coming back out tonight."

The young officer nodded his understanding of the statement.

"Why don't you go home for a few hours at least? Have dinner with your wife and kids and then I'll call you when I am ready to leave and meet you back here."

They exchanged cell phone numbers and after Spencer entered the hotel the officer drove off.

As she had promised, Spencer's date was waiting for him in the lobby as he entered. She was wearing a little black dress, medium high heels; a pearl necklace with matching ear rings and short black hair. In her left hand was a small black clutch purse. Spencer stopped cold in his tracks; she was a dead ringer for Audrey Hepburn. They had not met during the last conference that coincidentally they both had attended several months ago but she had picked up Spencer's business card and contacted him about her next trip to Chicago. They said their hellos with a hug and smiling at each other they walked into the restaurant.

Dinner was everything Spencer had hoped for, amazing food with a beautiful woman who seemed to be flirting with him. She recommended a chocolate dessert that they could take back to her room. Even though he was full from the meal at this point there was little that Spencer would have said no to. Back in her room she opened a bottle of red wine and though he wasn't really a wine person Spencer was more than happy to sip a little. The flirting soon became kissing and before long the sheets of the bed were being pulled back and two naked bodies pressed against the cool dry cotton. Several sips of wine and an hour of love-making later Spence finally crashed on the pillow exhausted. This date was better than he had even dared to dream. Lisa was an amazing lover. Why did she have to live so far away? This was the kind of woman he could get serious about; beautiful, successful and so many common interests to share. Before he could address the rest of the evening, wondering whether she wanted him to spend the night, she said that she had to get up early and suggested that he have a shower before he left.

His first thought was mild disappointment but New York was not that far away and he could arrange to have some extended weekend visits there. He jumped into the shower with a renewed vim and vigor.

Leaving her room Spencer didn't even bother to put his tie back on he just draped it over his shoulders. It was eleven thirty at night yet his step was light, his mind full of thoughts about Lisa and New York.

When he got outside the hotel he pulled out his cigarettes to finally have a smoke. He had been dying for one. Even though the new city wide ban had not eliminated smoking rooms Lisa was not a smoker. Smoking was one of the few things that he and Lisa did not have in common. He shook his cigarette package a bit surprised that there were only two cigarettes inside. He was sure he had almost a half a pack when he left Kelby to come on his date. Oh well he would just have to stop at a gas station on the way home and pick up another pack. He pulled out of the hotel parking lot and realized that he hadn't called the officer who was watching him. He will call him when he stops for smokes. He took the 290 West to the Ronald Regan Memorial Tollway and got off at Highland for gas and cigarettes. Before filling up his car with gas he called the young officer and suggested they meet at the restaurant and bar across the street from the gas station. Spencer parked at the far end of the bar parking lot so the officer would be able to see his car more easily and then got out to have a cigarette while he waited. He was still thinking about Lisa as he cracked open the new package of cigarettes. Frowning he looked at the package and wondered if smoking was enough to keep he and Lisa from having a relationship. He walked towards a garbage can to discard the cellophane wrapper when suddenly pain soared from his chest. At first he thought he must have be having a heart attack but when he clutched at his chest his hand touched something and he looked down to see an arrow sticking out of his torso. Now his mind was focussed as he turned to look for his attacker. He couldn't see her but she must be out there somewhere in the dark. The officer from Kelby would be here soon and they would catch her, but first he had to sit down, he was getting dizzy.

Wilson checked his watch and then looked at the clock on the wall of the bullpen. He had been waiting all night to hear something back from Chief Driscoll or Nelson. Twelve fifteen. Well, as the saying goes, no news is good news.

Then his cell phone rang. It was Chief Driscoll.

"Chief?" he answered anxiously.

"I am afraid she got Spencer."

"What? How?"

The Chief explained to Wilson how the young officer had found Spencer.

"Damn. I'll be there in fifteen minutes."

For the first time in quite a while Wilson used his portable flashing roof light on his way down the Tri-State Toll-way to Highland. His rental car did not have the special light package or the custom squawk horn that his SUV was equipped with. He had no problems locating the crime scene. Flashing lights from two cruisers and the ambulance showered the parking lot of the bar. Wilson jumped from his car towards Chief Driscoll.

Driscoll pointed at the ambulance as they closed their doors and drove away.

"She shot him in the back with an arrow."

"Damn," said Wilson. They were sure she would use a bow at some time in her attacks but this was off the grid.

"How did he get here?"

Chief Driscoll relayed the story about the date at the hotel and how Spencer convinced the young officer that everything was fine.

"That's like the tail wagging the dog."

"Yes. I informed him that he is under suspension until further notice."

"There aren't too many things he could have done worse than let the person he is guarding get killed because he went home for dinner," said Wilson.

Chief Driscoll, unlike his predecessor could remain calm during a crisis.

"I am pretty sure he is aware of that. I don't think this is a something that he is likely to forget. I sent him home after he gave his statement to the first officer on scene."

Wilson looked at the Chief and pondered the young officer's predicament. If Wilson had done something like this while under Captain Stone's watchful eye he would never have made detective. Perhaps the young officer will get a second chance to prove himself at some point in the future but now he will have to live with the circumstances and find out what he is made of. He will either never get over the regret of his actions and quit the police force or learn a valuable life lesson and become a solid police officer.

"She shot him from behind. The arrow went through the back," said Driscoll.

"Really? I would have thought that she would have shot him from the front so he could see her right before she killed him."

"I would have assumed so also."

Wilson chewed on this information while looking around the parking lot for the spot she shot her bow from.

"Wait a minute," Wilson said. "Think about this. She pushed Taylor down the stairs from behind. She caused the stampede that killed Dr. Brennan from in the barn. She was nowhere to be found when Chief Caswell crashed and she was absent when Murphy died."

"What are you saying?"

"She can devise an elaborate plan to kill her victims but doesn't have the stomach to watch them die."

"So she shot Spencer and just left him to die," responded Chief Driscoll.

"Yes. I would imagine that Dr. Devlin will have an opinion about that being a woman issue. I think most male spree killers would want to stand over their victims and watch them die."

"I don't have any experience with that other than what I have read but it does sound logical."

"Damn I hate this. She must have been following him waiting for an opportunity to take him down. I am glad we have our plan ready for tomorrow but now we don't know what she might use as her next weapon. The bow was our next choice so what weapon or accident is she planning for Webster."

"Judging from the fact that she trailed Spencer to this spot it appears she had eyes on him all night," said Chief Driscoll. "If the officer had been here at the time Spencer stopped for gas and cigarettes would she have skipped him or shot the officer also?"

Chief Driscoll's supposition gave Wilson a moment of thought.

"Let's assume that she was following him. How could she know that he would leave the hotel without a bodyguard?"

The Chief replied, "She would have had to have seen the cruiser leave and that gave her an opening."

"Yes. But how could she know that he was leaving the hotel. If Spencer sent the officer away thinking he might be staying the night why would she sit there and wait."

"To achieve her goal all she had to do was wait until midnight. If he didn't come out then she would miss her time frame."

"But she didn't miss. And I don't believe she does anything by chance," said Wilson.

"So how did she know when he was leaving?"

"The only way she could know for sure when he was leaving would be if she had arranged it."

"Unless there was a fire alarm, that caused everyone to leave the building, for Spencer to leave the hotel before midnight it had to have been orchestrated by her."

Chief Driscoll said, "But how?"

"I doubt that he was taking any phone calls while on his date so she didn't lure him outside with a phone call like she did with Ernie Taylor."

Wilson was almost steaming inside. She had out-smarted them again.

"She sent him outside herself," Wilson exclaimed. "She was his date!"

"I thought you cleared his date?"

"We did," said Wilson. "We cleared Lisa Raines. She is from New York."

Wilson walked over to the first officer on scene and told him to leave a copy of the report on his desk and then returned to where Chief Driscoll was standing.

"Come on Chief. Meet me at the hotel."

Wilson jumped into his rental car and turned on the flashing roof light for the drive to the Plaza Hotel. He could see the flashing lights of the Chief Driscoll's truck in his rear view. Wilson didn't bother parking at the hotel; he drove up to the front door and flashed his badge to the doorman. Chief Driscoll pulled up right behind him and they went to the front desk together.

Wilson flashed his badge again at the front desk and told the clerk to call Lisa Raines. After a moment of understanding the clerk called her room.

"I am sorry to bother you Miss Raines but there is a detective here that wants to talk to you."

"In person," Wilson said in case the clerk planned on handing the phone to him.

"No miss he says he needs to speak with you in person."

The clerk hung up, "She will be right down detective."

The moment that Lisa Raines entered the lobby from the elevator dressed in jeans and a tee shirt Wilson knew that they had been duped. The thick mane of red hair was marginally brushed but there was no doubt that this was the real Lisa Raines. She was wearing slippers and Wilson guessed that she was at least five-seven; too tall to be Susan Doyle. She walked right up to Wilson and Chief Driscoll.

"Miss Raines?"

"Yes."

"I am Detective Wilson. Where were you this evening?"

"I was having dinner here in the hotel with one of my clients. I can provide you with his name if you need it."

"Do you know a man by the name of Andrew Spencer?"

"No," she replied very abruptly.

"Do you know a woman by the name of Susan Doyle?"

"No."

"Thank you for your time."

Lisa Raines looked at both men and then turned and strode back to the elevators. The two men walked back to their vehicles.

"She has used fake names and now a real name. She adapts well," said Wilson as he looked up to the top of the building. "There are almost two thousand guests in this hotel and we have no idea of what she looked like today. She could be Dolly Parton one day and Princess Leah the next."

"It's a bit like Cinderella where she becomes herself after midnight."

"The difference is that Doyle is both the pretty sister and also the evil sister."

Chief Driscoll chose his words carefully, "Detective I was thinking that it might be a good idea to keep quiet about tonight's attack on Spencer. The people of Kelby are rattled enough as it is and we do have a big day planned for tomorrow."

"That might be a good idea for a several reasons. Other than the team we will keep it quiet for now. I'll see you in the morning Chief."

The evening's events were exactly why Captain Stone and Lieutenant Trentini are keeping their distance from Wilson's investigation. Another murder and this time, even though given the change in the circumstances it was almost unpreventable, it was close enough to Chicago to tarnish the image of the investigation team. Wilson was buoyed by the relief that Doyle would not get to Webster, yet disappointed that Spencer had made himself such as easy victim. The belief that 'it won't happen to me' is one that many victims of violence or accidents carry with them until it does happen to them. Some get a second chance but sadly most do not. The rest of Wilson's team will be shocked when they learn of what happened but that will have to wait for morning. There was no sense in ruining everyone's sleep tonight.

CHAPTER 28

THE PLAN WAS to have everything in place by eleven a.m. and finally do something that would affect Doyle instead of her doing things that affected them. The team minus Nelson assembled in the bullpen by seven thirty. Wilson called Nelson and put her on speaker phone and then he told them the news. The reaction was the opposite of 'you could hear a pin drop' as they showed their anger and frustration with both a verbal trashing of Doyle and also the kicking of chairs and the throwing of pens. Wilson fully understood their ire. All the work to protect the final people on Doyle's potential list and Spencer throws it all away in a single moment. Their discontent with Spencer was curtailed by the fact that he was now a victim and that Doyle had once again proven how cunning she could be. Once the news had registered and been accepted the business of the case began.

Campbell started the ball rolling, "I have commandeered a tow truck so we won't have to bring a civilian driver into the mix." Campbell had done some tow truck driving with the impound guys in case he ever had to fill in for one of them. "The car is covered in the impound yard right now."

"Mac is ready to go," said Anthony. "He will follow Campbell to the site."

"All's quiet on the western front," said Nelson over phone. "Webster has been surprisingly cooperative."

Wilson said, "Once the accident is finished I will go to the retirement home and pick up Mrs. Webster and bring her back to Webster's house. Insulating her in that way should reduce any stress she may feel. Ideally it would be great if Doyle was in Kelby when the sirens go off at the fire hall but if not she will get a blow by blow description in The Journal."

Anthony said, "Do you think it will be enough to stop her in her tracks?"

"I don't know. Even Dr. Devlin couldn't say definitively one way or the other. But I am sure it will give her cause to think and that should give us an edge."

Wilson turned to Detective Anthony, "After you call Chief Driscoll wait until you hear the sirens, and then call the Journal."

Campbell said, "Mac, Anthony and I will pick up the cadaver and put it in the front seat."

"Okay. Let's go do this."

"Good luck guys," said Nelson before she disconnected.

As expected Wilson was the first to arrive in Kelby. When he entered the Kelby Police Department he was instructed that Chief Driscoll was waiting for him in his office. "Good Morning Chief," said Wilson as he closed the door of Driscoll's office behind him. "Do you still have that file on the farm eviction?"

"Yes," said the Chief as he reached into one of his desk drawers, pulled out the red folder and handed it to Wilson.

"What are you looking for Detective?"

"I am not sure Chief," said Wilson deliberately as he opened the folder and scanned each page slowly before turning them over. "But after the attack on Spencer last night I was wondering if there was something that we missed. This eviction was four years ago, a year before you arrived in Kelby."

"That's correct."

"That is good for you. That should mean you are not on Doyle's radar." Wilson continued to carefully scan the pages in the file hoping for something to jump out at him.

He closed the file and slouched in his chair thinking to himself. Spencer wasn't in the picture of the ribbon cutting ceremony so why did Doyle go after him and in such a calculating manner? Spencer's carelessness on his date had signed his own death warrant. Suddenly he sat up straight.

"That's it," he shouted.

"What is it?" asked Chief Driscoll.

Wilson hurriedly flipped through the pages in the file.

"I was just thinking that about Spencer's death and then it hit me." Wilson held one of the pages staring at it. He handed the page the Chief Driscoll.

Wilson said, "Do you see it?"

Chief Driscoll shook his head and frowned.

"Look at the signature of the Justice of the Peace. It is not very clear but it should be easy enough to verify."

"It's Spencer's," said Driscoll.

"That was his connection to Doyle. He must have run for office in the last election."

"Yes I arrived right after the elections. I never witnessed him in a role as a JP. I was recommended to Chief Caswell to replace his previous deputy who had run against him and lost."

"If Spencer had told us about his connection to the eviction we could have prevented the attack and he might still be alive," said Wilson. "What was he thinking keeping it a secret?"

"Perhaps he felt his role in the eviction would never come to light or that somehow it might have hurt his chance of winning the next election."

"It proves once again how clever Doyle is and why she has been able to stay one step ahead us. But with a bit of luck that should change today."

Wilson's trip to the Kelby Police Department preceded the procession of three vehicles, now approaching Kelby, on a secret mission to an undisclosed destination. When the big white tow truck, towing a covered car, and driven by Officer Campbell, turned right at Pacific Road hardly anyone noticed. The two cars that also turned right and followed the slow moving tow truck were similarly unimportant to those standing at the corner waiting to cross the street.

Everything was moving on schedule. When Officer Campbell reached the bend in the road he pulled over and Mac and Detective Anthony did the same. They unhooked the car off the winch and then Campbell moved the tow truck to the other side of the road to lift the rear of the car and put it on the right angle to make it go over the bank and hit the culvert. Once they had it lined up on the edge of the road and with the gear shift in neutral the three men pushed it over the soft shoulder and watched it slide down the grassy slope to the culvert. It certainly wasn't as exciting as a real crash might have been but the already damaged front end of the car made it look like it had really happened. Mac instructed them to move the cars back further from the burn car and then he pulled out a tool box from the back seat of his car. He opened the trunk and removed a large red can of gasoline with a long spout and then after putting on a special pair of fire resistant overalls he walked down to the car. The hood was ajar about ten inches from the previous damage and it creaked loudly when he lifted it up. Mac removed a cell phone with two wires from the tool box and connected one wire to each of the battery terminals. He slowly closed the lid to its original position. The space was enough to allow him to pour gasoline onto the engine and battery. Then he opened the driver door and poured more of the gasoline on the interior of the vehicle and the cadaver. He closed the driver's door about halfway and then poured the rest of the gasoline over the hood and the driver's door.

Once he was back at the cars he took one more look at the burn car. Campbell and Anthony looked edgy as Mac pulled out his cell phone.

Mac smiled at them, "Don't worry the gas tank is dry so there won't be any explosion."

Mac dialed a number and a fire started under the hood. It quickly spread to the interior and the flames sported a black hue from the burning plastic in the dashboard and console.

"That's it gentlemen. Have a great day," said Mac as he got back into his car and drove away. Officer Campbell quickly followed while Anthony made a phone call of his own.

"Yes Detective," answered Chief Driscoll.

"It's done," replied Anthony.

Chief Driscoll disconnected and nodded to Wilson. The Chief called the fire department to advise them of the reported car fire on Pacific Road and advised them he would meet them there. Wilson left to go to the retirement home and pick up Webster's mother.

Anthony looked back at the burning car. It looked exactly like a car accident gone badly. He heard sirens in the distance and placed his call to The Journal. The only piece of the plan not yet in place is the call from Chief Driscoll to the Medical Examiner's Office in Chicago and then the arrival of Dr. Fred McLaughlin and his team to remove the body. The sirens grew louder and then a fire truck came into view heading right towards the fire. Right behind the fire truck was Chief Driscoll's Suburban truck.

A photographer and a reporter from The Journal arrived just as the firemen started dousing the flames. More cars followed shortly and soon a crowd had gathered to see what had happened. Anthony blended in amongst the onlookers waiting and watching. Would Doyle be here today as Wilson had hoped? Despite a decent description would Anthony be able to pick her out in this crowd? The murmurs he heard were 'What happened?' – 'Whose car is it?' – 'Was anyone hurt?'

People were taking pictures with their cell phones and calling to tell others in town what had happened. Anthony kept looking to see if any of the women, looking at the fire engulfed car, fit the size and height characteristics of Doyle. Then he heard new murmurs in the swelling throng, 'Oh no' – 'Are you sure?' – 'Is she okay'? so he listened closer.

To ensure that everything in the plan moved at normal rate the Medical Examiner's van carrying Fred arrived in thirty minutes. It didn't need to speed down the highway to beat the normal forty-five minute drive because they had left early and timed their arrival make it seem that they rushed to get here.

"Oh my god," a woman shrieked next to Anthony.

A startled Anthony said, "What is it?"

The woman, who was too old to be Doyle, turned to Anthony, "It's Ms. Webster from the Chamber of Commerce. They're saying that is her car."

This new information traveled like wild fire through the crowd. If Doyle was here she knew also.

Fred and his assistant with a gurney waited at the soft shoulder for the Fire Department to give them the go ahead to remove the body. They removed the body and strapped it to the gurney and hauled it back up the slope to the road. When the black tarp body bag on the gurney crested the hill it was the concluding evidence to the crowd that Deborah Webster President of the Kelby Chamber of Commerce had perished in the car fire. The Medical Examiner van pulled away as the firemen wrapped up their hoses. The people still watching were whispering in groups – 'I bet it was the killer' – 'was she on the list' – 'who is next'.

Gradually the crowd dispersed. Wilson had sequestered Mrs. Webster at her daughter's house where Nelson was still on guard. The Journal would have news of the death and pictures of the car accident on the front page of their paper on Monday morning. Even if Doyle was not in Kelby today she would soon know about the accident. Tonight they could all get a good night sleep knowing they were finally a step ahead of the killer. The plan was almost complete.

CHAPTER 29

THE CAR CRASH in Kelby made the early morning news in Chicago. Wilson saw the pictures of the firemen putting out the fire. Anyone in Kelby who were somehow not aware of the car crash yesterday would be reading about it in the morning paper today. Doyle had to be well aware of the circumstances by now. Wilson worried about what was going through her head. Would she finally break down and give up her fight or would she do the opposite and go postal on everyone involved.

Yesterday when he and Anthony had returned to the bullpen they spent a few hours replying to the pile of phone messages about a Doyle sighting. After three hours of listening to hotel and motel people looking for their fifteen minutes of fame they still had no luck. They finally called it a day at eight and Wilson took his girlfriend Jennifer out for dinner and a movie. Her daughters were home so after the movie it was just a kiss good night. She shares equal custody of her daughters with her ex-husband but Wilson never stayed overnight when the daughters were home with her. Instead he settled for the kiss and a whisper in his ear.

Doyle's consistent two-day schedule indicated that today was an attack day. The big question now is whether or not today was the day she was going to attack Webster and if it was, what will she do now knowing her next victim was already dead. The only other person left on the potential list was her brother, and even though he has an officer watching him all day and all night she has proven her ability to get her victims alone before she kills them. All this went through Wilson's mind before he had even left his condo for the drive downtown.

The bullpen had a sweet aroma this morning, the distinct smell of donuts. Detective Anthony was taking advantage of the fact that Nelson was in Kelby guarding the supposedly recently demised Deborah Webster and had purchased a box of his favorite types of donuts. There wasn't a plain one in the bunch and several of the other detectives in the bullpen were happy to be sharing in the deep fried delights. Even the trim and fit Officer Campbell had given into to the temptation and was nibbling on one.

Wilson smiled at the less than tense attitude in the bullpen this morning. Even though today was one of Doyle's target dates they were all feeling better about the investigation. To ensure that any attempt by Doyle would thwarted today Chief Driscoll had two officers with Frank and as an extra precaution an officer would drive by the Webster house each hour. Everything was in place and they were eager to get to the next part of the plan. The fake funeral for Webster would be on Wednesday.

By lunchtime there had been no change and although that was the outcome they wanted it wasn't the outcome they expected. The ability of Doyle to evade them and still trap her victims was a burden to their confidence. As each minute went by the anxiety in the detectives was like a clock spring and Doyle was the key winding them tighter and tighter one turn at a time. It was quiet, too quiet for all those working on the case. Wilson was pensive. There were no new sightings of Doyle at any motels or hotels and no new vehicles spotted in Kelby. How was she able to be invisible? What if her brother was never a target? If Webster was the last one on her list then was she finished? The issue that bothered Wilson was that they didn't know who was really on her list. Would she wait for Melissa Green to come back? Was she psychotic enough to keep going after all the people in the picture? Was Wilson's assumption that the people who were out of town were safe, a wrong assumption? Could she really be going after the Mayor of Chicago and the Governor of Illinois? The mind is an amazing thing. It takes a dozen positive thoughts to negate a single negative thought and Wilson had just thought of two very scary negative thoughts.

At four o'clock Wilson realized that they had not had lunch and he was about to tell Detective Anthony to go out and get his other favorite comfort food, pizza when Anthony's cell phone rang. It froze them in their tracks for two reasons. First, even though they were hoping against it in the back of their minds they were expecting a call so their nerves were on edge. And second, Anthony's cell phone was not the one they expected to ring. They froze and then unfroze. Wilson's phone was the one they expected to ring so Anthony's phone ringing was more confusion than apprehension. Anthony looked at Wilson almost apologetic, like he had interrupted something important going on in the bullpen. He looked at the number and a frown formed on his face. It was the Winnfield Police Department.

"This is Detective Anthony. Hang on I am going to put you on speaker phone. Okay, go ahead."

"Detective this is Officer Greg Milanowycz here in Winnfield. I am the one who called you with the phone number for Mr. Fisher."

"Yes I remember."

"Well I am calling because there has been an accident here in Winnfield."

"An accident?" The words jumped off of Anthony's lips in surprise.

"Yes sir, a welding accident. It was Mr. Fisher. That's why I'm calling you."

The bullpen was stunned into silence. An accident. The words of Officer Milanowycz were ominous and yet clear. The word accident and Doyle were synonymous and the fact that it was her ex-husband solidified the connection.

"Hello? Are you still there?"

"Yes Officer Milanowycz we are. We are just a little shocked at this news."

"I can understand that sir. The Fire Marshall said Fisher was using a plasma cutting torch to remove the tops of some scrap 55 gallon drums. Apparently the sparks and heat from the torch ignited some oil residue inside one of the drums. When the drum exploded, the top he was cutting off decapitated him. They said he died instantly."

More silence from the bullpen.

"Detective?"

"Yes officer."

"The strange thing is that the owner of the scrap yard swears that the drums were empty and dried out. All the rest of the drums the Fire Marshall checked were dry, exactly as he said."

"So only one barrel had oil inside," said Anthony.

"Yes sir."

Wilson said to Anthony, "I doubt there will be any finger-prints on the barrel."

Officer Milanowycz asked, "Finger-prints sir?"

Anthony replied, "If the barrel had been tampered with there would normally be finger prints left on it."

"You think someone put oil in the drum on purpose."

"Yes we do."

"But that would be murder."

"Yes it would and it was probably his ex-wife."

"Really? I will have to let our Chief know right away."

"If he has any questions he can reach us here," said Anthony.

"I am sure he will."

"Tell him to ask for Detective-Sergeant Wilson."

"Sorry to be the bearer of bad news sir."

"We understand Officer Milanowycz. Thank you for calling."

Click

The news of the death of Doyle's ex-husband was difficult information for the team to swallow. While it was good that no one in Kelby was attacked it marked the first time that someone not in the photo had become a victim. This added a new dimension to the profile Wilson thought; one that could have disastrous results. Did it mean that there were other people in Doyle's life who were now potential targets? It moved her brother to the top of the list.

"She knew he had that part time job today," said Campbell.

"Yes, he told us last week," said Anthony.

"But how did she know he would be killed?"

Wilson responded, "She was married to a welder for four years. He probably told her many times about the dangers of his job trying to make himself appear more macho. He might have even told her about this very scenario."

"Wow, he could have unintentionally given her the method the kill him."

"And she remembered it."

"It is possible she didn't care how he was killed but she must have known that he was unlikely to survive being that close to an explosion."

"Wait, if she was in Winnfield this morning then she had to have left here by eight last night at the latest. It's a twelve hour drive."

"But would she want to drive all night?"

"If she had this already planned for today then she might have been on the road to Winnfield before we staged the car accident so she could get a night's sleep."

"And that would mean she wasn't in the crowd watching it and that she hasn't seen the news yet."

"She must be on her way back here now."

"Well she's not going to find out until she gets back tonight. She won't hear about it on the car radio until she gets into Illinois."

"No she won't."

"The next questions are; Where is here? And how will she react when she finds out about Webster?"

"Now we know why we haven't had any Doyle sightings for the past two days. She hasn't been here to be seen," said Campbell.

"You know," said Anthony pausing for effect. "Maybe all these sightings that were not Doyle is because she never was there to be seen. Maybe, as most of them turned out, they just thought it was Doyle because we sent out the picture."

"Sometimes that is the situation," said Wilson. "In fact . . ." Wilson stopped in mid-sentence looked at the ceiling and then slapped his hand loudly on the desk.

"Damn!"

Campbell and Anthony looked at each other with quizzical expressions on their faces.

"What is it?" Campbell asked first.

"We are not in Kansas anymore Toto!"

This reply did nothing to bring clarity to Campbell and Anthony as they still looked bewildered wondering where Wilson was going with his comment.

"We have been looking for her in hotels and motels because we got one hit."

Campbell and Anthony said nothing, waiting for him to continue.

"That one hotel hit was closest to her next target that day. She wanted to be at the farm early, before sunrise, so she wouldn't be seen. She didn't want to take any chances of being late. But all the rest of her victims were attacked later in the day. There was no rush for the rest. How many times have we said that she doesn't leave anything to chance?"

Anthony looked at Wilson with raised eyebrows. He was pretty sure that was a rhetorical question so he didn't answer.

"She duped us again."

"How?"

"She probably knew that we would be looking for her in hotels and motels so she deliberately used the Liverpool Motel as bait. It kept us focussed in Kelby while she was hiding out somewhere else. She was here at least a month before the killings started. I sincerely doubt that she was dragging all her belongings from hotel to motel. I'll bet she has rented a house somewhere. She most likely put all her furniture and things in storage. We might be able to find out where but I don't think we have that much time and it won't help us too much. I doubt it will be anyplace that she visits regularly."

It amazed Anthony when Wilson started on one of his brainstorming breakthroughs. How did Wilson's mind sort through stuff so fast? Anthony considered that maybe his marriage and having two kids put a drain on his brain power that because Wilson wasn't married that he didn't have that to worry about. In his mind that was his story and he was sticking to it.

"I am going to call Nelson and Chief Driscoll to update them. I need you two guys to call all the real estate people that do rentals and find out if they have rented a house to a woman fitting Doyle's description. It would be roughly six weeks ago."

This was a breakthrough that they needed. If they were successful in finding the right real estate agent they might be able to find Doyle before the fake funeral.

"Hey stranger," Nelson said when she saw it was Wilson calling her. Her mood was light as she had not been expecting any bad news from Wilson and talking to someone other than Webster, who kept asking for more information about what was going on, was a nice change.

Wilson filled her in on the news.

"That poor man," she said. "And he had no idea that she was gunning for him."

"No he didn't. And neither did the rest of us."

Nelson said, "What now?"

"We're ruling out the hotel sightings. We think she had other ideas. We're looking for houses that were rented out about six weeks ago to anyone who looked like Doyle but we will need to get lucky we want to find her before the funeral."

"What if you don't? Do you want me to stay here or help out at the funeral?"

"You have to stay with Webster. Who knows what Doyle is capable of? She might have electronic eyes on the house. We can't take any chances on Doyle finding out that Webster is still alive."

"Gotcha."

"I know you want to get hands on but I can't trust Webster's safety to anyone else."

Nelson knew Wilson well enough to know that this wasn't a hollow compliment to pacify her but rather his matter of fact way of saying that it was a more important job than it appeared.

Next Wilson called Chief Driscoll and after explaining what had happened in Winnfield, he then discussed about the rental house possibility.

"If you could get your local realtors to check as well we could cover the area faster."

"I will have our people on it first thing in the morning," said Chief Driscoll. "This is an interesting idea. It would certainly better explain her ability to hide."

"That's what we thought too, especially if the house has a garage that could conceal her vehicle when she is there."

"And you don't think she is aware of the accident yet?"

"No. We expect she'll return here sometime this evening and then she might hear the news. At the latest it will be Tuesday morning."

"The funeral plans are all set for Wednesday at eleven am. There will be a reasonable turnout. Webster is quite popular here in Kelby. The majority of the businesses are shutting down for an hour to attend. If Doyle comes to the funeral the crowd will be large enough for her not to feel she will be conspicuous."

"We will have to find a way to be able to pick her out of the crowd."

"A single woman by herself would be more noticeable than a couple or group of women together."

"Doyle will figure out a way of blending in."

Chief Driscoll added, "She might even be smart enough to disguise herself as a man."

"I hope not. That would certainly make it even more difficult to pick her out."

"We can hand pick some people in the crowd and have them watch out for anyone they don't recognize as a local."

"That is a good idea. Doyle wouldn't be expecting that. I'd also like to get that photographer again. It didn't work out at Caswell's funeral but maybe it will work with Webster's"

"Will you be coming to Kelby on Tuesday?"

"If we have anything important to go over I will. I am trying to stay off Doyle's radar. I don't think she is aware of my rental car. At least I am hoping that she isn't. We need every edge we can get to be able to find her."

When Wilson finished his call with Chief Driscoll he opened his emails and sent off an email that was more a message in a bottle. He shrugged his shoulders and wondered if he was being realistic or just hoping for a miracle.

CHAPTER 30

A GOOD NIGHT'S sleep can help you start your day fresh. It can revitalize your mind and body and make you a healthier person; although it only works though if you actually sleep through the night. Staring at the ceiling as Wilson did however isn't considered the correct way to get a good night's sleep. He was normally able to sleep through the night irrelevant of what was on his plate but last night was an exception and he awoke feeling that he never slept at all.

A lack of REM sleep left Wilson feeling a disconnection with time. It was early Tuesday morning but it felt like he had only closed his eyes for a minute. He knew it was time to get up and get ready for work but his body was saying the opposite. The anxiousness of the approaching deadline had sent his brain and body into flux. Whatever sleep his body wanted or needed would have to wait until tonight. A hot shower was all he could give his body at the moment. Dressed in a brown suit today he was ready to head out but not before a quick call to Jennifer.

"Good morning beautiful."

"Aren't you sweet? I am not feeling all that beautiful this morning. I was painting the girl's bedrooms yesterday and I think there is still paint in my hair."

Ryan chuckled. "They sell painter hats," he said.

"I am not as organized at those kinds of things as you are. I sort of fly by the seat of my pants."

"I know. It makes life with you interesting."

"Just interesting," teased Jennifer.

"Very interesting and exciting. And for the record I like the seat of your pants too," Ryan countered.

"Well I like the seat of your pants also," Jennifer replied giggling.

"It might be a long day today and I wanted to hear your voice before I headed in this morning."

"I am glad you called. The girls thought, because you haven't been here since pizza night and because I was painting their rooms, that you and I had a fight. They thought the painting of their rooms was my way of dealing with it."

"And is painting your way of dealing with a tiff?" Ryan asked.

"Well you will have to wait until we have a fight to find out," Jennifer laughed. "And I said fight not tiff. A tiff means you show up the next day with flowers," she laughed again.

"I see," said Ryan with a smile. "Good to know."

"That's all the hints you get. The rest you have to figure out for yourself." Another giggle.

"Okay. Now I have to go find a photographer."

That statement threw Jennifer for a curve. "I don't understand. I am a photographer."

"Yes you are but this is for a funeral and not one I want you anywhere near."

"That sounds alarming," she said.

"It might be but I have said too much, now I must go. Enjoy getting the paint out of your hair."

"Anytime you want to come and help me wash my hair you are welcome."

"I think I will put that down in my notes for later."

"Well, here's hoping you have a good day and I will let you know when I am going to wash my hair again."

"Bye babe."

"Bye hun."

The previous blasé feeling of no sleep had been rectified with a shot of adrenaline after talking to Jennifer.

It was raining hard, low charcoal clouds moved quickly and rumbled without the flash of lightening. Traffic, as usual on a rainy morning, was slow but it gave Wilson time to think. Normally he did his best thinking behind the wheel of his SUV but this morning the rental car was still the substitute.

Sitting at a red light, watching one of the intersection cameras taking pictures of cars infringing on the amber light, gave Wilson an idea. Now he was eager to get to the bullpen and check his emails but the traffic on Skokie Highway was not cooperating so he detoured onto N. Lincoln.

Wilson booted up his computer to check on a response to the email he sent last night. He was hoping there was reply waiting for him that he could add his new idea to but when he explored his inbox the reply he was anticipating wasn't there. Wilson sat back in chair confused and disappointed.

He had emailed his friend at the FBI, Special Agent in Charge Mark Giordano about using his expert photographer at Webster's fake funeral and he was surprised that there had been no response back. Wilson reflected on the issue. Was Giordano on vacation? Would someone else reply back later today? Was the photographer not available? Wilson looked around the bullpen and noticed that he was the only one in yet so the coffee pot was empty. He got up to make a pot of coffee guessing the others would be here soon when his cell phone went off.

"Detective Wilson," he announced into his phone.

"Morning Wilson." It was Giordano.

Not an email reply, but a phone call instead. Something inferred to Wilson that this was not a generic 'How is the weather' call.

"To what do I owe the personal touch?"

"Decided to kill two birds with one stone. Your email was unexpected timing. I have some news for you."

That didn't sound like he was about to give some good news but Wilson couldn't think what the bad news could be.

"I am afraid that David Bay is dead."

Wilson was floored.

"Well that wasn't anything I was expecting."

This would not have been in the top ten things that he thought Giordano would have told him. After Bay testified in the trials of the two big drug companies that had manipulated Bay to steal company secrets he was moved to Statesville to serve the rest of his sentence. He was on medication to keep his negative alter ego "Jack', under wraps.

"What happened?"

"Apparently there was a confrontation in the yard and Bay attacked one of the gang members and he was surrounded by the rest of the gang and then stabbed with a shiv before the guards could react. It happened very fast. They didn't know why he lost it but after they tossed his cell they found over a week's supply of his meds in his pillow case. He was cheeking his meds and that allowed 'Jack' back in his life. Apparently the other inmates on his block knew about his other personality and were prepared for an attack."

"How does this affect the trials?"

"It doesn't. His testimony is in the transcripts and they are almost done with their posturing. There will be certain jail time for the two guys that paid Bay to steal and serious fines for the companies. Sorry to be the bearer of bad news."

"Do you want me to let his mother know?"

"She was at his trial but my people never spoke with her. I know you and Nelson went to see her, so if you want to break the news to her, feel free."

"Well I know Nelson is going a little stir crazy watching Webster so she might like a small diversion even one that brings bad news."

"Now about your other request."

"I was thinking about the other funeral and wondered if we could do it again."

"I don't see that as a problem. Although I am not sure that the result would be any different."

"I was thinking that also at first but this crowd will be substantially smaller and we know exactly who we are looking for, more or less."

"More or less?"

"We know she is female and that she is five-three unfortunately she has been very good at changing her hair and concealing her blue eyes."

"Morris is very good at identification techniques. That's his name by the way in case he didn't mention it. He usually doesn't. He has a few quirks like that but he is the best at photographing potential suspects."

Wilson said, "I had an idea this morning that might be even more helpful. Survey cameras measure while they scan and I understand that there are new digital cameras with a measurement program built in. It does the trigonometry for you and then displays the height of the object in the picture. If Morris has access to one he could tell us which women at the funeral are five – three. It would speed up our time frame for finding her in the crowd."

Giordano chuckled, "If they exist Morris knows how to get his hands on one. I will send your request to him and let you know if he can get one for Wednesday."

"Great."

"Are you sure you don't need any extra help at the funeral?"

"No thanks, it might turn into a too many cooks kind of thing and beside your black suits will still be too obvious even at a funeral."

"Perhaps you're right. Good luck with your trip to Pontiac."

"Thanks."

Click.

Wilson called down to the front desk to find out which female officers were on standby rotation today. The desk Sergeant gave him two names and he recognized the second one, Colleen Supinski.

"Send Supinski up to see me as soon as she arrives. Tell her no uniform today."

Campbell and Anthony entered the bullpen together and both turned their heads and smiled as they smelled the fresh made coffee.

Wilson called Nelson's cell. This time she was a bit more cautious with her banter in case he was delivering more bad news.

"I think you need a break."

"Really? I thought you said you wanted me here."

"I do but we have to go on a small road trip."

Now she was completely lost as to what Wilson was referring to.

"We're going to Pontiac this morning."

Nelson tried to decipher why they would need to go to Pontiac and could only come up with one answer; Mrs. Bay.

"Did something happen to Mrs. Bay?"

"No. She is fine at the moment. But that's who we are going to see. David Bay is dead."

"Oh no. The poor woman is going to be devastated."

"Yes. That's why I volunteered us to give her the news. She knows us, and that will be better than having a strange policeman dropping the bomb on her."

"Absolutely. When are we going?"

"I will be there in an hour. I am bringing your replacement with me."

"Who?"

"I thought you liked a surprise."

"I do like surprises in my personal life but not so much on the job."

"Okay. It's Supinski."

Nelson had met her, "Good choice. I think she can handle this situation here comfortably. Three women locked up in a house is not a cake walk."

Wilson laughed at her remark wondering if she knew its origin. Maybe he would ask her later.

"Well it is only for the trip today. I see you soon."

Click

After overhearing the conversation Anthony asked, "Where are you going?"

Wilson filled Officer Campbell and Detective Anthony in on the news about David Bay.

"So you're going to tell his mother that he is dead."

"Someone has to, and since we have already met her it will be less of a shock for her to hear it from us. I need you guys to really work the real estate people. Chief Driscoll will have the Kelby realtors check for renters. If you find anything close call me right away."

When Officer Colleen Supinski walked into the bullpen Campbell and Anthony pretended not to notice. It was difficult not to notice as she was a tall blonde with the broad shoulders usually given to an athlete. They evidently were not comfortable with a new member being added to the team. Wilson actually enjoyed watching the two of them being uncomfortable. They had accepted Nelson, she had seniority, but they still struggled with working with other women cops. Detective Anthony's issue came from a long line of family heritage that precluded putting the woman of the family in a position of danger. It didn't matter what that position was but being a cop was one of the jobs they frowned on for women. Protect the woman of the household to preserve the family. Perhaps it was an admirable stand in its time, but mildly archaic by today's standards. For Anthony it was a moral standing as opposed to a competition between the sexes. There was no grey in his life, everything was black or white. Exactly like his heritage.

"I was told to report to you sir," said Supinski.

"Yes. I have a short task for you. It requires a little bit of private babysitting."

"By babysitting you mean body guarding?"

"Yes."

"And no uniform means undercover."

"Yes."

"When?"

"We're leaving right now. I will fill you in on the way." One of the reasons Wilson had chosen Supinski was that she had similar personal characteristics to Nelson. If she decides to go that route she might even make detective faster than most of the men in this precinct. He turned to Anthony and Campbell, "Remember, anything even close call me. I should be back after lunch."

They left the bullpen quickly and were soon in Wilson's rental car on their way to Kelby.

"Where are we going?" She knew about the case, but not any of the details.

"We are heading to Kelby. We have a person to protect. Her mother is staying with her also."

"Sounds more mysterious than difficult."

"Good evaluation. One of the people you are guarding is technically dead."

"Technically sir?"

"Her death is a ruse to disrupt the killer's agenda."

"Fantastic," she exclaimed.

Wilson chuckled at Supinski's keenness, "Her mother is not aware of the big issue. She thinks that it is just a short vacation from her retirement home."

"And I should not mention anything."

"No. The mother knows about the killer and the possible danger but believes that we have it under control."

"So, positive attitude no frowns."

"Yes. But stay on your toes. Webster doesn't go anywhere near a window or a door."

"Got it."

"And last thing, if anything seems strange outside call Chief Driscoll first. He has an officer on patrol just in case. But remember only the Chief knows about Webster, the officers are in the dark about her death. They think she is really dead, so if you do call one of them into the house, make sure you keep Webster upstairs and hidden."

He parked a few houses away from Webster's and made the exchange of Supinski for Nelson while staying in the car. Anyone watching would only see a tall blonde going inside and a brunette coming out, as if visiting the grieving mother to share condolences. As soon as Nelson was in the rental car Wilson pulled away from the curb and drove straight to Thirty-Nine South.

"How did the boys take it when you told them you were bringing in Supinski?"

Wilson tried not to smile but it still came out as a smirk.

Nelson saw this reaction, "That bad?"

"Let's just say that I think they will be more focussed on the task of finding Doyle's rental house now."

The drive down Reynolds Street was a slightly different view from the half bare trees they saw last fall to the full flowering blossoms of early summer they were seeing now.

The leaves of the trees partially obscured the grey house they were looking for but when Wilson saw the white birdbath on the front lawn he knew that they were in the right place. The two large flower pots on each side of the front porch that were empty on their last visit were now stuffed with Pansies and Peonies. Wilson opened the screen door and knocked.

"Who is it?" echoed through the wood door.

Wilson answered, "Mrs. Bay, its Detective Wilson and Detective Nelson from the Chicago P.D."

He could hear the floor creak and then the door opened. No unlocking of the door required in Pontiac at ten thirty in the morning.

Instead of a look of surprise they were greeted with, "Good morning detectives. To what do I owe the pleasure of your visit this time?"

This time? Mrs. Bay remembered their visit last year. Wilson looked at Nelson.

"We're here about David Mrs. Bay," said Nelson.

"My son is in jail now so I am not sure what good talking to me can do."

Wilson said, "May we come in please."

"Oh of course. Where are my manners?"

Mrs. Bay directed them to the same couch they sat on the last time they were here and she sat in her chair.

"I just made some tea would you like some?"

"Yes please," said Nelson.

Wilson held up his hand, "Not for me thank you."

Mrs. Bay left to go to the kitchen and fetch the pot of tea. Except for the reason of the visit it had a feeling of déjà vu. The tray of tea and cups Mrs. Bay returned with was accompanied by digestive biscuits.

"What is it about my son that brings you here again?"

Wilson said, "Mrs. Bay, were you aware of David's personality disorder?"

"No not at all. I didn't find out until the trial. That's when all the secrets came out."

"So you know he was on medication for his disorder when he went to prison."

"Yes. He didn't like it much. He said it made him feel numb but that was what he needed to do. He needed to take the medication to prevent any more outbursts."

"That might explain something we were confused about."

"What is that?"

"David recently stopped taking his meds."

"Are you sure?"

"Yes, they found a batch hidden in his pillow case."

"Oh my. I hope he's okay."

Nelson said, "That is why we are here Mrs. Bay. I am afraid David had another attack because he didn't take his medication."

"He did? Is he okay?"

"No Mrs. Bay David was swarmed by a gang in the yard and he was stabbed. He didn't survive his wounds."

Mrs. Bay dropped her china tea cup onto the tray. Her hands were shaking trying to right the cup on its saucer. Her mind was processing that David, her son, was gone. Up until today she had resolved that he would most likely spend the rest of his days in prison and she would see him once a month. Now in a heartbeat he was gone. She would not be seeing him again except at his funeral.

"Here let me help you with that," said Nelson as she put the tea cup back on the saucer. Mrs. Bay's body was trembling and tears began to wash down her cheeks.

"Is there someone we should call to come and be with you?" Wilson asked.

Mrs. Bay looked at Wilson confused, "Pardon me?" She had not understood what he had said to her.

"I said is there anyone we can call to come and stay with you?"

"Oh . . . yes. Mildred lives next door at number seventy seven."

Nelson gathered up the tray and took it into the kitchen and then left to get Mildred.

Mrs. Bay had settled back into her chair and dabbed at her tears with a white cotton handkerchief. Watching her expression it now appeared to Wilson that her son's death did not come as a total shock to her, but she had hoped that if he kept taking his medication, he would have been okay in jail.

Wilson gave her a minute to herself and looked around the room. The same pictures on the mantle, some of David and others of her and David together. He had barely noticed them before, but they were more evident now that David was dead. It seemed strange to Wilson that there were only pictures of David, none of his brother but today was not the time to bring that subject up. Many families have a black sheep that is rarely seen or heard from.

Nelson returned with the next door neighbour, Mildred. She was white haired and similar build to Mrs. Bay. Side by side they could have passed as sisters. Mildred hugged Mrs. Bay and held her hand.

"Mrs. Bay do you need us to contact anyone?"

Mildred and Mrs. Bay looked at each other before she replied.

"I will call my other son Dustin, he will take care of everything and Mildred is here now so I will be okay."

Wilson and Nelson exchanged a glance, the tough part was over.

"Thank you detectives, for coming all this way to tell me in person, I imagine this was difficult for you."

"We just wanted to be sure you would be okay. If you have any more questions you know how to get in touch with us."

"Yes, I still have your cards. You are fine representatives of the police force. Thank you again."

That was their cue to leave and they did.

Wilson stopped for lunch at the same deli that they stopped at the last time they were here and they both ordered the same corned beef sandwiches. They hadn't spoken since they left Reynolds Street, both wrapped up in their thoughts.

Sitting at the table enjoying their lunch Wilson finally broke the ice.

"Humph," he mumbled.

Nelson said, "What?"

"I didn't really pay that much attention to it the last time we were at her house but this time it was very obvious."

"What was?"

"The pictures on the mantle."

Nelson reached back into her memory to visualize what he was referring to.

Wilson continued, "They are all of David or David and Mrs. Bay. There are no pictures of Dustin."

Nelson thought for a moment, "Yes, you are right. That is very strange."

"He lives in Michigan. Maybe he is the black sheep in the family?"

"That might explain it but a mother usually has a picture of every child, even the bad ones."

"One of life's unsolved mysteries I guess."

"Possibly," said Wilson wiping his mouth with his napkin. "Let's get back."

When Wilson dropped off Nelson and picked up Supinski there had been no news from Campbell, Anthony or Chief Driscoll and that started to make him edgy. It was not just the lack of results but also the time ticking away that was bothering him.

CHAPTER 31

THE BULLPEN WAS quiet when Wilson walked in. Officer Supinski was not with him. She had checked back in with the front desk Sergeant and changed into her uniform for street duty. Campbell and Anthony were on the phones desperately trying to find a real estate agent that would have the lead they needed to find Doyle. When Wilson opened up his emails he was pleasantly surprised to see one from Giordano, *'Morris has the camera you need'.* Outstanding, Wilson thought, finally some good news.

He typed in an additional request and replied back to Giordano, *'We will also need earplug microphones. Can Morris bring them?'*

Send.

Time was still ticking away so the elation of Giordano's email was short lived, and anxiety began creeping back into his thoughts.

Wilson's cell phone rang. It was Chief Driscoll.

"Yes, Chief. What do you have?"

Campbell paused to listen; Anthony was still talking to someone.

"We have a hit just south of Kelby. It's a farmhouse that is being rented out by the estate. The farm is still being run by the estate until it can be put up for sale but they have rented out the house supposedly to a couple but the realtor only met the wife. She said that her husband travels a lot for work. It would be a perfect spot to hide in plain sight."

"Yes it is, but you can't go out there in police vehicles she will see you coming from a mile away and who knows what she has done to protect herself from a siege."

"What do you suggest?"

"We need someone that she would not have already seen even if she has been watching us."

"Yes, that would make sense but if we use anyone in Kelby she might recognize them."

"Correct, and we can't take any chances on that happening." Wilson paused and then said, "I have an idea Chief; let me get back to you."

"Great. I will await your call."

Wilson picked up his desk phone and called the officer on the front desk.

"Please have Supinski paged to get back here immediately."

"Yes sir."

Click.

Campbell stopped staring and went back to working the phones.

Fifteen minutes later Officer Supinski arrived still in uniform.

"Get changed quickly and meet me at my car."

Supinski didn't even question why. To be able to work with the special task team twice in the same day was a dream coming true for her.

"Yes sir."

Wilson asked Campbell to take a break and waited for Anthony to finish his call.

"Okay. We might have a hit south of Kelby. I am going to go check it out. I am taking Supinski with me as the lead since Doyle would not have seen her yet. It might not be her but if it is Doyle we will call you right away. Otherwise keep after those realtors and call me if you get anything promising."

Quiet affirmation from both as Wilson left the bullpen.

Supinski was nervously waiting for Wilson at his rental car. Wilson threw the car keys to her, called Chief Driscoll on his cell and got in the passenger side.

"Chief, we are on our way. Where is the farm?"

"Take the highway to Peace and go south, turn right on Gorley and the turn south on Universal. The farm is on the right after you cross Elmer. It is only five miles south of Kelby, you can't miss the house it's a big two story red brick. We will be waiting for your call on Universal on the north side of the highway just two minutes away."

"What's the plan?" Supinski asked.

"You will drive up to the house. That's why I gave you the keys. Ask her for directions to highway Thirty Nine South. It's about ten miles west of the farm so it will sound like a reasonable request."

Supinski needed more information, "Where will you be?"

"When you turn south on Universal I will get in the back seat."

"How will you know if it is Doyle or a real renter?"

"I am not going to determine that. You are."

"How do you want me to do that?"

"First thing you look at is her height. She is five-three so you will be able to determine if the person who answers the door is taller or shorter than that. If she seems too tall check her shoes. Next she has blue eyes. Hopefully she isn't wearing colored contacts around the house. Her hair colour could be anything. It was blonde but she has appeared with brown hair so either she is sporting wigs or dyed it."

"How do I let you know?"

"Before you get out of the car you are going to call my cell phone and put your phone in your jacket pocket so I can hear the conversation."

"Cool."

Twenty minutes later Supinski pulled over facing south on Universal Road and Wilson moved to the back seat.

Wilson called Chief Driscoll and told him that they were close and heading to the house.

"Slow down after you cross Elmer. You have to make it look like you are lost."

Supinski turned the rental car onto the farm house driveway. There was no car visible but the garage door was closed as it would be if this was really Doyle. She stopped the car near the house and turned off the engine.

Wilson said, "The order of checkpoints will be her height, the colour of her eyes and then description of her hair."

"Yes sir," she said as she dialed Wilson's cell phone and then slid her cell phone into her pocket and after his phone rang she exited the car and headed for the front door.

Wilson was hunched down in the back seat with a slightly obstructed view of the front door. His heart was pumping faster now, like when he was standing on the tee of the eighteenth hole with a one shot lead. So close to the end and yet you still have no idea how it will end.

He heard Supinski's knuckles rap on the door and then the sound of the door opening and from his viewpoint Wilson could see a side view of a woman in the doorjamb.

"Hi. Sorry to bother you but I think I am lost," said Supinski.

"Where are you going?" was the reply in a woman's voice.

"To highway thirty-nine. I thought I was following the directions but I don't have a GPS. I wasn't too far south so I thought I was okay."

Supinski had just said that the person answering the door is the right height to be Doyle.

"I'm not sure I can be of much help. I am not very good with directions," the woman at the door said.

"Maybe I missed the road sign I was looking because the sun was in my eyes." Supinski raised her hand above her eyes in a manner that shielded the sun from her eyes like a visor on a hat. She pretended to look up and down the road.

"They said to look for a blue sign but I didn't see it. There was a green one. But I am pretty sure it wasn't blue."

She had just told Wilson that the woman had green eyes.

"Let me call my husband he will know where you need to go."

The woman turned her head and called her husband to come to the front door. "Carl, can you come here please."

A man appeared in the doorway and she repeated her lost story to him.

"Keep heading south and turn right on Sperry and that will take you to thirty nine."

The woman was not Doyle. Wilson disconnected the open line to Supinski's phone and called Chief Driscoll.

"False alarm Chief. It's not Doyle. This woman has her husband in the house."

"I am not sure if I am relieved or disappointed."

"I know what you mean."

Supinski got back in the car and waited for Wilson to finish his phone call and give her further instructions.

"I will see you in the morning Chief."

Click

Supinski was staring at Wilson waiting for instructions.

"Let's go home," he said exasperated.

After a few minutes of silence Wilson said, "We may have to do this again. Are you up for it?"

"Yes sir."

"Good. You did a terrific job of talking in code."

"Thank you sir."

For some reason when Supinski called him 'sir' was not as irritating to Wilson as when Campbell called him that.

Wilson phoned Nelson.

"We took a look at a rental property but it didn't pan out."

Wilson gave her the summary while Supinski drove and listened.

"We need to have everyone in position by ten tomorrow morning and that includes you."

"Who is going to relieve me, Supinski?"

"Yes."

Supinski smiled. Hearing that she was being included in tomorrow's agenda made her day.

They had heard no news from any of the other realtors that everyone had talked to. With all the computerized systems, for buying and selling houses, Wilson thought there would have been several hits by now. Perhaps the good news is that they were prequalifying the leads so his team would not be chasing all over the greater Chicago landscape for nothing. None the less, no news in this case was not good news.

Wilson and Supinski picked up burgers and fries for all four of them from Wally's Burger Emporium, one of Detective Anthony's favorite food stops, before his wife put him on his new diet. Wilson decided that a little comfort food could go a long way to relieving the stress of chasing Doyle, and the look on Anthony's face when he saw the logo on the greasy walled paper bags, said it all.

With their stomachs full Campbell and Anthony eased their previously stiff mood towards Supinski, and any tension they had was now gone.

"We are all going to be meeting at the Chamber of Commerce building at ten. The Chief, and three officers in plain clothes, will meet us there. Nelson is coming also; Supinski will take over for her at Webster's. The Chief and one officer in uniform and four others will be pall bearers. The three plain clothes officers, with you two and Nelson, will be our eyes in the crowd. You will all have an earplug, and I will be directing you towards people who may be Doyle, to confirm whether or not from Kelby. If we get confirmation on Doyle, the six of you will close ranks on her."

Supinski listened nervously from the edge of her chair. This was the most exciting thing that had happened to her in just her second year on the force. Being involved in an undercover operation, even though her part was small, was more than she had ever expected at this point in her career. If she had any doubts about her future they were now laid aside, the decision in her mind had been made. She was going to become a homicide detective and she couldn't imagine a better person to learn from than Detective Wilson.

After their meal was finished, they discussed more minor details of the operation. Wilson wanted any question discussed, so there wouldn't be any confusion at the funeral.

"I will be in the van with Morris, scanning the crowd and giving you directions. It will be difficult to pick her out of the crowd at the church; she can mix in with the other women. And even more difficult, if she is wearing all black, and a hat and sunglasses. But, there are only two exits at the cemetery, so if she goes to the grave she will be trapped. Chief Driscoll and two cruisers will arrive at each end of the road to the cemetery ready to cut off the road once everyone is in the cemetery."

"It sounds like we have all contingencies covered," said Campbell.

"Normally I would agree with you Andy, but Doyle has been managing to stay one step ahead of us so I am still cautious."

At eight o'clock Wilson surmised that they had done enough for the day. Realtors were either heading home or showing houses and not really interested returning calls that weren't going to make them money.

"See you all back here at eight."

Even though they had been straining hard all day to dig up something on Doyle, and they were mentally drained, they were reticent to leave feeling that they had not accomplished the goal.

"Now get out of here now," Wilson chided. "I need you all to be fresh tomorrow, so get a good night's sleep. We have to be sharp and prepared for absolutely anything. A mental lapse might mean the difference between winning and losing, so go home now!"

They shrugged their shoulders like children trying to defy a parent who was asking them to go to bed, but crept out of the bullpen knowing Wilson was right.

CHAPTER 32

A SILENT BULLPEN greeted Wilson on Wednesday morning, but there was nothing silent about the thoughts in his brain. Trying to mesh all the intangibles into to one seamless plan was the problem that was filling up his mind.

Worrying about something is rarely an effective way to solve a problem, so instead Wilson was going through each part of their plan, and extrapolating possibilities. Even though it was proactive, and positive, it was still a tax on the nerves.

He had arrived even earlier this morning than he anticipated due to his mind racing. A quick visit to see Jennifer last night had soothed his soul and allowed him to get to sleep. That was until his subconscious suddenly woke him at four in the morning, posing a predicament that he was not ready to address. What if they didn't catch Doyle at today's funeral? The answer of course, is that Captain Stone would be raking him over the coals, and wanting to know how he was going to catch Doyle before she killed again.

Everything they were doing was predicated on Dr. Devlin's assessment that Doyle will want to see Webster buried. More accurately, Doyle would want to see the body, but that was eliminated from her choices by the ruse that it was burned so badly it had to be a closed casket. Wilson checked his emails and saw a confirmation from Morris. A good start to the day.

Supinski arrived only seconds before Campbell and Anthony, but if her punctuality was designed to impress Wilson she had succeeded for the moment, and it took his mind off of the issue that awoke him.

No donuts this morning, only coffee and awareness. Residual questions were discussed informally, no room for omissions, any and all subjects relating to the funeral were raised. After every topic had been picked to the bone, Anthony and Campbell logged onto their computers and checked their emails.

"Holy shit," Campbell exclaimed staring at his computer screen.

Everyone looked at him and Anthony laughed because Campbell was a religious man and never swore in public.

"What is it," asked Wilson.

"We have a live one."

They all knew instantly what he meant. He had been given a lead to a rental house and he was sure was Doyle.

"Confirmation?"

"Yes."

"How?" Wilson asked wondering why he was so sure.

"It is rented to a Phoebe Ann Moses from North Star, Ohio."

"And how is that confirmation . . ." Wilson said waiting in anticipation of Campbell reply.

"Phoebe Ann Moses really is from North Star, Ohio," said Campbell as he turned slowly to face him, "But she is better known as *Annie Oakley*."

"Damn!" said Anthony.

"Good. She's out smarted herself this time," said Wilson.

Campbell said, "The house is rented for 3 months. The owners are on a round the world cruise they won."

"Where is it?"

"In Naperville, exactly halfway between here and Kelby."

"So she placed herself in the *Neutral Zone*." Wilson was an avid Star Trek fan.

"Just outside of both the Kelby and the Chicago investigation areas."

"Lucky for her," said Anthony.

"Nothing that she does is by luck," said Wilson. "That was all part of her plan to have the ability to be close to everywhere she needed to go, and Naperville is five times the size of Kelby, so she would be invisible to the locals. Let's take a look at the street on your computer map."

Campbell punched the keys and a map of the street came up on the screen. The street the rental house was on was just two blocks south of the highway giving her quick access to either Chicago or Kelby; however it ended in a cul-de-sac. Whether it was because she was rushing or just oversight she had made a tactical mistake. There was no secondary exit. No way out if the street was blocked. Either she had been over confident of her ability to hide, or she never foresaw a showdown at the rental house.

"Judging from this location we won't need much to trap her. She probably isn't expecting visitors, so I don't think this house will be booby trapped, but we will take all the right precautions. Anthony, call Mac and tell him we need his services right away."

Supinski had been mum taking in the interaction but then she blurted out, "How do we approach the house?"

Wilson looked at her, "Well we can't pretend to be lost this time."

Anthony said, "What about a door to door salesman?"

"Hmm." Wilson considered his idea.

"Or a municipal survey with a clip board and sheet?" said Supinski.

Wilson nodded at her, "That would work. She wouldn't know if it was real or not. Print something out with Naperville as a header."

"Andy, you will drive your cruiser to the cut off street that leads to the highway, right here," Wilson pointed on the computer screen. "Mac can wait there with you. I will park my rental at the opening to the cul-de-sac ready to cut it off any vehicle that leaves the house. Anthony will park over here," Wilson pointed to another side street. "In case she somehow gets her vehicle by me."

"Anthony, get a hold of the Chief in Naperville and let him know that we will need his men to seal off the perimeter of the area as soon as we get there. We don't want to leave her any access to the highway. Tell him we should be there in thirty minutes."

"Andy, load your cruiser with the riot gear. Let's cover all our bases."

Wilson and Supinski arrived at the intersection a block from the cul-de-sac and waited for everyone to arrive before moving into position. Anthony called his contact with the Naperville Police Department to advise them they were ready, and then drove past Wilson's rental car to a spot further down the street.

Wilson watched Anthony drive by through his rear view mirror as he sat facing the cul-de-sac.

He looked over at Supinski, "Ready?"

"Yes sir," she replied while holding her clip board and fake survey sheet.

"Okay same as before, height, eyes, and maybe hair."

"Got it."

"I can see you from here, but if I use the binoculars, for a close up view of who answers the door and it is Doyle, she might see a reflection and panic so the open phone is our only communication."

She dialed Wilson's cell phone and then exited the rental car and walked down the street towards the house with a clipboard in one hand and a pen in the other. She paused on the sidewalk in front of the house next door to the target house and looked at her clip board pretending to check some information. Wilson smiled at her casual improvisation.

She stopped briefly at the empty driveway of the rental house looked at her clip board again and then strode to the front door and rang the bell. She stood and waited looking at her clipboard again and then rang the doorbell one more time.

Wilson heard the doorbell ring both times. He watched her stand on her toes and look through the small glass partition at the top of the door.

"No lights on in the house," she said facing the street.

Was Doyle hiding in the house, or was she already on her way to Kelby? Or worse, was she out shopping and about to show up while Supinski was waiting on her doorstep.

Wilson wanted to be sure he made right call. He called Anthony, "Come and take my spot and if anyone turns into the cul-de-sac, cut the street off."

"Okay"

He drove up and parked in front of the house next door and got out and walked to the front door.

"Stay here," he said to her as he walked down the side of the house. A small wooden gate blocked access to the back yard but he reached over it and unlatched it. The back of the house had a wood deck leading to a set of patio doors. He peered through the patio doors and confirmed that there were no lights on. The kitchen was spotless and the other room he could see was also tidy. It almost looked like no one lived here. It appeared that Doyle's organizational skills extended to housekeeping.

Wilson walked to the front door and took out the key that Campbell had picked up from the realtor on his way here.

"Wait in the driver's seat of the car. Call me if she shows up. I can slip out the back if I need to." He waited for her to get into the rental car and then entered the house and locked the door behind him.

Similar to his view from the rear the front entrance displayed the same immaculate condition; it was as if no one had been here. If this is where she had been hiding then the next question that crossed Wilson's mind was whether or not she was coming back. It appeared at first sight that she had meticulously cleaned up before she left. Was she gone to a new secret lair? Had they missed their golden opportunity? His body was pumping with adrenaline, so close and yet so far. He crept down the hallway towards the back of the house. Between the front room and kitchen was an open door to a washroom on the right, it too was spotless. On the left a closed door caught his attention. He paused and listened but there was not a sound in the house. He reached to his hip unclasped his gun and brought it in front of him as he slowly turned the door handle and opened the door. It was a den.

Wilson opened the door fully and then froze. As much as he should have been prepared for it he was still shocked at what he saw. There was no one in the room but it was the first evidence that they were right about Doyle. The right wall of the den was a wall of books, so many that the shelving was almost indiscernible. A desk with a computer and a lamp faced the middle wall. The left wall was the one that had made Wilson stop dead in his tracks. The wall was covered with pictures and sticky notes. It was a chronological picture calendar of the killer's exploits. Wilson stood perfectly still and looked around. He didn't want to contaminate the scene and he certainly didn't want Doyle to know he had been here. Now he knew she would be coming back. He took out his cell phone and snapped some pictures of the room and then backed out of the room closing the door.

Once outside the room his mind returned to the present. He turned and walked to the front door but stopped at the bottom of the stairs leading to the second floor and decided to check one more thing before he left. He ran up the steps and in the first bedroom he looked into he saw a suitcase on the floor. The bedroom closet was empty; she was packed and ready to leave as soon as needed. He ran down the stairs lifted with the knowledge that for the first time, they were one step ahead of the killer. She was now following their lead. Doyle was already on her way to Kelby.

Wilson stopped his car beside Detective Anthony's.

"A small change of plans Anthony. I want you to stay here and watch the house. If she comes back, call your contact at the Naperville Police Department and tell them to seal off the perimeter again. Then call me." Wilson lowered his voice to a serious tone. "And under no circumstances do you approach the house. Wait for us to arrive. Is that understood?"

"Yes sir."

CHAPTER 33

WILSON AND SUPINSKI drove to Kelby with Officer Campbell and Mac close on their heels. After the two women changed places, Wilson and Nelson rendezvoused with everyone in the back parking lot of the Chamber of Commerce building. Once inside the building, they went to the conference room, where Wilson brought the group up to speed on the house in Naperville.

"When I got up this morning, I had a nagging thought that she might not be here, but now we know for sure that she is."

Wilson introduced a shy Morris to the group.

"Morris has a camera that will give us a person's height to within a quarter of an inch. Five of you will have the ear plugs and I will be doing the directing, during to funeral, towards women who fit Doyle's profile. That will be Officer Campbell and Detective Nelson from Chicago PD, and Officers Scott, Warner, and Yang, from The Kelby PD."

"We do not want to challenge Doyle in a crowd. I don't think she is armed with a conventional weapon. By that I mean not a gun, but she might have a Taser or mace or even a paralytic drug."

Officer Warner raised his hand, "What do we do if we identify her."

Wilson pointed, "Do nothing. Act natural, and wait for my signal, and do not stare at her. Remember, we are dealing with a very smart, but possibly psychotic person. She has demonstrated in her attacks that she is detailed, organized, and dangerous. I don't expect anything different today if she feels confronted."

Another raised hand. This time is was Officer Yang.

"I am hoping your answer will be no, but is there any chance she is carrying a bomb?"

"Good question. We have discussed this previously, and even though we ruled it out as a possible aspect of her attacks, we can't rule it out completely. We don't believe she is suicidal, it doesn't fit the profile, but in the event that it she goes that route we have Mac with us from the bomb squad to help us out."

Wilson looked around the room.

"Your question Officer Yang, also addresses our main concern, the safety of everyone at the funeral. That is why we want to make our attempt to isolate her, at the cemetery, when she moves away from the crowd. We are going to keep the parking spaces at the cemetery a hundred yards from the grave site. If we can get her when she is walking back to her car we should be able to catch her off guard. Right now we have the upper hand. We don't think that she will be prepared for our trap and we will be hiding in the crowd just as she is. If she believes that she will not be noticed, she will be playing right into our hands. And if we can pick her out of the crowd before we leave for the cemetery it will make it even easier to snare her before she gets to her vehicle at the cemetery."

Heads in the room nodded in confirmation.

"That being said, I want to reiterate that we are dealing with an unstable personality, and that she could do anything. One last note the ear phone is a one way microphone. You can hear us but we can't hear you. It is good up to two hundred yards so we will never be out of range."

Another raised hand; Officer Yang again. "Why is it only a one way mike?"

"I don't want to take a chance on anyone being seen talking into their sleeve. That's the kind of thing that would give us away to Doyle."

"Okay"

"One last thing on the ear piece. If we identify Doyle before the cemetery make sure you keep your ear piece opposite of her, it will prevent her from hearing anyone potential feedback and noticing it in your ear."

More nodding of confirmation.

"Okay let's go to church."

Morris parked his custom beige colored surveillance van across the street from the church, just a couple of parking spots away from the front steps. The angle was not an issue as they were well within a decent visual distance. He and Wilson were in the back seats, and the darkened windows made it look like no one was in the van.

As each of the surveillance team reached the steps of the church they were given a verbal test signal and turned and nodded towards the van. Chief Driscoll and one other officer attended the church eulogy in full dress. They would sit together in the church as if paying the respects for the Kelby Police Department. If no police had shown up it might have made Doyle suspicious.

The majority of the people going into the church were bunched closely together to get a picture measurement from Morris's camera. Women tend to cluster while it was the men who would stand alone. Two women were alone momentarily, but one was too short and quite old while the other was far too tall to be Doyle. The first part of the stakeout was a waste. Hopefully when the people are coming out of the church there would be more separation amongst the crowd. Another issue was that the majority of the women were wearing black, and although it wasn't raining it was overcast and cooler, so most of the women had sweaters or full length coats covering up their more distinctive dresses.

Wilson commented to Morris that even though Chief Driscoll had mentioned that Webster was well liked and the town would be taking time for her funeral he was still surprised at the size of the turnout.

"I never permit myself the luxury of surprise. It allows an emotional reaction to distract me from my task at hand," said Morris.

Wilson looked at Morris and remembered Giordano's remark that Morris was a strange character. Indeed he was.

When the crowd departed the church Morris was able to get a read on three women, fitting Doyle's profile, but getting to them now was still dangerous, and if those persons did not go to the cemetery then in all probability they would not be Doyle. Wilson relayed the information to the team.

"Attention team, we have three potentials. The first is a woman in mostly black wearing a black hat with green trim on the headband. The second is a woman is in a dark brown suit with black purse and black hat. The third is also in black but with a long navy sweater, no hat. Let's confirm who is a resident of Kelby as soon as possible when we get to the cemetery."

Morris, with Wilson inside the surveillance van, left to get the required position in the parking lot of the cemetery. Not all the cars that came to the cemetery were able to park in the parking area that was deliberately made smaller to make people walk a substantial distance to the grave. Some of the cars had to be parked along the road, but as Chief Driscoll would have the road blocked at both ends Wilson was not worried.

Officer Yang was the first to act on the three women they needed to identify. He signaled to the van that the woman in brown suit with the black hat and black purse was a resident of Kelby. It turned out that she was the owner of the candle store next to the Chamber of Commerce.

Morris picked through the crowd as they made their way to the grave and one more woman made the checklist. She was wearing a black pant suit with a distinctive short black jacket, black hat and sunglasses. Wilson felt his pulse quicken when he thought to himself that this woman might be Doyle. Once she reached the throng at the grave site she disappeared into a wall of black.

Officer Scott who had been quiet all day made his way towards the woman with the green head band on her black hat. He cautiously moved to her left side following Wilson's instructions to keep his ear piece on the opposite side of Doyle. Gingerly he stepped forward to get a look at her face, his heart pumping and his palms sweating. As naturally as he could, he leaned forward, and keeping his head facing straight ahead, he looked at the woman out of the corner of his eye. In all his years of serving on the force, standing beside a potential murderer suspect, and eye-balling her, was never on his list of things he thought he would be doing. Officer Scott turned his head ever so slightly for a better view of the woman's face, and then exhaled a deep breath when he recognized her ear rings even before he saw her face. The woman was one of his wife's friends and the ear rings she was wearing were a birthday gift from his wife to her. He turned back to face the van and nodded slowly.

Wilson had been watching intently, "Two down, two to go." Morris said nothing.

Wilson called Chief Driscoll, "We are down to two choices. A woman dressed all in black and another one with a navy sweater. I am leaning towards the one in all black; she has a very distinctive outfit. Almost too snazzy for a funeral. You can let the others through when they leave if you know them, or they don't fit that description."

"Will do."

Then Wilson spoke to the team. "Scott you come back here to the exit and watch everyone leaving. Yang and Warner follow the women in the navy sweater. Andy, you and Nelson follow the woman in the nice black outfit with the short jacket and hat."

Wilson liked working in teams of two; they were easier to communicate with.

Wilson watched Nelson and Campbell walk slowly behind the woman in black towards the cars. She got into a white two door.

"Andy you pull out behind her and make sure she can't turn around on the road."

It was time. Wilson called Driscoll.

"Chief, she's in a white car and Andy will drive behind her to cut her off."

"Okay Detective."

Click.

"Okay Morris, follow Andy."

The procession headed towards the road block where Chief Driscoll was waiting.

Nelson and Campbell were behind her car and several Kelby police officers in front of her, no place for her to go. Wilson watched keenly as Chief Driscoll approached the car and then leaned over to speak with the woman driver. Campbell and Nelson got out of Campbell's cruiser and walked towards the white car with their right hands on the holsters.

Chief Driscoll stood up and waved the white car through the road block. Wilson jumped from the van and ran towards Chief Driscoll.

"What the hell?" Wilson said as he reached Driscoll.

"What's the matter detective?"

"That woman was the one I was telling you about."

"Sorry detective, but she is the wife of one of our councilmen. She is not Doyle."

"What? No." Wilson turned around and looked for Officers Yang and Warner. They were walking towards him. "Where is the woman in the navy sweater?" He yelled at them.

Yang replied, "That's what we were going to ask you."

"No woman in a navy sweater passed me," said Officer Scott.

Wilson was as close to panicking as he could get. He ran back to the van, grabbed the camera out of Morris's hand and started flicking through that pictures that Morris had taken of people leaving the cemetery. Then he saw it.

"Shit."

"What?" Nelson asked.

"Look at this one."

Wilson held the camera out so they could see the picture that had made him swear. It was a woman in a black outfit with sunglasses and a black beret.

"This is Doyle."

"But how?" asked Campbell." You mean we all missed her?"

"No. She was at the church and came to the cemetery wearing a long navy sweater but she left dressed like that.

"God she is smart," said Yang.

"But we didn't let anyone through that was wearing black that we didn't know," said Chief Driscoll.

"She's a chameleon. She must have had another outfit in her car. Think Chief was there anyone that you can recall that sticks out in your mind."

Chief Driscoll looked at the other two officers standing at the road block hoping for some clarity.

"Wait there was a woman in red. I thought it was a strange color to wear to a funeral."

"What was she driving Chief?"

"Umm"

"Think hard."

"It was a navy SUV."

"She is heading back to Naperville. Andy Let's go!" Wilson yelled at Officer Campbell.

Officer Campbell didn't even have to ask what Wilson wanted him to do. In a split second he was in his cruiser, Wilson in the passenger seat and they tore off heading to Naperville. Officer Campbell was in his element now. While other officers and detectives might have sharper crime fighting skills than Campbell, no one in the Chicago Police Department could match him in driving skills. Campbell had worked in a racing pit crew before joining the police force and his driving prowess was renowned amongst fellow officers. If any officer could catch up to Doyle's SUV it would be Campbell.

Nelson jumped into the beige van with Morris; they followed behind.

Campbell turned onto Route Thirty-Eight which ran parallel to the highway to Naperville with one important exception. It dipped south towards the highway in about five miles and this little detour would save them valuable seconds in their chase of Doyle's navy SUV.

Wilson called Anthony.

"Anthony here, no sign of her yet."

"Don't move. She's on her way."

Wilson filled him in on what had happened.

"Tell the Chief in Naperville what is happening. If we don't catch up to her first she should be there in about ten or fifteen minutes. We can't endanger her neighbours. Ask him to put his men in her house. She won't be expecting that."

"Right away sir."

Wilson could tell by the number of times today that he been called 'sir' that everyone was getting a little tense.

Campbell had skilfully sped down the highway to Naperville without using lights or a siren to pass dozens of cars. Knowing that Campbell was an accomplished driver did not make his moves any less frightening for Wilson.

Wilson was the one getting tense now. They were almost at the first cut off for Naperville and they had not seen Doyle's vehicle yet, then Campbell weaved around a van and there it was, a navy SUV. Campbell accelerated the police car and the navy SUV put on its right turn signal, indicating that it was getting off the highway. The cut off Doyle had taken was a long shallow ramp that ended at a 'T' in the road, and a stop light. Campbell continued at full speed, but the navy SUV stopped at the light, still with its right turn signal on. She was turning south towards the rental house. The south bound lanes were separated from the northbound lanes by a grass median.

"Hang on," said Campbell.

Wilson knew what Campbell was going to do, but the image and the reality of it was more than he had ever experienced.

Just as the SUV started the right turn Campbell rammed the cruiser's ram-bar into the right rear of the SUV near the tire. The collision set off the air bags and the SUV spun around until it was facing north. Campbell stopped his cruiser and backed up so he was facing the side of the SUV, and then drove the police cruiser into the door panel forcing Doyle's vehicle onto the curb and pinning it against a streetlight pole.

They jumped out and ran to the driver's door with their guns pulled. Campbell whipped the door open but before they could say anything they saw Doyle had been knocked unconscious. Blood trickled from the side of her forehead but her seat belt held her in place. Both of them were breathing fast as they looked at her. Time seemed to standing still, or at least moving very slowly.

They were thinking, 'This is it?' – 'Is it over?' The reality of the situation was hard to accept. It had happened too fast. Doyle was trapped in her vehicle. The chasing was done. Their hearts were pounding in their chests.

With his gun still pointed at Doyle, Wilson pulled out his phone and called Detective Anthony.

"We . . . ," he sucked in air. "We are at the Winfield Road cut off. We need medics. Doyle is down. Repeat. Doyle is down."

"Yes sir," Anthony replied.

Campbell pulled out his handcuffs and cuffed Doyle's hands to the steering wheel. Even unconscious she was not to be trusted, but once her hands were secured Wilson holstered his weapon. Seconds later sirens sounded somewhere nearby. The Naperville PD and Fire Department had been waiting at the ready. Wilson heard a noise behind him. He turned around to see the beige van pull up to the light and Nelson jumped out and ran towards them.

"Holy shit," she said. "Are you guys okay?"

Wilson said, "Yes. We're fine."

She looked at the person handcuffed to the wheel. Doyle was wearing a red outfit as Chief Driscoll had described. Something about it looked strange to Nelson and when she touched the sleeve she noticed it was navy inside. Doyle had been wearing a reversible sweater/dress that she must have flipped inside out, so that no one would have a clear sighting of her. Blue, then black, then red. Every person describing her at the funeral would be describing her in a different colored outfit. Nelson looked at the unconscious woman in the navy SUV. She shook her head, such brilliance wasted. It was hard to believe that this woman, sitting in the driver's seat, was the one who had committed six murders.

She looked at Wilson and said, "I can't believe that this is it. That it's over."

Wilson understood exactly what Nelson was thinking. It wasn't that she couldn't believe that the chase to catch Doyle was over, that was not the issue. It was the way it ended. The case started seventeen days ago, and the team had discussed every possible way of capturing Doyle, but not once was a car crash an idea on the table. It was a sudden unexpected end to their quest, and Wilson knew it would take time for everyone to absorb the finality of it.

Campbell was motionless, still looking at the woman he had handcuffed, trying to comprehend what he was seeing.

Sirens came to a screeching halt at the accident. Detective Anthony appeared from behind a fire truck and ran up to Wilson and then looked back at Doyle in the damaged vehicle.

"Holy crap. Are you okay?"

"Yes, the damage is worse than it looks."

"Campbell did this?"

"Yes. The cruiser is designed for ramming and he is quite good at it. Although I don't recommend it for the faint of heart." Wilson injected a little humor to deflect the shock of the circumstance.

"You were in the car with him."

"Yes."

"Wow."

Now it was detective Anthony's turn to begin accepting the end of the chase. He stood and stared at the wreck while the paramedics moved

Doyle to a gurney. Officer Campbell re-cuffed her hand to the rail of the gurney.

"Andy, go with the ambulance and make sure she stays cuffed."

Campbell nodded and climbed into the back of the ambulance.

The second set of paramedics at the scene gave Wilson a quick check over to be sure he was not suffering from a concussion.

Wilson called Chief Driscoll, "We have her Chief."

"Terrific."

He briefed Chief Driscoll on the details.

"Wow." It was the classic response for the moment.

Wilson asked Chief Driscoll to send a Kelby police officer to pick up Nelson and drive her back to Kelby to rescue Wilson's rental car from the Chamber of Commerce parking lot.

"Not a problem," replied Chief Driscoll.

"I will call you in the morning with any final details."

"Thank you."

Click.

Next Wilson sent a simple text message to Lieutenant Trentini, 'Doyle captured.'

Then he called Captain Stone.

"Yes Wilson," Stone answered in his typically gruff voice. He was expecting more bad news. He anticipated Wilson was going to say that Doyle did not show up for the funeral.

"We have her sir."

"You have her?" Stone said in mild surprise.

"Yes sir. She is on her way to Naperville Hospital in an ambulance, with Officer Campbell guarding her."

"Hospital. She's hurt?"

"Yes sir. She was knocked out in the car accident."

Captain Stone did not ask about the accident, "Any other issues."

Wilson knew that he meant injuries to the team, or any of Doyle's targets.

"No sir. We are all clean here."

A pause.

"That is good news. Well done detective."

"Thank you sir."

"I look forward to seeing your report."

Click.

CHAPTER 34

DOYLE WAS UNDERSTANDABLY less than cooperative when she awoke in the hospital and was questioned by Wilson. She was still besieged with her obsession that she had a quest to finish. She did not seem to understand the gravity of her situation and struggled to free herself. After a consultation between Dr. Devlin and the Head of Internal Medicine at the hospital it was decided that they would give Doyle a small injection of Thiopental Sodium, for both the safety of the patient, and the ability to interview her. Ten minutes after the injection was administered, Doyle awoke in a more compliant mood.

She readily admitted to her crimes, but she was not mentally able to understand that she was doing anything wrong. Her vendetta was against those responsible for her father being removed from his farm. Her mind had twisted the facts, and now to her, the eviction was the cause of her father's death. She truly believed that everything would be okay soon, even if she didn't understand how that was going to happen. While she did not seem to know who worked at the Genesis Research Lab, giving credence to the idea that the other scientists were never targets, she admitted that Melissa Green was on her list. The only reason she had not been attacked, was that Doyle had just not been able to figure out where Green was. Her brother was not a target either. This time, blood was thicker than water.

The evidence they took from Doyle's wall of pictures in the rental house, backed up everything she was saying to Wilson. If she didn't come out of her psychotic breakdown, Doyle might never know that Webster was not dead, and they might never be able to determine why she killed her victims in the order that she did. Additionally, she may never be ruled sane enough to stand trial. Catching a murderer isn't about winning; it just means the losing stops.

Once in Kelby the officer driving Nelson dropped her off beside Wilson's rental car. She then headed over to Webster's house to pick up Supinski and deliver the news. There was no more need for a bodyguard.

On the way back to Naperville, the two policewomen barely said two words to each other. It wasn't out of dislike but rather from the enormity of the day. The last twenty-four hours were filled with ups and downs in the chase to find Doyle, and now the conclusion of the day's activities was finally hitting them.

The Naperville Police Department would be posting a guard on Doyle's room until she could be released from the hospital for transport to the Cook County Jail. Officer Campbell and Detective Wilson had been checked over twice for any possible neurological symptoms that might have stemmed from the accident. Both were cleared.

Wilson sat down in one of the metal chairs, near the Nurse's station at the entrance to the wing where Doyle was being detained, and thought about the day. The ploy had worked, though not as precisely as he would have liked; Doyle would not be attacking anyone else. Now his job was to connect all the information they had acquired from Doyle, and the wall in the rental house, to the people she had murdered.

He opened his phone and scrolled through the pictures he had taken of Doyle's wall. The third and last picture he had taken had the information he was looking for. The picture confirmed that today was the day that Doyle had planned to attack Webster. The fake funeral had in fact saved Webster's life. Wilson wondered, if they had continued protecting Webster in her house, how Doyle was going to get to her. Would Doyle tell them one day how she planned to get to Webster, or would she have no memory of her plan, if she breaks down and reverts back to her previous self. If they had been able to send away everyone on her list, what would Doyle have done? Would she have stewed for a few days, and then lashed out at an innocent bystander? Would she have resorted to blowing up buildings to get at her prey?

All of Doyle's mental skills had made her an intimidating adversary. The woman went from ordinary scientist to mad scientist in a New York minute. Why? Wilson shook his head. All this tragedy put onto one person's shoulders. Why did she snap? What made her choose this path over suing someone, or protesting in front of the bank, or digging up all the dirty secrets she could find and exposing them?

The woman in the room at the end of the hall, was as far from a murderer, as Wilson could imagine. She was an attractive blonde with soft features who had dyed her hair brown and cut it short. She should be attending PTA meetings, and shopping with her girlfriends, and watching soap operas. Instead, she would be going to prison for the rest of her life, and worse, she may be regretting deeds that she might not even be able to remember. Perhaps that might be better for her than if she does remember what she did.

The human brain is the most complex machine known to man. Chemical compositions control its ability to function. Change those compositions, and you might have an idiot savant who can play Chopin flawlessly, by ear on the piano, but not be able to tie his own shoe laces or someone who can remember every detail of every day of their lives and yet not be able to hold down a job. Sometimes it turns someone into a great inventor, like Leonardo Da Vinci, who could write backwards with his left hand and then sometimes, sadly, it turns someone like Susan Doyle into a modern day Dr. Jekyll and Mr. Hyde.

Wilson was disturbed from his thoughts when the entrance doors swung open and Nelson and Supinski walked in.

He stood up and they stopped in front of him. They both looked at him and without speaking; they came to the same conclusion. He looked older.

Detective Anthony and Officer Campbell were talking to the Naperville police officer who was assigned to guard Doyle. Wilson waved at them to come over to him.

"We have a ton of paperwork to do and we can't do it here. Anthony, take Andy back with you. We'll see you in the bullpen."

Wilson looked at them. No one had moved. "Let's go," he said and led the way out the doors.

CHAPTER 35

MELISSA GREEN THANKED Wilson when he called her to let her know that it was safe for her to return. As much as she enjoyed visiting her husband's parents the thought of spending another week there was pushing her patience to its limits.

Wilson put down the phone and looked at the clock; eight-fifty. This morning in Kelby, Chief Driscoll would have the unenviable task of telling his officers that Webster was still alive and why they were kept in the dark. Wilson felt a tinge of regret that they had to do it that way, but the only true way to keep a secret is to never repeat it. Wilson decided he would call Chief Driscoll later after the dust had settled.

He was staring at the report on Susan Doyle. It was finally finished, although there were still some loose ends to tie up, but none were critical to the case.

"Good morning Wilson."

The bright cheerful retort was an unusual greeting for the bullpen. Wilson looked up to see Dr. Fred McLaughlin, the Medical Examiner.

"Morning Fred. You're in a chipper mood. I wouldn't have thought climbing three flights of stairs would do that."

"I do a lot of hiking so a few stairs isn't much of a challenge Wilson."

"I see. To what do we owe this auspicious visit?"

"Well, I'm the bearer of good news today."

"Really," said Wilson.

"Yes. I think I solved a riddle attached to your case."

After hours of writing up the report on the Susan Doyle case Wilson was at a loss to figure out what Fred was referring to.

"Enlighten us please." Wilson gestured with his arms towards the other members of the team.

"Okay. Remember the first murder, Tom Murphy.

"Yes."

"We couldn't find any water matching the water sample we tested that was in the neti pot."

"Correct."

"Well, when you found out that Doyle had lived in Winnfield Kansas, I started looking for bodies of water there and I came across a news article from last year. Two people died of flu symptoms after swimming in Timber Creek. It was later confirmed to be P.A.M. They had either swallowed or snorted the creek water."

Anthony said, "So Doyle brought the water with her."

"It is a logical assumption. A sample of the creek water will confirm that. I will get one sent to me from the ME in Kansas and add that to your report later."

"Oh my," said Nelson looking at her copy of the case report.

Campbell said, "What is it?"

"The road that you rammed into Doyle on, in Naperville, is called 'Winfield', but with one 'n'."

Wilson raised his eyebrows, "Just a coincidence."

"I thought you always say that there is no . . ." Wilson finished her sentence.

". . . Such thing as a coincidence in a murder investigation. Okay, happenstance then. Better?"

"I don't know," said Fred in a jovial tone, as he waved and left the bullpen.

Wilson made the call to Chief Driscoll.

"How did it go?" Wilson asked.

"Better than you might have expected Detective. It wasn't a total surprise to them. They are a not just a bunch of country bumpkins, and they had, as you say in poker, an ace up their sleeve."

Wilson was thrown for a moment that Chief Driscoll remembered that he played poker, but what was this ace he referred to?

"I hope I never gave them the impression that I thought they were bumpkins."

"No. Not at all Detective. It's just a saying."

"So what was this 'Ace' you were referring to?"

"Well I'm afraid it is my turn to tell you a secret."

Wilson was intrigued by that statement.

"Go on."

"Technically it is an omission of the truth. I never actually told you a lie. I led you to believe something that seemed quite credible at the time."

"Well you certainly have me stumped so far Chief."

"Spencer is not dead."

"What?"

"Yes. I told you that she had shot him, and the ambulance took him away before you could see him."

"Yes they did."

"I decided that if everyone thought he was dead, there wouldn't be any attempt on his life in the hospital."

"What hospital?"

"Naperville."

Wilson laughed.

"What is so funny Detective?"

"You hid Spencer in the same hospital that Doyle is in right now."

"Ah, I see the irony now."

"I wonder what Dr. Devlin would say about her reaction to seeing a man in the hospital that she thought she had already killed."

"That could be a major influence on her psyche."

"I think her psyche has had more than enough influence on it Chief."

"I am afraid you are right Detective. Thank you for all your help. Drive careful."

Click.

At two p.m. Captain Stone, and Lieutenant Trentini, addressed the public and press.

"We are pleased to announce that Susan Doyle, the Kelby Killer, has been apprehended. A special combined task force of the Chicago Police Department and the Kelby Police Department arrested her in Naperville at twelve-forty today. I cannot reveal the names of the task force but suffice to say that their efforts saved the lives of several people on her hit list.

It is with great pride that I thank those men and women, through this press conference for their effort on this case. A great debt is owed to them. It is sad and regrettable that others could not be spared. The Chicago Police Department is committed to the welfare and safety of the citizens of Chicago and I am proud that I am working with police officers who give their all every day to that end."

Captain Stone stepped back and let Lieutenant Trentini take questions from the press. Wilson watched from the wings, and then retreated to the bullpen to finish up the loose ends that the state prosecutor would want tied up.

Wilson's cell phone rang surprising him out of his funk. It was Giordano.

"Good afternoon Wilson."

Wilson replied, "Thanks again for the loan of Morris. He's as strange as you had said."

"I am glad he was able to help. I must say, that was a bizarre ending."

"Yes, very odd."

"I see you got your pat on the back from Stone."

Wilson smiled, "Yes, he does that well."

Silence.

Wilson said. "What is it?"

"I'm afraid I have called with some bad news. Mrs. Bay passed away last night."

Wilson slumped in his seat.

Giordano continued, "They think she had a heart attack in her sleep. Her next door neighbour found her this morning, when she went over for a morning cup of tea."

"She was a very nice person," said Wilson. "Perhaps it was too much too fast."

"Perhaps," said Giordano. "These things are out of our hands."

"Yes."

"Anyway, I thought you would want to know."

"Thank you."

Click.

Wilson told Nelson the news about Mrs. Bay.

"She was such a sweet lady and mother."

"Yes she was."

"It's strange how sometimes bad things keep happening to one family."

"Usually they happen in threes."

"There isn't much chance of a third bad thing now."

"No, I guess not."

"We're done here now guys, so go home."

Supinski and Campbell left while Anthony cleared off his desk and shut down his computer.

"Not me," said Nelson.

"Pardon?" Wilson said.

"I'm not going home. I have a dinner date," she replied proudly.

Anthony waited at his desk listening to the conversation.

"Someone new?"

"Yes. The concierge at the Plaza."

"Well then have fun," said Wilson smiling at her.

Anthony walked out with Nelson.

A moment later Wilson shouted after them, "And drive careful."

3699189R00151

Printed in Great Britain
by Amazon.co.uk, Ltd.,
Marston Gate.